Running From A Rock Star

Brides on the Run, Book 1

A Novel

by

Jami Albright

Copyright

Running From A Rock Star
Brides on the Run, Book 1

Copyright © 2017 by Jami Albright

First Edition.

Editor: Serena Clarke
Designer: Najla Qamber Designs

To Jennifer

You're my romance partner in crime, and the reason this book was born. If you hadn't had a birthday, I would've never started writing. It's a few years late but…Happy Birthday! I love you and I miss you every day.

Chapter 1

Light seared through Scarlett Kelly's eyelids. She buried her face in the cool pillow to block the glare, but even that slight movement caused an explosion of agony. Pain and nausea crashed into her like a train on fire.

After several minutes of panting through her symptoms, the misery subsided long enough for her to peel open her dry, sticky eyes.

Her conservative dress and equally unadventurous bra stared at her from a condemning puddle on the floor.

Stomach tight, she slid her gaze slightly farther to the right to identify the black pile in her peripheral vision. A motorcycle jacket. Combat boots. Black jeans. And…a guitar? Yes, a beat-up guitar leaned against the wall on the far side of the room. And poker chips littered the carpet like crushed confetti after a wild party.

What the—

Suddenly, something warm cupped her naked breast. She peered down at the large hand connected to a tattooed arm, connected to a…

Oh. My. Lord.

She rotated her head, and a stifled gasp jammed in her throat as she stared into the sleeping face of the man who shared the bed.

Gavin Bain? A thrill skittered through her. The sunlight shone on his raven hair. His smooth bronze skin. Fascinating tattoos. Bam! A memory surfaced through her

1

muddled brain. She'd traced the lines of one of those tattoos, the ninja star on his chest. She'd touched and then kissed her way... Oh, heavens, had she done *that* with this rock god?

She, Scarlett Kelly, children's author and poster girl for responsible living, had sex with Gavin Bain. Gavin Bain, the rock star, AKA *The Delinquent*.

Her brain tried to piece together the previous night. She rarely drank and certainly not to excess. Even during the worst time in her life, alcohol hadn't been involved.

An acute case of bed-head made pushing her red curls from her face a painful challenge. Why had she drunk so much? It all came back in flashes of utter dismay. The Children's Writer's Conference in Las Vegas. Nervous anticipation of signing the contract that would save her family financially. That dream blowing up in her face. Then the added humiliation of overhearing herself described as a No-Fun-Nun.

She'd shown them. Look at her now, naked in a strange man's bed, the absolute picture of wholesomeness.

I've got to get out of here.

She held her breath as she removed his hand and slid from the bed. Moving unsteadily, due to her pounding head and sour stomach, she searched for her clothes, careful to be as quiet as possible.

The purse, bra, dress, and boots were easy. But where were her panties?

A panic attack threatened, and her whole body trembled. Could she have removed her underwear before she got to the room? If so, she hoped that memory stayed hidden. She gave up on the lost undies and headed for the bathroom.

Lord, she needed to pee, but after a prolonged study of the toilet, decided it would be too loud and leaving an unflushed toilet was just bad manners. Even though she'd become, by all appearances, Slutty McSlut Slut, she couldn't bring herself to be impolite. So she dressed as fast as her shaking hands allowed.

The reflection in the mirror caught her eye, and the blood pounding through her veins turned to ice. Her head jerked toward her image so fast her brain vibrated. For the briefest of seconds, she saw her mother. A tiny whimper cut through the silence, and she ran trembling fingers over her face. People always said she looked like her mother, but now, while making the walk of shame, the resemblance was uncanny. The mental mantra she'd been repeating her whole life reverberated in her head. *I am not my mother. I am not my mother. I am not my mother.* She grabbed her purse and fled the pristine bathroom.

A cool breeze from the air conditioner drifted up her dress and skimmed her bare bottom. She didn't ever go commando—too much freedom. Restrictions were safe. Without restraint, a girl could find herself hung over, panty-less, and on the verge of a nervous breakdown while covertly fleeing a rock star's hotel room.

Oh, wait. That already happened.

She glanced at the door. Nine feet, and she'd be free of this disaster. Logic screamed escape. Compulsion kept her rooted to the spot, and it became imperative that she find her underwear.

I cannot leave without them.

Where could one pair of basic white panties hide? The chandelier was blessedly free of them. Nothing on the drapery rod. But a photo on the desk made life as she knew it come to a screeching halt.

A gaudy cardboard frame held a picture of her and Gavin under a red neon heart. *The Valentine Wedding Chapel of Love* spelled out in rhinestones around the frame's border.

It couldn't possibly mean what she thought it did.

Nooooo.

3

Next to the picture, the condemning proof—a marriage license issued by the State of Nevada, signed by Gavin Michael Bain and Scarlett Rose Kelly. Her vision blurred, causing the letters on the certificate to dance like cartoon characters.

She wrapped her arms around her middle and glanced back to the gorgeous sleeping man in the bed. A wave of vertigo slammed into her, along with the memory.

She'd told him she'd only have sex with her husband.

With shaking hands, she grabbed the evidence of their reckless night and shoved it into her purse.

While her hard-won reputation exploded into a million pieces, her inner wild child made a victory lap around the room. If that hussy had been driving the bus last night, then she was the reason for this catastrophe.

How could she have been so irresponsible? What was she going to do? No good answer for the first question, but she knew the response to the second. Find the panties and get the heck out of Las Vegas.

She dug through the comforter at the foot of the bed. She kicked at his pile of clothes. She checked behind his guitar.

Nothing.

Nothing.

Nothing.

They had to be under the bed.

Crap.

Not interested in waking The Delinquent, she cautiously made her way to his side and quietly lowered herself to the floor, ignoring the sweet smile he had on his face while he slept. The white material peeked out between the headboard and the mattress. Hallelujah. She reached in and yanked them free.

All the extra movement pounded dizzying pain into her skull. She bent forward and rested her head on the soft carpet, and waited for the room to stop spinning.

"Are you praying?" asked a sleepy male voice.

She squeaked, then slowly turned her head without lifting it from the carpet. Amusement sparkled in Gavin's smoky gray eyes.

"Yes, I'm praying you're a very bad dream."

He rolled his eyes as if that couldn't possibly be true. "Good one. Why are you really on the floor?"

"I, uh, I…" The marriage certificate hidden in her purse and the cacophony of self-condemning thoughts made it hard to focus.

Suspicion darkened his handsome face. "What are you hiding under the bed? Is there a recording device under there?"

"Are you serious?"

He leveled her with a deadly serious glare. There was no trace of the formerly amused man.

"Actually, there's a reporter from TMZ under here, would you like to say hello?"

When his features went from dark to thunderous, she knew she'd made a critical error with the sarcasm.

"I was just…um…looking for something." She forced herself to meet his eyes.

"Looking for what?" Titanium coated every word and drilled into her hungover brain.

Time to go.

She scrambled to her feet. An increased heart rate, combined with residual alcohol pumping through her system, made the room spin. She swayed and toppled cheek first into the side of the dresser, dropping the panties in the process.

"Ouch!" She covered her face with her hands.

Sheets rustled, and suddenly, he was in front of her. "Shit, are you okay?"

She slowly lowered her hands and…hot mother of a freakin' cow. A very naked Gavin squatted in front of her with all his dangly bits…well, dangling.

"Fine, thanks." That's it? That's the best she could come up with a gorgeous naked guy in front of her. So much for clever repartee.

She honestly did try to keep her eyes above his shoulders, but—come on. This was her last chance to see a rock god in all his tattooed, naked glory. One quick peek, then she rose unsteadily to her feet.

"It was nice to…um…meet you, but I should go." She inched toward the door.

"Wait. You're not going anywhere until I have some answers." He made a grab for her arm. Fear and adrenaline lit her up like a rocket. She forgot her injury, made an evasive move, and sprinted to get away.

When she got to the door, she glanced over her shoulder. Gavin hopped on one foot trying to yank on his jeans. The last thing she saw was her husband as he fell, legs tangled in the fabric of the jeans.

She bolted down the hallway toward the elevator. "Come on, come on, come on." She jabbed the down button repeatedly. A small, logical part of her brain, not currently recovering from near alcohol poisoning, wondered what she hoped to accomplish by running. But the larger, wholly irrational, part of her psyche screamed, Married? I'm freakin' married? I've got to get out of here.

Gavin stumbled from the room and into the hall, still struggling with his jeans. They were over his hips but not buttoned. He strode down the hall toward her.

The indicator bell dinged.

"Stop. Do not get on that elevator."

The sight of him stole the air from her body. Magnificent—scary as hell—but totally, completely magnificent. For a crazy instant, she almost complied, but then the doors slid open and broke the spell. She lunged forward, but relief made her clumsy. She tumbled head over heels into the elevator, dress flying over her head as the doors slid shut.

Great, she'd just mooned her husband.

***

Gavin thanked the security guy for opening the door. His half-naked trip into the hall had ended with him locked out of his room. Once inside, he leaned against the smooth wood and burst out laughing. The last thing he'd seen before the elevator doors closed was her bare ass with a brand-new tattoo that read "Gavin."

He could almost forgive her for running out on him. After all, she'd have to live with his name tattooed on her butt for the rest of her life.

The laughter made his head throb. God, he was hung over. Most of his memories of the previous night hid behind a coagulated haze of alcohol.

He'd gone to one of the Bellagio's bars to have a drink and unwind. The frustrating phone call with that damn private investigator had left him in desperate need of diversion. And the pretty redhead with the Texas twang and innocent blue eyes had offered the perfect distraction.

They'd had a few drinks. More than a few, actually, and he was paying for it this morning. He massaged his temples then dug in his bag for pain relievers. He didn't do this shit anymore and dammit, in light of recent events, he didn't need to do it again.

After the second scotch, or was it the third, the memories got hazy. But he definitely remembered falling into bed with her, her soft hands on his body, her sweet, if slightly boozy, breath in his ear as she snored gently…wait, what?

"She fell asleep." Relief flooded his body. He didn't have to worry about a recording device. There was nothing to record. Good thing too—the last thing he needed right now was an internet scandal.

7

What had she been looking for under the bed? He moved to where their ill-fated confrontation took place, and picked up a scrap of white material. It was a pair of women's underwear.

He wouldn't call them granny panties, exactly, but they weren't sexy. They were...sensible. He shook his head. He'd never been to bed with a woman who wore sensible panties.

SCARLETT KELLY was written in permanent marker on the tag. She wrote her name in her panties?

Eight-year-old boys going to camp wrote their names in their underwear, not grown-ass women who sleep with rock stars in Las Vegas.

His phone alarm sounded, nearly giving him a heart attack. He cursed his throbbing head and the piercing tone as he crossed the room to silence the thing.

He stared at the lock screen on his phone like it was a two-headed dragon. Appeared he and the girl—Scarlett—had taken a selfie. That was a first. He smiled at a sliver of memory.

Gavin.

Yeah?

I want to kiss you.

Nobody's stopping you, sweetheart.

Her hand trembled as she brushed the hair off his forehead and then slid it around to the back of his neck. She gently pulled him to her.

The kiss had been soft and tentative. He couldn't remember a better kiss, which was saying something. He'd snapped the picture as their lips touched.

The alarm gave a reminder screech. Time to get moving. His stomach churned at the thought of returning to California.

He'd never considered Los Angeles the City of Angels. The whole town was overrun with pretentious, phony people who were completely self-serving. He'd stuck it out as long as he could, but after Johnny died a year and a half ago, he'd given it all up and moved to Seattle.

But to salvage his career, L.A. was the place to be.

He pulled the letter from Johnny out of his wallet. It was a morbid talisman guiding his every move. The damn thing had changed his whole life. Holding it shot his anxiety through the roof.

He pulled oxygen deep into his lungs and unfolded the letter. Every time he read his friend's rambling words, they blew back at him like a hurricane. It was a gut shot from the only person he'd ever trusted.

Gav,

Remember when I went back to Memphis to lay down a few more tracks for the album? When I was there I saw Tara, you remember Tara, y'all partied together when we recorded the album back in September. Well, she was pregnant, man, I mean fuckin' big pregnant, and she said it was yours. I totally freaked. So, I paid her off, man. I paid her off and she went away. I don't know why I didn't tell you. Fuck, the guilt's been eatin' me up inside. She said it was a boy, but that doesn't matter. Who knows if it's really yours? Right? It's probably not. The last thing you need is a paternity suit. But, I know you would've wanted to know, and I didn't tell you. I know I screwed up. AGAIN. Shit, I'm so sorry. Don't hate me, Gav. Please? Screw this, I need to tell you in person.

He smoothed the creased piece of paper on the nightstand. Was there a kid out there with his DNA? He'd be almost two by now. Wouldn't he?

He leaned his arms on his thighs and cradled his head in his hands. "What the hell were you thinking, Johnny?" He raised his gaze and stared out the window at the Las Vegas skyline. "I love you, man, but I'm so pissed at you right now. I still can't believe you kept this from me."

Was the pretty, self-absorbed blonde, who lived to play, a good mom or still a party girl? The possibility this baby might have the same kind of life he'd had…he wouldn't wish that for any kid, especially his own.

He plowed his fingers through his hair. Hopefully, the private investigator he'd hired could find Tara. Gavin didn't even know her last name, or if she was actually from Memphis, but his manager said this guy could find anybody.

Thinking about Johnny, Tara, and this baby wasn't accomplishing anything except to spike his blood pressure. He returned the note to his wallet, scrubbed his face, and headed for the shower.

While the hot water ran over his aching head, he felt a lot older than his thirty years. He was so over the sex, drugs, and rock-n-roll, but they'd definitely left their mark.

With a towel around his waist, he moved to the sink and wiped the steam from the mirror. He ran a hand over his face, trying to decide if he should shave. A glint of gold caught his eye.

He froze.

There, on the third finger of his left hand, was a gold band.

What the hell?

He squeezed his eyes shut. Tried to shuffle and rearrange the puzzle pieces into place.

His eyes snapped open.

"Son of a bitch!"

Chapter 2

Scarlett jumped at the ding of the microwave.

"What's wrong darlin'?" Aunt Honey asked. "You've been as skittish as a newborn colt ever since you got back from *Lass* Vegas."

That was the truth. Her nerves were a frayed tangle of anxiety. After she'd fled Gavin's hotel room the day before, she'd high-tailed it home to Zachsville, Texas, to try to figure out how to get out of this colossal mess.

Honey ran her soft fingers across Scarlett's cheek. "Your face looks just terrible. How'd you say it happened?"

Well, you see, Honey, I got spooked when my naked rock star husband growled at me, and I fell into a dresser.

"I'm fine. I stumbled into a door when I got up in the middle of the night, and its Las Vegas, Honey, not *Lass* Vegas." She tried to assume a nonchalant lean against the kitchen counter only to jerk upright because of her sore backside. Who knew tattoos hurt so much? It was unfortunate that she'd discovered the tattoo in the plane's lavatory and proceeded to lose her ever-lovin' mind. Evidently, screaming like a woman possessed while at thirty thousand feet is frowned upon by the FAA. The ensuing conversation with the air marshal was not an experience she cared to repeat.

Honey gave Scarlett a pointed look and adjusted the jacket of her rhinestone-studded velour track suit. On her round body, it stretched like plastic wrap around an overly full bowl of pudding.

"Okay, fine." Scarlett folded a dish towel and placed it on the counter. "I'm a bit jetlagged and I guess it's made me jittery." She took a deep whiff of Mr. Clean, fresh laundry, and banana-nut muffins. Exhaling, she relaxed into the comfort of the kitchen. The bright white walls, red counter tops, and yellow gingham curtains blowing in the Texas breeze embraced her as a mother would, and for a moment she was safe in the warm bubble of home.

"I'm still mad at you for not taking me with you to Sin City." Honey spooned sugar into her coffee. "I bet that's what's wrong with you. You brought a little bit of Sin City home with you." She winked one blue-shadowed eye.

And just like that, the bubble burst, and Scarlett's vital signs ratcheted off the charts.

The concealed marriage license, like a matrimonial time bomb, ticked away. She could almost see the illuminated numbers counting backwards while she stood frozen in indecision, not knowing if she should cut the red wire or the blue. She had no idea what to do.

Some young women who decide to throw caution to the wind for one night get fired, or arrested, or contract a nasty STD—lucky girls. Not her. She got a husband. A notorious rock star husband.

For the last twenty-four hours, she'd done nothing but obsess over what had happened.

She'd been in Vegas for the Nevada Children's Writer's Conference, and more importantly, to finalize a deal with the Carousel Network to make her Fiona books into a weekly television show. The money would be a huge boost for her family. She'd been excited, but also a little apprehensive about signing her baby over to the network.

Imagine her surprise when she walked into the meeting to find Sarah Belle, author of the Molly Mayhem books, sitting at *her* negotiating table.

Honey set her coffee cup down with a thud. "I'm so mad at those Carousel people I could spit fire. They're a bunch of idjits."

Scarlett reached for the coffee pot and poured her aunt another cup. "I think they're *idjits* too." She grinned at Honey.

"Tell me again what they said."

"They said they loved Fiona and all of her antics, but they wanted to make her more contemporary…more street smart."

Honey scowled. "I don't know why they would want to change that precious little thing."

"Me either, Honey." Scarlett wiped up a spot of spilled coffee. "So now they're considering Sarah Belle's books, along with mine, for the television series. Sarah's main character lives in the city and is sassier than Fiona." She was also crude and disrespectful, but Scarlett didn't mention that to Honey. "They've decided to do some focus group testing to see which character appeals to the widest audience. We're supposed to come up with changes we can make to our stories that better meet their criteria."

Pressure built in Scarlett's head every time she thought of turning her industrious, precocious, innocent Fiona into a cell-phone toting, slang spewing, sarcastic tart. She wanted to tell them to *shove it*, but in the end, she'd agreed. What choice did she have?

"Scarlett darling, you are the most creative, hardworking person I know. If anybody can do it, it's you." Honey gave her hand a squeeze. "I know what will cheer you up. Let me tell you about my last trip to the casinos over in Shreveport."

"Okay." Scarlett pulled up a chair and, chin in hand, gave Honey her full attention. Honey's stories were entertaining. Maybe it would help keep her mind off her own problems.

"Well, me and Birdie were havin' a drink in the bar, and Wardell Pritchett came sniffin' around me like I was a dog in heat, when all I wanted to do was listen to the band and drink my margarita."

Perfect. Switch the margarita for an apple martini, and she was back in Vegas at the Bellagio's bar being seduced by the baddest bad boy in rock-n-roll.

"Did you hear what I said, Scarlett?"

"What? Oh. No, I'm sorry. What did you say?"

"I *said*, Wardell, if you don't get your gnarly hand off of my backside I'm gonna yank your ten remaining hairs from your head. I don't know what the dickens he was thinkin'—I would squash the man in any intimate situation. I like my men with some meat on 'em." She cackled and toasted Scarlett with her cup of coffee.

Scarlett laughed and laughed until she realized she was crying. She was now officially hysterical. Before Honey could see her, she stood to face the window. Thankfully her aunt had switched on the TV and wasn't paying attention.

"Looks like you're not the only one who had a wild time in Sin City," Honey said.

"I didn't have a wild time." The words clawed their way through tears. She yanked a paper towel to blot her face and pulled off half the roll. "What are you talking about?"

Honey laughed. "That fellow there got married in *Lass* Vegas, and his new wife got a tattoo on her derriere."

Scarlett whirled around so fast the room tilted. When she regained her equilibrium, she saw a split screen on the television. One picture was of a girl in a white sundress, cowboy boots, and a straw cowboy hat strolling arm in arm with Gavin into a tattoo parlor. The other picture was of the same girl and Gavin exiting the tattoo parlor. He had his arm around her shoulder, and her head was down so you couldn't see her face. Thank God Gavin had bought her the hat after they left the Bellagio.

She plopped down in the kitchen chair. "Turn it up, Honey."

"Gavin Bain, the bad-boy front man of the multi-platinum band Wolfe's Bain, tied the knot in Las Vegas last night with this unknown cowgirl. She marked the occasion by having Gavin's name tattooed on her backside at *Leave Your Mark* tattoo parlor. The two were seen earlier in the evening drinking at the Bellagio Hotel. There is some speculation the two did not know each other prior to the meeting. A hotel employee has reported seeing the bride run from the hotel the morning after the wedding, which would explain rumors that the bride fled Las Vegas the following day without her groom."

The reporter shook back his artfully tousled hair and changed his posture to speak into a different camera. "Bain has been out of the spotlight since the untimely death of his bandmate and friend, Johnny Wolfe. Wolfe died in an alcohol-related car accident seventeen months ago. After the death of Wolfe, and Bain's reckless antics both on and off stage, Blast Records discontinued their association with Wolfe's Bain. Rumor has it Bain has been shopping around for a solo record deal."

A deafening roar in Scarlett's ears drowned out the Hollywood Reporter, while small black spots danced at the edge of her vision. She bent and put her head between her knees to keep from fainting. Thankfully, Honey was engrossed in the program and didn't notice.

Scarlett knew Gavin was famous, but it hadn't occurred to her that their marriage would be all over the news. It wouldn't be long before everyone knew what she'd done. Her thoughts careened into each other.

Will the media show up at the farm?

How will I explain this to my daddy?

What will people say?

Do I need a lawyer?

My legs look awesome in those pictures.

"Scarlett?"

The sound of fingers snapping intruded into her panic attack.

"Scarlett, did you lose something under the table?"

"What?" She rose to an upright position, blinking furiously. "Sorry. What?"

The doorbell chimed.

"Are you gonna get the door, or do you want me to?" Honey's drawn-on eyebrows furrowed.

"Huh? Oh no, I'll get it." She smoothed her red curls from her clammy face and rose. "I'm expecting something from UPS."

"Okay, I'm going to take a nap, then I'm gonna start your daddy's supper." Honey got to her feet, deposited her dishes into the sink, and made her way out of the kitchen.

Scarlett's panic tripled at the thought of her sweet father. "Where is he?"

"He had an appointment this afternoon. He won't be back for several hours."

The doorbell rang again, accompanied by insistent knocking.

"Coming." Geez, the UPS man needed to take it down a notch. She was a woman on edge and there was no telling what she would do if someone gave her attitude today.

She opened the door to a handsome thirty-something man wearing a red power tie, a tailored white shirt, and a gray suit that cost more than her car. His attire had probably been crisp and starched before it took a butt-kicking from the Texas heat. Now his clothes looked like the face of an aging movie star, still attractive but a bit droopy.

"Can I help you?"

If he was a salesman, he was out of luck.

"Scarlett Kelly?" He handed her a card. "My name is Jack Avery, and I represent Ga—"

"Honey, I'm home," Gavin said as he stepped up onto the porch.

"Gavin, I thought we agreed you would wait in the car until I had a chance to speak to Ms. Kelly." He spoke like one might speak to an overindulged child.

"No, Jack, you decided that. I didn't agree to anything."

Scarlett made a strangled noise and quickly stepped onto the porch. The door frame rattled as she firmly closed the door behind her. Right. As if she could keep this calamity from the inhabitants of the house with two inches of wood.

"What are you doing here? How did you find me?" Her vision went slightly wonky and sweat trickled down her face.

"Do these look familiar?" He dangled her white, *sensible* underwear around one finger. Her name, like a brand, clearly visible on the tag.

"Oh, my Lord, give me those." She lunged and snatched the undies out of his hand, then shoved them into her pocket.

Betrayed by her granny panties.

***

Gavin pulled in a huge breath and had to remind himself to exhale. His memory had not done her justice. She was beautiful, or she would be as soon as all the blood returned to her face. Her curly red hair, the color of a new copper penny, hung past her shoulders. The yellow skirt she wore and long, tan legs were hot as hell. But it was her sapphire eyes that held him rooted to the spot, a good thing, too, because he was finding it hard not to pin her against the wall and lick her up one side and down the other.

He frowned when he saw the bruise on her cheek that stood out in stark contrast to her freckles. That must have happened when she fell. He didn't like that he'd played a part in her injury. This protectiveness and his attraction to her were definitely a complication he didn't need.

Scarlett clearly didn't share his feelings. She looked at him like he was her worst nightmare come to life. Not the usual reaction he got from women. Maybe he should have waited in the car until Jack had talked to her. She looked like she might keel over, and they needed her cooperation to take care of this disaster.

"You have to leave. Right now. I...I will meet you anywhere, but we can't talk here."

Her gaze darted from one man to the other.

"Well, Scarlett...may I call you Scarlett?" Jack asked.

"I don't care if you call me Lady Gaga as long as you leave right now. I'll call and we can meet somewhere else."

"I don't think that's such a good idea, Scarlett." Jack stood his ground. "We're here, and I think it's in everyone's best interest if we discuss this now."

"No, no, no. You have to leave." She dragged her hands through her hair.

Gavin could see the man was losing her. Awkward, emotionally uncomfortable situations like this were exactly what he paid his people a buttload of money to avoid. He nudged Jack and hissed, "Handle this."

His attorney squared his shoulders and put on his scariest Hollywood power face. "Scarlett, I need you to calm down. You have an obligation to deal with this situation. You married my client, a very wealthy and famous man. For all we know, you took advantage of him in his inebriated state, and you did it with possible nefarious intent. Then you disappeared with the marriage license, which makes us question your character. We're here to ensure you do not try to use this marriage for self-promotion and in the process harm Mr. Bain's career. We also need to discuss the best means by which to dissolve this union."

She stopped fidgeting and focused all her attention on Jack.

Gavin saw the self-satisfied expression on his friend's face that clearly said, *You're playing with the big boys now, little girl.*

She gave Gavin an assessing look. "This is your representation?"

He nodded.

"Then you're an idiot." She crossed her arms under her world-class breasts. "You should never let him speak for you. Ever."

She narrowed a glare at the attorney. "Did you expect to get my cooperation with that condescending speech? You arrogant ass."

"Ms. Kelly—"

"You listen to me, Mr. Avery. I couldn't give two flips about who either one of you are." She pointed one elegant finger in Jack's face. "My life is as screwed up as his." Her finger jerked toward Gavin. "In fact, I'd venture to say I'm more screwed than he is because I'm not a rock star with a bevy of lawyers to do my dirty work for me."

Her frosty eyes stayed fixed on Jack. "I will say this once and use small words, so you don't misunderstand. Go. To. Hell."

She directed her gaze at Gavin and her expression softened. "I panicked, and I ran, but it's not every day I wake up married to a rock star I don't remember marrying. I'm deeply sorry for my part in this entire mess. This situation can't have been any easier on you than it has been on me. I will do whatever I need to do to make this right, but can we *please* not do this on my family's front porch?"

Gavin nodded, fascinated. One minute she'd been a scared, intimidated mouse, the next she'd grown fangs and claws and gone toe-to-toe with one of the most ruthless lawyers in Hollywood. He couldn't decide what was more remarkable, the fact that she'd put him and Jack in their places, or that she'd taken responsibility for her actions.

"Good, because if either one of you does anything to upset my daddy or my aunt, I'll castrate you both."

Ouch. Note to self: don't piss off the redhead.

Chapter 3

If the wall hadn't been behind her, Scarlett would've slid to the porch. Her legs quivered like Jell-O. Confrontation always made her feel this way. She'd used profanity. She hated when she did that. It was so…improper. One more thing to lay at Gavin Bain's feet and another reason she needed to get rid of him.

Before she could, a shiny red convertible careened down the dirt driveway, kicking up dust like a crimson tornado. It skidded to a stop, spraying gravel into the air. A diminutive dynamo, in a power suit and Jimmy Choo heels, sprang from the driver's seat and marched up the sidewalk. Her short black tresses fluttered with every step she took.

Scarlett closed her eyes and exhaled the lungful of air she'd been holding since Gavin and his attorney arrived. She'd never been so happy or surprised to see anyone in her life. Everything would be okay now.

"Scarlett Rose Kelly, don't say another blessed word." Her best friend and attorney climbed the three steps to the porch and nodded to both men as she handed them a card. "Luanne Price. I'm Scarlett's attorney."

She zeroed in on Scarlett's bruised cheek. "What the hell happened to your face?" Her mouth thinned, and she shot Gavin an accusatory look.

Scarlett took an involuntary step in front of Gavin. "Calm down, Luanne. I fell."

A warm hand slid over her hip and lightly patted her behind. A soft whisper blew across her neck. "How's your butt, tattoo girl?"

Her humiliation reminded her it was boys against girls, and he was the enemy. A low masculine chuckle chased her back to the ladies' side of the porch.

When she looked at Gavin, he shrugged and grinned. How could a man as unholy sexy as him manage to look like a little boy with his hand caught in the cookie jar?

"Ms. Price, I'm Jack Avery, Mr. Bain's attorney, and manager." He extended his hand and offered her a professional smile. "I'm sure you understand this situation is time sensitive. The story is being reported by the media, and your client's erratic behavior has only served to fuel their curiosity. My client's reputation could be irreparably damaged because of this marriage and its inevitable conclusion."

Luanne snorted. "Your client once tried to drown Paris Hilton and kidnapped her dog. By comparison, a quickie marriage in Vegas seems somewhat tame."

"To be fair," Gavin interjected, "I only provided the diversion, Johnny stole the dog."

"You call a near drowning a diversion?" Scarlett was appalled.

"No." He chuckled and rubbed the back of his head. "Johnny hated that chick. He especially hated the way she carried that poor dog around all the time. It made him nuts, I mean, he was *really* obsessed. So, we were at the same party as Paris one night, and he decides to rescue…what was that damn dog's name?" He snapped his fingers a few times. "It doesn't mat—"

"Tinkerbelle!"

Gavin grinned at Scarlett. "Yeah, Tinkerbelle."

His remarkable eyes crinkled at the corners when he grinned.

"Like I was saying, we see Paris at this party, and Johnny says he's going to rescue Tinkerbelle, but he needed a diversion. So I pushed her into the pool. Johnny grabbed the dog and ran. I tried to help Paris out of the water, but I was load—um, not at my best and kept losing my grip. By the time they got her out, Johnny was halfway to Tijuana with Tinkerbelle." His self-deprecating smile was so adorable she couldn't help but smile.

She was in so much trouble.

Luanne looked at Jack. "I think we can agree Mr. Bain's reputation precedes him."

"Be that as it may, your client ran from Mr. Bain's hotel room with a marriage license and wedding photos. She's uncooperative, argumentative, and irrational. Not to mention her ridiculous threat of castration."

Luanne looked to Scarlett for confirmation.

Scarlett nodded, and Luanne winked at her.

"Good God. There are two of them," Gavin muttered.

"Don't worry Mr. Bain." Luanne fixed her gaze on the other lawyer. "Only one of us is truly capable of castration."

Jack zeroed in on Luanne like a hungry lion who'd found a playmate. "Ms. Kelly's emotional outbursts have cost us time, and she's refusing to meet with us."

"That's not true. I said I would meet you somewhere other than the front porch of my family's house." Scarlett's voice rose with every word.

Jack gestured to Scarlett, as if to present exhibit A. "Do you see what I mean?"

"I'm curious Counselor, how exactly is she supposed to act? You've accosted my client at her home, insulted her, and if my guess is correct, intimidated her. I wouldn't be surprised if you threatened to huff and puff and blow her house down, Mr. Avery." Luanne crossed her arms and gave Jack the stink eye. "Am I right?"

Jack smiled slightly. It appeared he was enjoying this little sparring match. "I assure you Ms. Price, Mr. Bain and I only want what's best for Ms. Kelly."

The flash of guilt in Gavin's eye told Scarlett an ambush was exactly what they'd intended.

"I'll worry about what's best for my client," Luanne said. "You worry about yours."

Jack leaned his butt against the porch railing and crossed his arms like he hadn't a care in the world. "Ms. Price, you bring up a good point. You see, the intricacies of this case are very specific. How much experience do you have in matters such as this? Ms. Kelly's interest might be better served if her attorney had a skill set that includes something other than the litigation of a stolen mule."

"Mrs. Bain." Luanne matched his nonchalant pose as she leaned against the outer wall of the house.

"I beg your pardon?"

Luanne looked down her nose at the other lawyer, which was no small feat. Even in her five-inch heels, she was still four inches shorter than him. "My client is now Mrs. Bain."

"I suppose so—"

"Also, I have every confidence in my ability to understand the 'intricacies' of this case. I have a great deal of experience dealing with complicated matters of law, Mr. Avery. For example, I've done a quick mental analysis of the Texas Penal Code and have deduced that your sorry hide isn't worth twenty-five to life. So, you get to live." She smiled her best man-eater smile.

Jack ducked his head but not before Scarlett saw a grin and flash of teeth.

Gavin uttered an obscenity that blistered the air. He stood with hands on hips staring at the ground like it had just occurred to him that he was actually married.

Welcome to my world, dude. Now run around Las Vegas without your panties and tell me how you feel after that.

Jack tipped his head in Luann's direction.

She reciprocated. Evidentially they were calling this round a draw.

"I need a moment to confer with my client." Luanne took Scarlett by the arm and ushered her toward the front door. "Make yourselves at home. The porch swing is very

23

comfortable." She waved her hand in the direction of the swing. "Water's in the mini fridge over there."

Both men gawked, and Scarlett stifled a ridiculous giggle. Anyone who mistook Luanne's elfin features and extravagant style as a sign of weakness would be sorry. Honestly? She was sort of scary.

Without waiting, Luanne took Scarlett by the arm, shoved her back through the front door, and closed it soundly behind them.

***

Gavin hadn't been able to look away from Scarlett. She was all buttoned-up good girl on the outside, but he'd experienced the wildness within her. She was a puzzle he wanted to solve, and it screwed with his determination to get her out of his life as soon as possible.

Jack chuckled. "That Luanne's a pocket-sized spitfire, isn't she?"

Leave it to Jack to view what happened between him and Luanne as entertainment.

Gavin shrugged. "I guess."

Jack loosened his tie and unbuttoned the top of his shirt. "Damn, it's hot out here. I need to make some phone calls, and I have a feeling those two are going to take longer than a moment to confer. They're probably doing each other's hair, painting their nails, and plotting how to take all your money."

"You think?" Great, just what he needed. Something else to worry about in this increasingly fucked-up situation.

"I have no idea. They both seem a bit unpredictable." With a shake of his head and another chuckle, Jack sauntered away. "I'll be in the car with the air-conditioning. Let me know when Thelma and Louise emerge."

***

"Holy freakin' shit," Luanne shrieked. "That's Gavin Bain. Is he smokin' hot or what? I wanted to take a big ol' bite." She twisted to peek out of the blinds.

Scarlett would have laughed if her life weren't circling the toilet. "Yeah, he's pretty good-looking." Even to her own ears she sounded less than enthused.

Luanne turned from the window and gave Scarlett an appraising look. "You, on the other hand, look like crap."

"Makes sense, 'cause that's how I feel." Luanne's image wavered a bit as tears pooled in her eyes, and she swallowed a Texas-sized lump in her throat. She'd never been so happy to see anyone in her whole life. "How did you know I needed you?"

"I had the TV on in my office and saw the report on Hollywood News. You know I love that show. Shay Wallace is my favorite. It's embarrassing. I'm such a fangirl—"

"Luanne. Don't make me hurt you."

Luanne cleared her throat. "I caught a glimpse of the dress the woman wore and knew it was you. Remember? I was with you when you bought it, *and* I recognized your cowboy boots. By the way, those boots make your legs look a-maz-ing."

Scarlett brightened. "I know, right?"

"So, I picked up the phone to call you, but before I could, Mandy, my secretary, who is Becky Koontz's sister...you remember Becky? She works at the Stop-n-Shop." Luanne sat down on the arm of the nearest chair and slipped off one of her Jimmy Choos to inspect it. "Well, Becky called Mandy who called me to say that a good-looking man in a fancy suit—that's a matter of opinion—and another guy who looked a lot like Gavin Bain came into the Stop-n-Shop to buy gas. They also asked how to get to the Kelly farm." Luanne returned the shoe to her petite foot and stood to smooth her skirt into place. "I put two and two together and deduced that my best friend was in deep doo-doo. You want to tell me what the hell is going on?"

"No." How could she explain something she didn't even understand?

Luanne arched a perfectly sculpted black brow. "Try again."

"Okay, fine." Scarlett flopped onto the nearest chair like a petulant child.

"Get a grip and grow up, Scarlett. Your rock star husband is out there, and he isn't going away, which means you need my help. Also, if you haven't told *me* about any of this, I know you haven't told your father. He's not home?"

"No." She dropped her gaze. Her insides petrified when she thought of the conversation she was going to have to have with her father.

Luanne glanced around the room and whispered, "Where's Honey?"

"Napping, so there's no need to whisper. You know once she's asleep a nuclear bomb wouldn't wake her."

"Why didn't you tell me, Scarlett?"

The hurt in Luanne's voice made Scarlett look up. "I'm sorry. I don't know why I didn't tell you. I guess I thought if I didn't tell anyone then it wouldn't be true." She picked up a throw pillow and hugged it to her chest. "It's so embarrassing. I got drunk and got married in Las Vegas, Luanne. I'm such a cliché."

"I forgive you. And you're not a cliché. Don't talk about my friend that way."

Scarlett smiled and wiped her wet lashes with the back of her hand. "Thank you."

Luanne removed her suit jacket and laid it on the back of the chair. "Alright, now tell me what the hell happened. I thought the big news would be your TV deal with Carousel, not your marriage to Gavin Bain."

"Yeah, well, so did I." She picked at the fringe on the pillow. The dejection she'd kept at bay, since her meeting in Vegas, wrapped itself around her like fog on a cool, wet morning.

"You got drunk?"

"As Cooter Brown."

"I've only seen you drink one glass of wine maybe a handful of times." Her fist went to her hips. "Again, what the hell happened?"

"When I walked into the meeting another author named Sarah Belle was sitting at the table. Carousel informed me they loved my books and Fiona, but they want her more street-smart. They said Sarah's characters are too edgy, and they want her to soften them up some. They've given us two months to revamp our concepts, then they'll choose between the two of us."

"Like a contest?"

"Sort of."

"Bastards."

"Totally."

Luanne paced in front of Scarlett. "So...what? You decided to drink your troubles away?"

"Not exactly."

"What exactly?"

"As soon as that awful meeting was over I couldn't get out of the room fast enough. I was so mad and upset."

"Understandable."

Scarlett blew her bangs from her eyes. She could feel the heat crawling up her neck. "I left so fast I forgot my sweater. I ran back to the room to retrieve it."

She fought the urge to cover her face. Humiliation smothered her at their remembered words. "They were laughing. I could hear Sarah's laughter above all the men even before I got to the room." A deep breath in and a long breath out. "One of the men said I was the most repressed, uptight, frigid woman he'd ever met, a real No-Fun-Nun. I should have stopped when I heard him, but I was

27

practically in the room. I crossed the threshold just as Sarah said I needed a stiff drink and to get laid."

"What did you do?"

"I stood there with my mouth hanging open and my face probably the color of a stop sign, looking as pathetic as they thought I was. After several long seconds, Sarah giggled and said, 'Oops, sorry.'"

Luanne's features turned to stone. "That bitch."

"Yes, she is." She could count on Luanne to always be on her side.

"So how did Gavin get involved?"

"I got my sweater and ran to the bar at the Bellagio. They were right about one thing. I did need a stiff drink. I'd barely sat down when I heard this guy ask if he could buy me a drink." She shivered at the memory of Gavin's warm lips at her ear. "I turned to politely decline and about swallowed my tongue."

"I'd like to swallow *his* tongue."

"Really, Lou?"

"I'm sorry. You're right." Luanne fanned her face, then covered her mouth with one hand. "That was completely inappropriate for the moment. Please continue."

"Anyway, with *Scarlett, the No-Fun-Nun* still ringin' in my ears and this gorgeous man in front of me." She shrugged. "I let him buy me a drink. I mean, would an outrageously sexy rock star want to buy a sexually repressed woman a drink? No. He wouldn't. So...I said yes."

He'd ordered her an apple martini and a whiskey for himself. She knew good girls didn't talk to strangers, but she moved to a dark corner booth with him anyway. Over the next hour, they talked, laughed, and unfortunately, drank a lot.

Fueled by apple martini courage, she'd kissed him. It was a life-altering kiss. When he kissed her back, she was lost, totally and completely lost. Her sensibly constructed, meticulous world popped like champagne bubbles on New Year's Eve.

She gently touched her lips. That kiss had been the beginning of the end for her.

"Okay, I get that. But how did you get from, *Can I buy you a drink* to *Let's get married?*"

Scarlett looked away and chewed her bottom lip. "I told him I would only have sex with my husband."

She braced herself for her friend's response, but nothing came out of her mouth. She'd done the impossible—struck her sassy friend speechless.

"Oh, Lou, I know! It's insane." She cringed when she remembered him leading her out of the casino. "Did it occur to me to ask him if he was off his meds? No. Did I say *I can't marry you?* Not one time. I didn't even bother to state the blatantly obvious. *I DON'T KNOW YOU!* I didn't do any of that. Noooo, I said, *Okay*, and trailed behind him like a happy puppy."

Luanne held up her hands. "Wait. It was his idea to get married?"

"Yes."

"Shut up."

"I know." Scarlett bit the inside of her cheek to keep from smiling. Because as messed up as this whole thing was, there was something dream-worthy about a rock star dragging her off to get married.

"And then you got a tattoo?" Luanne couldn't quite hide her incredulity.

"Evidently." She readjusted her position to take the pressure off the inked side of her bottom.

"The news report said someone saw you running from the hotel."

"Yes, and I didn't stop running until I got onto the plane. Sadly, the humiliation continued."

"What happened on the plane?"

"I went to the bathroom because the right side of my behind was hurting. I thought maybe I'd hit it during my escape."

Luanne pressed her lips together but not before Scarlett saw her grin. "What'd you do?"

"The lavatory was so small I had to contort my body around to see my backside. About the time I lowered my yoga pants and saw *Gavin* written as big as Dallas on my butt cheek, the plane hit a pocket of turbulence. I screamed and was slammed against the door at the same time."

She rubbed her temples. Wished she could dislodge the memory. "It was just the last straw, you know? I pretty much lost my mind. I kept screamin' and cryin', and the next thing I know a man is banging on the door. He demanded I open up or he was coming in after me. Before I could get myself together and pull my pants up, the door flies open, and an air marshal is standing there with a .357 Sig aimed at me. Nothing says your life has veered off track quite like that."

"Are you shitting me?"

She tried for a reassuring smile. "It all worked out. He was actually very nice, all things considered. I told him what had happened, and he let me go back to my seat. I don't think he knew what to do with me. I doubt he'd had much training in runaway brides who discover unknown tattoos at thirty thousand feet."

Luanne's eyeballs nearly bugged out of her head. "Holy shit...just...holy shit." She started to say something else then stopped. She furrowed her brow and ran dainty fingers through her short raven hair. "I wonder how Gavin found you so fast."

"My underwear." The pillow she clung to absorbed the words but not the mortification.

"What? I didn't hear you."

"My underwear." She didn't know she could actually speak without moving her lips.

"You're unaware? Huh?"

"MY UNDERWEAR!" She pulled the wadded up white cotton material from her pocket and stretched the waistband between two fingers, the black lettering proclaiming their owner. "I left them in his hotel room."

"You wrote your name in your underwear?" Luanne snorted. "Why would you do that? You're twenty-five years old, for cripes' sake."

"I wore them on the church retreat last month, and I didn't want to lose them."

The look on Luanne's face screamed disbelief.

"They were new." She silently begged her friend to understand.

Luanne lowered her head while pinching the bridge of her nose. Her shoulders shook with silent laughter which gave way to huge guffaws. "Let me get this straight. You seduced Gavin Bain, the bad boy of rock-n-roll and sex on a stick, wearing underwear you wore to a church retreat. Isn't that sacrilegious? I mean, isn't there a commandment that says, *Thou shalt not seduce rock stars while wearing your Sunday undies?*" She howled with laughter.

"Luanne, I..." All the stress, all the shame, all the sheer ridiculousness of the entire situation avalanched down on her. She was married. To a rock star she barely knew. And she'd done it wearing big mama panties. Giggles escaped her clenched jaw. Once the dam broke, there was no holding it back. She laughed until her sides hurt, and tears streamed down her face.

"I love you, Luanne." She wiped her cheeks with the sleeve of her shirt. "Today has been just horrible, and you've made it a lot more bearable. Thanks."

"You're welcome."

"So what do we do now?"

Luanne held up her finger. "Keep your panties on and let me think." There was a beat of silence and then they were laughing again.

***

Gavin put both hands on the porch rail and took several minutes to absorb his environment. Jack was in the air-conditioned car, gesturing excitedly and talking on the phone. Annoyance at his friend made him grip the railing so hard he nearly broke the wood.

Damn attorneys. They were ridiculous. It was like watching a prequel to murder…or foreplay. The only thing they were worried about was who had the biggest package. His money was on Luanne. She was a tiny thing, only a buck five soaking wet, but he'd bet ten pounds of that was her balls.

He stepped off the porch and made his way to the car for the only thing that gave him comfort when his world spiraled out of control—Patsy, his guitar.

Johnny called her a giant pacifier. He smiled at the memory.

Patsy had been a constant companion for fourteen years, his most prized possession. The best $87.50 he'd spent in his whole life. He'd written his first song with her, played her for tips when he was living on the street. When they recorded their first album, it was Patsy he'd slung across his chest and made some of the best music of his life. After Johnny died, he'd wrapped his body around her to stop the agony. She'd been with him through the best and the worst times of his life.

He glanced back at the house and thought of Scarlett Kelly Bain. Best or worst?

Only time would tell.

***

"How long have they been here?" Luanne said.

Scarlett picked at a hangnail and made it bleed. She pushed down on the wound with her other hand and glanced up at her friend. "They ambushed me twenty minutes ago." She saw Luanne covertly peeking out the window again. "Luanne, I'm in trouble here. Will you stop ogling him? Tell me what to do."

Luanne turned from the window and didn't even have the decency to look embarrassed. "He has a guitar," she whispered. "Where do you think he got a guitar?" She turned back to the window and sighed.

She actually sighed.

"He probably brought it with him." She pressed hard on the still bleeding cuticle. "He told me..." She stopped as another lost memory hit her square in the face.

"I grew up in the system, so I never had a pot to piss in. The first guitar I ever bought was the only thing I owned for...well, forever. I worked my ass off, roofing houses to get the money to buy her. Her name's Patsy," he'd said, affection coating his voice. "I have more expensive guitars, but I keep Patsy with me all the time. I never go anywhere without her."

"He told me he never goes anywhere without the guitar."

Her heart stuttered. Gavin was someone she could like.

***

Gavin made his way to the swing hanging at the end of the wide front porch. He lowered himself onto it with Patsy on his lap. This place was like something out of a Hallmark movie he'd happened upon while channel surfing in a hotel room.

It had white clapboard siding, sturdy round columns, and pitch black shutters. A fat, lazy tomcat stretched out on a lounge at the other end of the porch. The heat made the air shimmer, but there were ceiling fans, and with the breeze it was tolerable. The only thing missing was Granny hand-churning ice cream.

He rocked back and forth while softly strumming the guitar. The smell of fresh-cut grass floated on the air and locusts rattled in the distance. A horse whinny and a couple of mooing cows from the pasture behind the house added to the sense of peace that settled over him. He liked it here. This place was a real home.

A tree house rested in the branches of a huge tree in the side yard, and in the distance, he could see a small pond. It was a great place for a kid to grow up. That thought led him to check his phone for a message from the private investigator.

Nothing.

His was strangely unconcerned about the estrogen party taking place within the house, probably because he had a bigger issue to deal with. The marriage could be resolved by signing some papers and throwing some money at the problem. The thing with Tara and the baby wouldn't be so easy to take care of.

The melody from his guitar mixed with the summer sounds. His fingers danced along the neck of the instrument. Lost in the music, he let go of everything and played. The more he emptied his mind and fed off the peace of this place, the more in sync he was with the notes pouring through his hands. His breath hitched and he toed the wood porch to stop the swing. Was there more?

Sweat that had nothing to do with the heat rolled down his back. His heart faltered as he plucked a few more chords. Patsy was singing. He thought he might never hear her like this again. Seventeen months. It had been a year and a half since he'd written anything. Why now? Why here?

Needing to capture the song, he pulled his phone from his pocket. The picture of Scarlett and him kissing came up as soon as he pressed the power button. Was she linked to this? He swiped the screen and thumbed on his recording app.

Tired of his own thoughts, he turned off his brain and played.

***

Scarlett closed her eyes and listened to the music coming from the porch. It was her favorite Wolfe's Bain song, a ballad that never failed to break her heart. Then the familiar song morphed into one she'd never heard before. The music wrapped around her, tugging her toward him.

Get a hold of yourself, Scarlett.

She needed to focus. "Where's the lawyer?"

"That asswipe's sitting in the car. He's on the phone, no doubt insulting half the free world with his bullshit." The blinds clicked as Luanne let them fall back into place. "Okay, tell me what you want."

"You have to ask? I want a divorce, and I want him gone." That sounded so final. She ignored the tiny hiccup beneath her breast bone. It was for the best.

"Are you sure you don't want to keep him? He's sooo pretty."

Gavin wasn't pretty. She could have ignored pretty. But the sexy, thrilling, sentimental, beautifully dangerous man on the front porch was impossible to ignore. He called to her inner wild child and begged her to come and play. Even now, she could feel the little beast rattle her cage trying to get free while the humiliation of her previous escape was plastered all over the television and the internet. And her playmate sang songs on her front porch. That was not acceptable.

"He's got to go."

Luanne stared at her for a moment then nodded. "Okay. I can do that. But just one thing before we go."

"What?"

Luanne rubbed her hands together. "Let me see that tattoo."

***

Gavin finished the song and stowed his phone away. The swing swayed as he slumped against it. His eyes stung like he was about to cry. What a pussy. Before he could embarrass himself, Jack appeared, cell phone in hand. "Gavin, we've got to talk."

"What is it?"

"I just got off the line with the guys at Storm Side records, and they are not happy." Jack pulled up a patio chair and dusted dried leaves out of the seat.

"Why?"

"Well, Gavin, let's recap." He began ticking off items on his fingers. "You met a woman in a bar. Four hours later you married her in a Las Vegas wedding chapel. Ten hours later she's seen running from your hotel in a panic. And thirty-six hours later it's plastered all over the media. Does that ring any bells?"

"What the fuck do they care? I didn't marry any of them."

"Gavin, they see this as an indication of a pattern of behavior. You have a reputation for being impulsive and making bad decisions that lead to negative consequences. They are not excited about investing time and money into an artist who may piss it all away."

"That's ridiculous. A quickie marriage in Vegas doesn't have one damn thing to do with my ability to make music. I mean, it's easy enough to fix, right? We sign some papers and it all goes away."

"That's not the point." Jack gave him an *are you really that stupid?* look.

"Why don't you tell me the point, then?"

"I assured them you'd grown up and learned from your mistakes. A week later you're all over the news with a runaway bride you barely know." Jack reached over to the mini fridge and grabbed a bottle of water. He took a long pull and looked at Gavin. "I'm worried they're going to withdraw their offer."

"What? You've got to be shittin' me." Gavin fiddled with the gold wedding band. He didn't know why he was still wearing it, but he was.

"I'm absolutely serious."

Gavin squashed the impulse to tell them all to go to hell, that he'd do what he wanted when he wanted. If it were only that simple, but Johnny's letter changed everything. He draped his arm over his guitar. "What do I do, man? I mean, I can't undo it, and it's not like I can stay married and sell this as a legit marriage."

Jack stared at him. "Why can't you stay married? There's no law against it. It would solve your problem with Storm Side and go a long way toward redeeming your public image."

"Dude, are you crazy? First of all, you've completely lost it if you think she'll agree to this. Have you seen how skittish she is? Second, what makes you think I'd go along with it? I mean, I don't want a wife. You know I have a lot of shit going on in my life right now." He laid Patsy in his lap and ran his fingers through his messy hair.

"Gavin, when you and I first discussed a comeback, you were on a mission. You knew exactly what you wanted, and how you wanted to get it. I don't think that's changed."

No, the goal hadn't changed. He needed gainful employment, and the only thing he knew how to do was make music.

"Maybe if we offer her money she'll agree." Jack's shark's gaze narrowed in calculation.

The firecracker who said she didn't want a damn thing from them and accepted total responsibility for this mess. Not a chance in hell. "She'll never go for it, she has too much integrity."

"Everyone has a price, Gavin. Let me handle it."

"Alright, but you might want to dial back the intimidation. They don't respond well to being bullied."

Jack feigned innocence. "I'm a regular pussy cat."

Gavin snorted. "Yea, you're a real prince."

"Don't worry. We've got this." Jack slapped Gavin's knee and gave him a cocky grin.

Gavin glanced at the front door of the house and chewed his bottom lip. It was likely the only thing they would get from these two women were their asses on a platter.

Chapter 4

"Are you out of your mind?" The words exploded from Scarlett's mouth.

"No, Scarlett, I am quite serious." Jack's voice was annoyingly calm.

They'd moved the impromptu arbitration to her home, about four hundred yards up the drive from the big house. Still on the property, but far enough away that she had some privacy.

The honeysuckle and lemon scents of her small, cozy gingerbread house on the water failed to sooth her as they always did. She loved this place with its eclectic décor and comfy reading nooks. It was her safe place, where she retreated from the world. Resentment burned through her at having her sanctuary invaded by these two men. Her home. Her space. Her life.

"You want us to stay married?"

Jack nodded. "It's in my client's best interest if this marriage appears as a legitimate union. His reputation is negatively impacted if the public believes the wedding was an impulsive, drunken mistake."

"That's exactly what it was!" Didn't this idiot understand anything? The urge to pound her head against the wall overwhelmed her, but she wouldn't give this guy the satisfaction. A better idea would be to smash *his* head against the wall. That violent thought should have soothed her, but he kept talking.

"Scarlett, nothing can be accomplished if you continue with these emotional outbursts. If you can compose yourself, I'll explain." Jack moved to the table where his briefcase lay.

Luanne rubbed tiny circles on Scarlett's back. "Take a breath, sweetie, and try to calm down."

Scarlett whirled on Luanne. "You think this is a good idea?"

"No. I told you I would get you out of this. However, Mr. Avery does have a point. For me to successfully navigate you through these waters, you will need to stay calm."

"Well said, Ms. Price." Jack had the nerve to smile.

Luanne shot him a withering look. "Zip it, Counselor, we are not on the same side. I think your idea sucks balls, but I'm willing to hear you out. It's in Scarlett's best interest for me to have all the information."

Gavin leaned forward in his seat with his elbows on his knees. He hung his head and hissed. "This is such a shit storm, fu—"

"Oh. My. Gosh." Scarlett directed her fiery words at Gavin. "Do you have to use such filthy language? Seriously, you have to be more imaginative than that." She seethed at the use of the "F" word. To her, people who used it were intellectually lazy.

His *Delinquent* stare drilled into her. "I'm sorry, princess. Have I offended your delicate sensibilities? Maybe you should have thought about that before you married me."

"Gavin," Jack rebuked.

Gavin flipped him off and slumped back onto the couch.

Anger swirled and gathered at her vocal chords. She opened her mouth to give a scathing retort, then closed her mouth. Luanne was right, she needed to be calm and get control of her anger. With a Herculean effort, she schooled her expression and turned to Luanne. "I'll listen to what he has to say, and then I want them both to leave."

"Okay." Luanne looked at Jack. "Mr. Avery."

"We are in the process of securing a recording contract for Gavin with Storm Side Records. This marriage comes at a precarious time in the negotiations. In the past, Gavin's had a reputation for reckless behavior and the events of the night before last have not improved that perception. If the executives at Storm Side believe Scarlett and Gavin married after a brief courtship and with genuine affection that would go a long way in quelling any misgivings they may have about Gavin's reliability."

Luanne cleared her throat. "Mr. Avery, I sympathize with Mr. Bain's plight, I do." She put her hand to her chest in the universal sign for *my heart goes out to you*. "That being said, my client should not be expected, nor is she obligated, to participate in the rehabilitation of his image. Mrs. Bain is not interested in remaining married to your client." She looked at Scarlett for confirmation and Scarlett nodded. "We will be seeking a divorce as soon as possible."

Scarlett couldn't believe this was happening. Movement from the other side of the room caught her eye. Gavin leaned his head against the back of the sofa with his hands over his face. He dragged them down to rest on his chest and stared at the ceiling. A fist squeezed her heart. He was all alone. He needed her. Unconsciously, she took a small step toward him but, thankfully, regained her senses before her foot hit the ground. He wasn't her problem, a truth she'd do well to remember.

Jack shoved his rolled cuffs up his arm. "Mr. Bain will not give his wife a divorce."

"Mr. Bain won't have a choice. He can't stop Scarlett from filing for, and being granted, a divorce."

"Maybe not, but we can tie it up in the courts and make it as expensive and painful as possible for your client."

"To what end, Counselor? When all is said and done, your client's image will be damaged, and my client will be divorced. Also, I'm sure the media would love to hear what

Mr. Bain has put this poor woman through when all she wants is her life back."

Luanne's words faded into a rhythmic drone of legalese as Scarlett's heartbeat pulsed in her ears. It drowned out everything but a high-pitched squeal that could quite possibly be signaling an aneurysm.

No time to dwell on an impending stroke. There was a bigger problem to deal with.

Her daddy was home.

***

Gavin was hyper aware of Scarlett. So he knew the moment she moved toward the front door and slipped out.

Oh, hell no. You're not getting away this time.

Surely the lawyers would call her back, but they were too invested in their argument. Screw it, he'd go after her. He marched out onto the porch.

Her yellow skirt swayed as she strode away from another confrontation. "I can't believe you're running again."

Gravel crunched under her feet as she spun to face him. She shaded her eyes from the sun. "I'm not *running* anywhere, Gavin. I need to talk to my father."

He made his way toward her. The Texas sun made him squint and wish for his Ray-Bans. "You and I are the ones who need to talk."

"There's nothing to say."

"I want to talk to you about staying married."

"You're wasting your time. It's a ridiculous scheme, and I won't participate."

He shook his head and brushed a hand over the back of his neck. "You know, Scarlett, I'm still kind of choked up from the speech you made earlier. The one where you apologized for running and said you'd do whatever you had to do to make this right. Well, staying married would make it right."

Her hands went to her waist, and steel daggers shot from her eyes. Why did he find that so adorable? He seriously needed to have his head examined. He didn't do complicated, highly emotional women, but this fiery redhead had him reconsidering that stance.

She crossed her arms and popped her hip. "I meant I'd give you a quick divorce."

"I don't want a divorce."

"You're insane."

"Probably, but I want to stay married."

"No." *Step.*

"Yes." *Step.*

"No." *Step.*

They were nose to nose. Both were breathing harder than was necessary. Gavin lifted his hand and ran his index finger lightly over the bruise on Scarlett's cheek. Raw desire flared, scorched, and tore up his arm. "Does this hurt?"

"Not too much," she whispered.

"I hate that I caused this."

"S'okay."

He continued to gently stroke her cheek. She allowed it for several long heartbeats. But Gavin saw the exact moment when the spell broke. Her black brows furrowed over her lids and she took a few stumbling steps back. "You're such a pig."

"What'd I do?"

"You can't seduce me into going along with this ridiculous plan. I'm not changing my mind."

"What? That's not what I was doing."

"Sure it wasn't. I'm filing for divorce in the morning." She turned and made her way down the path that led to her father's house.

His pounding heart rattled his ribs. Desperation had him by the balls. Fear shoved words from his throat. "I'll pay you." They were out and there was no calling them back.

Everything stopped. The birds didn't sing, the cows didn't moo, Scarlett stopped dead in her tracks. She slowly turned to face him, like a gunslinger in an old western. Cue the tumbleweeds. "What did you say?"

The glare she gave him made him briefly reconsider repeating himself, but at this point, he had nothing to lose. "I said I'll pay you. Name your price." The disdain in her eyes made his gut hurt.

She stayed mute. But her ocean-blue eyes, now the color of rough seas, said a thousand things—none of them good. The pain in his gut migrated to his chest.

He needed to grow a pair. This wasn't the time to puss out. "Scarlett, did you hear me? I said I'll pay you to stay married to me."

"I heard you." She turned and marched away.

"Scarlett."

She never slowed down. The last thing he saw before his Sunday-school-teacher wife disappeared behind a crop of trees was her delicate hand as it shot into the air and flipped him the bird.

***

Scarlett stomped up the path to her father's house. "Pay me. He wants to pay me. I shouldn't have flipped him off. I should have turned around and said it to his face. Unbelievable, who does he think I am? *What* does he think I am?" she muttered. Her anger escalating with each step.

She stopped outside the barn when her phone rang. Crap, her agent.

"Hello, Marie."

"Scarlett Kelly, or should I say Scarlett Kelly Bain, you've been keeping secrets," Marie cooed.

Scarlett's legs nearly went out from under her. She gripped the phone, praying she'd misunderstood Marie. "What did you say?"

"Now don't play coy with me. It's all over the news."

"Th...the news?" She dropped down on the side of the horse trough.

"Well, not the world news, but it is all over entertainment news. They're calling you the *Renegade Bride*. Isn't that adorable? You know, to go with The Delinquent? I can't believe you didn't tell me."

A tear slid down Scarlett's cheek. Along with any hope this would all go away quietly. She brushed it away with the back of her hand. "We were trying to keep it private." She bit her bottom lip and blinked furiously.

Marie laughed. "If you wanted to keep it private, you shouldn't have gotten married in Vegas."

"Well, if that's all you called about, Marie, I need to go. Thank—"

"No, that's not the only reason I'm calling. Your identity was revealed an hour and a half ago, and since then I've taken calls from two of the largest children's publishers in the country. They're very interested in your books. I also received a call from Richard Graves, the Carousel Network's bigwig. He wanted to confirm the rumor."

"Was he upset?" She hadn't even thought about how this marriage could affect her relationship with Carousel.

"On the contrary, he seemed quite intrigued. I don't know if you're aware, Scarlett—and I only say this because I love you—but you're a tad bit uptight, dear. It can be off-putting. And I'm afraid—again because I love you—people might find you a teeny bit boring."

"I'm not—"

"But marrying a rock star in Las Vegas is the exact opposite of prim and proper, you naughty girl. Now, hopefully, they will reconsider this ridiculous contest between you and Sarah Belle."

Scarlett struggled for words, picking one then discarding it for another. How was she supposed to respond to that? "Marie, I'm going to need to call you back. Ah…Gavin needs me."

Marie gave a throaty laugh that reminded Scarlett of a bordello madam.

"Okay…well, bye." She couldn't get Marie off the phone fast enough.

"Bye-bye, Renegade Bride."

Scarlett hung up on Marie's delighted chortle. Boring? Since when was decorum and good manners boring?

She was suddenly bone weary. Nobody understood the energy it took to maintain her propriety. Constantly fighting against her mother's reputation, the town's expectations and her own inner wild child was exhausting.

Those vultures didn't care about her or her books. They were only interested in capitalizing on the publicity this insane marriage generated. She stomped up the back steps of the house, gripped the handle of the screen door and jerked it open. It banged behind her, causing Honey to drop a soapy plate into the dishwater.

Her aunt turned from the sink, her veined hand covered her heart. "Good-night, Scarlett, you scared the livin' daylights out of me."

Scarlett went to the older woman and wrapped her in a hug. "I'm so sorry. I guess I don't know my own strength." It was a lame attempt to cover her irritation.

The warm arms that enveloped her helped to chase away the memory of Gavin's proposal and Marie's call. She sniffed in her aunt's Jungle Gardenia scent then kissed her plump cheek. "I heard daddy's truck. Is he in the barn?"

"No darlin', he's in his study." Honey placed her soft hands on Scarlett's face and lifted it to the light. "Baby, you don't look well." She moved one hand to Scarlett's forehead. "You don't feel feverish, but maybe I should rub some Vicks on your feet tonight before you go to bed."

Scarlett smiled a real smile and stepped away from the comfort of the warm embrace. "I don't think Vicks is going to cure what's ailing me, but thank you." With that cryptic statement, she went in search of her father.

Her life flashed before her eyes. Moments caught on film hung on both sides of the hall. Humperdink, Honey's cat, wound his way around her legs. She bent to scratch behind his ears. "Are you going to be my back-up, Humperdink? I could sure use one."

Bile burned her throat at the sound of her dad's voice. The dread of confessing her recklessness in Vegas made her muscles go limp. Those details weren't anything a father wanted to hear, no matter how much he loved his daughter. Especially when that daughter had a mother like hers.

Her mother—she would've *loved* this whole situation, every sordid detail. Drama had been Mary Kelly's middle name. She'd been the talk of Zachsville, and not in a good way.

Like mother, like daughter?

Not if she could help it.

From the kitchen, Humperdink's food clattered into a bowl, and in an instant, she was alone in the hall. So much for backup. She'd been dumped for Kitty Boodle.

She stood outside the partially ajar study door, and summoned her courage. She raised her hand to knock but stopped dead at the sound of her father's voice.

"Poppy, this is Floyd Kelly. Honey told me you called. How's your daddy enjoying his retirement?"

After a moment, he chuckled. "I bet he is drivin' your mama crazy. So, what can I do for you, Poppy?"

Poppy Sims, Zachsville's golden girl, had recently moved back to run the local bank. Scarlett hadn't seen her yet. Thank God.

The worst night of her life and the former head cheerleader were forever tied together.

A shudder ran over her body as she remembered being instructed on the finer points of homemade tattoos, in a filthy holding cell. Scarlett could still smell the stale urine while sharing a bench and communal toilet with a gangbanger named Lil Roxie.

Her father's aggressive tone called her back from that terrible night. "What in the hell are you playin' at, Poppy?"

What was happening? It was something bad if her father was cussing. She plastered herself against the wall behind the door and strained to hear over the thundering blood pounding in her ears.

"Yea, I'd say you damn well need to explain."

Explain what?

"Poppy, I've known your daddy for fifty years. He knows I'm good for it. This damn drought's put me a little behind."

Scarlett knew she should leave, but she couldn't make her feet move, especially with her big, rough father practically begging. Now she wasn't even pretending not to listen.

"Yes, I do understand that Hartley isn't runnin' the bank anymore. But how is it possible I have to pay fifty thousand dollars in thirty days, or the bank's gonna take the farm? Poppy, be reasonable. This will ruin me. I'll lose everything."

Scarlett clasped her hand over her mouth to stifle a gasp.

"No, I realize it's not your problem. But that's how we've always done business around here, like neighbors."

"Yea." He breathed out. "I'll be in touch."

The phone clattered to the desk, and she ventured a look through the slit in the door. Floyd Kelly, the strongest person she'd ever known, had his head in his hands, and his shoulders were shaking. With a sense of horror, she realized he was crying.

What should she do? Risk her father's dignity and go to him, or give him privacy and pretend she hadn't overheard his conversation.

In the end, she left him alone. She leaned against the wall and closed her eyes. Fifty thousand dollars? How would they ever come up with that kind of money? It was impossible.

Then her eyes snapped open, and she ran down the hall and out of the house. Once she was outside, she pulled her cell phone from her pocket.

"Scarlett, you didn't ne—"

"Marie, I want to make a deal."

"What kind of deal, sweetie?" Marie practically purred.

"A deal. You know, a deal. Call another network. If Carousel's not interested, then someone else will like all this publicity. I need it finalized in the next thirty days."

"That's not how these things work, Scarlett. These sorts of agreements can take months. Besides, I'm holding out for the best offer. We don't want to appear too eager."

"No. I want you to find a taker today, and I want the money..." She looked at her calendar app and counted thirty days out. "By the twenty-third."

Marie's laughter felt like road rash to her frazzled nerves. "Oh Scarlett, that just can't be done. Don't worry. I've got this under control. I'll be in touch." It was Marie's turn to hang up on her.

She stood there staring into space, her arms limp at her sides and her cell phone grasped loosely in her hands like a deflated life preserver. What was she going to do now?

She chewed on her nail and paced back and forth. Her father didn't have that kind of money and the only hope she had of helping him just evaporated. She stopped. And looked back toward her house.

Or had it?

***

Gavin sat on Scarlett's front porch as a couple of dragonflies flew around her small garden. Guilt weighed on him. He shouldn't have offered the money. He'd known there was no way she was going to accept payment to stay married to him. Even though it meant trouble for him he was pleased she'd turned him down. He smiled when he recalled her dainty hand shooting him the bird. It was nice to know not everyone in the world could be bought.

A bee dive-bombed his face. He swatted at it and saw Scarlett striding toward him. Her expressive face was blank, and it looked like she'd been crying. Guess things hadn't gone well with her dad. He didn't like the idea of someone making her cry.

She stopped directly in front of him. "Fifty thousand dollars, payable immediately."

Disappointment swamped him, but he quickly schooled his features. "You and your old man come up with that number?" Bitterness oozed around each word.

"I didn't talk to him. He doesn't know anything about this, and I never want him to know I took the money from you for this purpose."

He believed her. She was easy to read. "What are your terms?"

"I will stay married to you for three months, and we will live here at the farm. I have no intention of leaving my family for this outlandish scheme."

"One year. I intend to get my money's worth." He looked her up and down. It was a dick move, and he knew it, but damn it, how could he have been so wrong? She was just like everyone else, out for what they could get. People sucked. On the other hand, he was getting what he wanted, so he reined in his anger.

She crossed her arms. "Four months."

"Eight months." He matched her stance.

"Six months. Final offer."

He nodded. "Deal."

She blinked back tears.

"It won't be that bad, Scarlett. If everything goes as planned, I'll be back in L.A. in a few weeks to start recording. We'll be seen together in public smiling and happy for the paparazzi. You'll make a trip to see me, I'll come to see you, then...we'll drift apart. Everyone knows how hard a musician's life can be for a relationship, so the record company won't be surprised when we divorce and go our separate ways."

She didn't say anything, only nodded.

He glanced around the farm. "The good news is there are two houses, so you can stay at your dad's, and I'll stay here. Technically we won't be living together."

All the color drained from her face. She raised her head, her blue irises stark against the paleness of her face. She dropped down onto the porch step. "We'll have to live together."

"Why?"

"Honey."

"What?"

"My aunt Molly Jean lives in the house with my daddy. She can't hold water."

When she looked up, the confusion must have shown on his face because she translated. "She can't keep a secret."

"Even if we ask her not to tell?" He made a note to buy a *hick-to-English* dictionary ASAP.

"Oh, she won't mean to tell, but yeah, we can't trust her to keep this to herself. Daddy says if the terrorists, North Koreans or Russians want to know all our national secrets they should kidnap Honey because she'd tell them everything they wanted to know. Like, who was sneaking out of Grace Holcomb's house at three in the morning, why the Abernathy's youngest really went to live in Canada, and what caused the food poisoning at the Methodist pot luck last month."

"I get it, she can't keep a secret." He stood and leaned his butt against the porch rail and crossed his arms.

"Not if her life depended on it. Oh, and there is also Joyce and Brody."

"Who are Joyce and Brody?" His head began to throb.

"Joyce is our housekeeper. They live in the big house too. She takes care of Daddy and Honey. Brody's her fifteen-year-old son. Monday is Joyce's day off and Brody's still at school. They could keep a secret, but it's a moot point because of the Honey factor."

It was like a damn chicken-fried commune. "Fine, I'll stay here."

He examined the dark circles under her eyes and knew his own looked the same. They'd both been through the wringer. Sympathy warred with contempt. His feelings toward her were so confused. He exhaled and extended his hand. "Six months."

She took his hand. "Fifty thousand dollars."

He pulled her to her feet. "Let's go tell the vampires."

Chapter 5

Gavin rubbed dry, scratchy eyes. Barely blinking for an hour had taken its toll.

Scarlett was still a flight risk, so during their interaction with the attorneys he'd kept his gaze glued on her like the warden at a women's penitentiary.

Dirty thoughts of playing *escaped prisoner and bounty hunter* took root in his brain. Desire rolled over him at the image of frisking Scarlett against a wall. He needed to strap that shit down. Sex in this screwed-up situation was a recipe for disaster.

Damn. Now she was wearing nothing but an apron and a smile.

Stop. Think about baseball or your current marriage contract. That'll kill your sex drive, Bain.

After they'd shared the terms of their agreement with Luanne and Jack, a quick contract was drawn up. Jack left before the ink dried. Luanne lingered for a bit then reluctantly left as well. No doubt she'd be on the phone with Scarlett as soon as possible to find out why her goody-two-shoes best friend agreed to this deal. He'd like to know the answer to that question himself.

"Well, that's that." He knocked his knuckles on the table.

"Yep." She rubbed her temples. "The money will be deposited into my account tomorrow?"

"Yes."

"Good."

It pissed him off she was so unaffected by the fact that she'd let him buy her. He ignored the voice in his head that called him a hypocrite. Yes, he'd offered her the money, but she didn't have to take it. Stupid.

He'd wanted her to be different.

She wasn't.

Move on.

He slapped his hands on his thighs and rose. "Well, I guess we should go meet your father and Billy Jean."

"Molly Jean," Scarlett said.

"Okay, whatever."

"Not whatever." She jumped to her feet, got right in his face, and punctuated her words with a finger poke. "If this farce is going to work you're going to have to play your part, buddy." *Poke.* "Which means you will remember my relative's names and not get into a fight with my father." *Poke.* "Or anyone else in my family." *Poke.*

He looked down at the finger jabbed into his chest and gently brushed it aside. "I am not going to hit your father. He's got to be what, sixty?"

"He's fifty."

"I don't go around hitting old men, Scarlett."

"Really? Because I distinctly remember an incident in which you punched a sixty-year-old man during an altercation at a coffee shop. I saw it on *Entertainment Tonight.*"

"You can't believe everything you hear or see on TV."

"So, it's not true?"

"Well, yeah, it's true. But that was eight years ago, and if the guy had minded his own business, he wouldn't have gotten hit. I was throwing a punch at the guy in front of me."

"How old was he?"

"I don't know, maybe fifty-five."

She stared at him longer than he thought completely necessary. "Well, clearly you've been misrepresented in the retelling of the dispute." She shook her head, pursed her lips, and did a great impression of a disapproving headmistress. "No wonder they call you The Delinquent."

"He hit me first. What was I supposed to do? Not protect myself?" Why was he defending himself? For some incomprehensible reason, he wanted her to understand. Ridiculous. He didn't explain himself to anyone. There'd only been one person whose opinion mattered to him, and he was dead.

The sound of gunfire interrupted their conversation.

Gavin ducked for cover. "Holy shit, what was that?"

"It sounds like Honey's gun." She went to the window and pulled the curtains back to investigate.

"You recognize the sound of your aunt's gun? Wait. Your aunt has a gun?"

"Yes, she has a handgun, it's a revolver because a semi-automatic is too hard for her to handle. Daddy carries a shotgun with him on the tractor, but that was definitely a handgun, not a shotgun."

"How old is she?"

"Seventy, why?"

"No reason." *Why? She had to ask why?* "Are you packing too?"

"Yes." She repositioned the bun she'd thrown her hair into and turned back to him. His incredulity must have been evident. "Gavin, this is Texas. We have the right to carry concealed. When a Texas child is born, they're given a birth certificate, a social security number, and a gun permit—not necessarily in that order."

When she saw his face, she laughed. "I'm just kidding. We're not that cliché."

Her deep, throaty laugh was infectious, and he laughed too. "Out of curiosity, what kind of gun do you carry?" His pretty little wife packing heat was hot.

"I carry a Springfield XDS, 9mm. It's small, lightweight, and fits nicely in the built-in holster of my purse. Also, the grip safety makes the trigger pull very smooth."

"Of course it does."

"We better go see what happened with my aunt, *Molly Jean.*"

They stepped out onto the porch as Floyd strode into Scarlett's small yard. "You heard Honey?"

"Yes, what was she shootin' at?"

"Reporters."

"What? She didn't hit any of them, did she?" Scarlett stumbled a bit but caught herself on the porch rail.

"No. Evidently, there was a commotion down at the gate, so she took the four-wheeler and went to investigate." He mounted the stairs to the porch and moved past them, tipping his head to Gavin when he passed on his way into the house.

They followed him inside the house. "Daddy, you've got to start hiding the keys to the four-wheeler. She has no business driving that thing."

"Agreed." He removed his cowboy hat and wiped his forehead with a bandana. "Anyhow, once Honey got down to the gate, she told them this was private property, and they needed to stay out. They didn't seem to understand what she meant was, *Stay off this property, or I'll shoot.* But she cleared it up for 'em."

"Where is she now?" Scarlett asked.

"Over at the house startin' supper. You know her, watch TV, read a little, shoot some reporters, and make dinner. All in a day's work."

"Good God, hillbilly gangsters," Gavin whispered. The family being armed hadn't been a consideration when he'd insisted on accompanying Jack to Texas. A laugh stuck in his throat as Scarlett's words about babies getting gun permits came back to him. He had a ridiculous picture of a cherub-faced child with a cigar hanging from its mouth and a gun belt around its tiny waist, a bottle in one holster and a baby-sized semi-automatic in the other.

Floyd set his hat on the coffee table and folded his bandana before putting it in his back pocket. "Scarlett, darlin', you want to tell me why reporters are trying to trespass on my property?" He rolled up one sleeve of his denim shirt and then the other. "Would it have anything to do with this fella?" He jerked a thumb toward Gavin. "Sally Pruitt called to tell me I have a new son-in-law and I'm guessing this is him."

Gavin's pulse stuttered when the older man leveled a glare at him. Clearly, Luanne wasn't the only person who'd happily castrate him. He fought the urge to cover his crotch, but shifted slightly to the side to protect the family jewels. The last time he'd been this obsessed with his balls was in middle school. Then, as now, you never knew who might kick you in the nuts for the sheer hell of it.

"You know Sally Pruitt is the biggest gossip in town."

Floyd turned to Scarlett, and his face softened some, but Gavin could see he wanted an answer. Her father didn't say a single word, and she folded like a cheap suit.

"Yes, he is."

What a wuss. It was time he took control of this situation. He looked Floyd in the eye and extended his hand. "Mr. Kelly, I'm Gavin Bain."

A flash of movement was the only warning he had before the older man's fist connected with his jaw, and the lights went out.

***

"Daddy," Scarlett yelled, and dropped to her knees at Gavin's side.

Floyd flexed his fingers, stepped over Gavin's prone body and headed for the kitchen. "He'll be fine, I barely tapped him."

"You knocked him out."

"Only because I knew where to hit him, he'll come around in a minute."

"How do you know?"

"I just do. Stop worryin'."

57

Scarlett lightly slapped Gavin's cheek and his dark stubble tickled her palm. A scar ran from his temple to below his left ear at his hairline. She gently traced over it, feeling the bumps and ridges. Her fingers drifted into his hair, and she cupped his head. The feel of his hair triggered another lost memory.

The lights of the Las Vegas strip barely penetrated the heavily tinted windows of the limousine. Swaddled in the cocoon of the dark limo, she hiked her dress up and straddled his lap. Her fingers tunneled through his soft tawny hair. "I love your hair." She held his head at the perfect angle for a heart-stopping kiss. "Your lips." She made her way to his eyelids and kissed each tenderly. "Your eyes."

He leaned his forehead against hers, holding her face in his hands. "I've never known anyone like you. I could drown in your sweetness."

"Don't worry. I'll save you if you do." And she kissed him again.

She'd sat on his lap—in a dress. Her cheeks flamed. Apparently, when Gavin was around, uninhibited Scarlett took control. This was going to be a long six months. Because the more she was with him, the harder it was to remember why that kind of behavior was inappropriate.

Ice clattered from the dispenser in the refrigerator door, making her jerk her hand away. She cringed when his head bumped against the floor. Oops.

There was something she needed to say before Gavin woke up. "Daddy, I know you're worried, but I want to assure you this is not me turning into mama."

He dropped some of the ice onto the floor, and it skated under the refrigerator. "We don't talk about your mother."

"But—"

"Scarlett." The way his face closed down let her know the subject was closed.

The tiny fissures in her heart widened at her father's immediate dismissal. It had been like that since the day her mother left. Her wanting, needing, to talk about things, and her father's unwillingness to discuss the subject.

"Where's your mop, Scarlett?"

"In the utility room."

"This floor's wet, so be careful."

The man loved her. She never doubted it. But sometimes she'd catch him watching her like she might spontaneously dance naked in public or do some other irresponsible, Mary Kelly thing, kind of like he was doing now.

He handed her a baggie of ice and placed another on the knuckles of his right hand.

As soon as she placed the bag on Gavin's jaw, he sat straight up, eyes crazed. "Jesus. What the hell happened?"

"Don't take the Lord's name in vain, son. I just welcomed you to the family. Count yourself lucky my shotgun is in the truck." Floyd folded himself onto the sofa and looked at each of them. "Now, you two want to tell me what the Sam Hill's going on?"

Gavin held the ice to his jaw and looked at her. She looked at him, and they had a complete conversation in that split second.

Go ahead, daddy's girl, tell him.

Oh no, pretty-boy, this is your show, you tell him.

You saw him hit me, right?

This was your idea.

He's your father.

You forced me.

Really?

Fine.

"While I was in Las Vegas I met Gavin and…well…it was love at first sight." That was sort of true if you substitute lust for love.

59

"Did ya now?" Floyd leaned back and crossed one leg over the other, resting one booted ankle on his knee.

She sat next to her dad and attempted her best grade-school-photo smile. "Yes."

***

Gavin bit his cheek to keep a straight face. She tried to communicate matrimonial joy, but her appearance was less happy bride and more clown-with-a-knife. Eyes wide and a slightly wild, a gigantic smile combined with smudged mascara and riotous red hair added up to clown on a killing spree.

"Then why am I just now hearing about this, and from Sally Pruitt of all people?" Gavin didn't miss the knife-edge tone in Floyd's voice.

"Well, we...we were—"

"We wanted to tell you together," Gavin interjected.

Scarlett gave him a grateful smile and took her dad's hand. "Yes, we wanted to tell you together."

Her father leaned forward and placed the bag of ice on the coffee table. He looked at them both. "Are you happy?"

"Yes."

"Alright then."

They embraced, and she wiped a tear on his shoulder then pulled back to look into his face, with a genuine smile this time. "I love you, Daddy." Gavin relaxed. He hadn't been sure she could sell the lie.

Floyd extended his hand to Gavin. "Welcome to the family, Gavin."

Gavin flinched. Who could blame him? His jaw hurt like hell. He cautiously took the proffered hand. "Thank you, sir." Floyd's grip of death communicated three words clearly—*watch yourself, son*. It was clear the man knew something wasn't right, he just hadn't figured out what yet.

"Okay." Floyd nodded his head like that was settled. "Now, tell me why Honey's got all those reporters to use for target practice."

"I'm afraid that's my fault. I'm a musician, and I've had some success. The media seem to be interested in the story, must be a slow news day."

Self-deprecating, nice touch.

"Where's Lindsay Lohan when you need her, huh?" Gavin chuckled, and Scarlett laughed hysterically. Not the *oh, that's so funny* hysterical but more, *I'm bat shit crazy* hysterical. She needed to calm the hell down, or her father was going to be more suspicious than he already was.

It was clear Scarlett's father didn't have a clue what Gavin was talking about. Still trying to read his daughter's situation, Floyd turned to Scarlett, and then glanced back at Gavin. His eyebrows arched and his lips pursed when he took in tattooed arms, messy hair, and muted rock star attire for the first time.

"Know anything about horses?" Floyd asked.

"Not a thing." Unease crawled up his back at the wicked gleam in the other man's eyes.

"Well, that's okay. You can learn." Floyd sat up straight and narrowed his eyes. "You aren't planning to take my girl away from her family are you?"

Gavin wasn't, but if he was, he might think twice about it. Floyd Kelly was not a man you messed with. Scarlett said he was fifty, but he didn't look it. Thick brown hair, void of any silver, framed a rugged face, and the right hook and muscled forearms indicated he was in great shape. The only sign of aging was the sun-beaten wrinkles at the corners of his eyes. Those suckers only made his hard-eyed stare more menacing. Gavin had been on the wrong end of that kind of stare before, and he'd put Floyd's up there with the best.

All the menace and wrinkles disappeared when he laid his hand on his daughter's cheek. "You're happy, darlin'?"

She leaned into his touch. "Truly, Daddy, I am." She was good, Gavin almost believed her. Of course, fifty thousand dollars was enough to make anyone happy.

When the two embraced again, Gavin gripped the arm of the chair to keep from sprinting from the room. Watching this scene made him uncomfortable and confused the hell out of him. Floyd had to be hurt to find out about the marriage from someone other than his daughter, so he should be mad or upset. But all Gavin saw was love and acceptance.

He didn't understand parent–child relationships—it was like deciphering a foreign language he knew he should be able to speak but couldn't comprehend. Hell, his dad was no more than a drive-by sperm donor and his mom a drug addict who forgot she had a five-year-old at home, alone. He'd grown up a ward of Washington state, unloved, undisciplined and unimportant.

Envy punched him in the gut so hard he almost doubled over. An old bitterness, like a sleeping dragon, roused and stirred to life.

He'd been such an idiot as a kid. How many times had he watched families and wonder what it'd be like to have one of his own? Or he'd fantasize his mom got clean and came back for him.

His sober mom wouldn't pick her skin until blood-crusted sores appeared, or ignore his existence. She'd be beautiful, with clean, shiny hair, clear skin, and warm, laughing eyes, eyes that looked at him and really saw him. Sometimes he could even imagine her waiting for him when he got home from school with fresh-baked cookies, and she'd ask him how his day had been. They'd talk, do homework, and his life would be pretty close to perfect.

When reality predictably came crashing down, he'd cry like someone had died.

Gavin made a promise right then and there to the stupid little bastard he'd been back then. If Tara's baby was his, he'd move heaven and earth to make sure that when the boy was thirty years old he wouldn't sit around grieving a family that never existed.

Hey, you play the hand you're dealt, man.

Even if it's a crap hand. For him, it was a string of foster families, beatings, a screwed-up system, and weird-ass women who thought he was stud meat by the time he was fifteen. It wasn't pretty, but he'd survived. His best songs came from that well of pain and anger, so it wasn't a total waste.

That's what he told himself, anyway.

He rubbed the dull ache in his chest. It scared the shit out of him. Either he was in cardiac arrest, or he was beginning to wish for things he could never have. He hoped it was a coronary, because that long-forgotten desire for a family had the power to shred his soul. A heart attack would only kill him.

Chapter 6

Scarlett gulped sweet Texas air as she, her husband, and her father made their way to the big house. The crunching of the gravel underfoot helped to ground her. Another deep inhalation and the chaos of her life abated slightly. She clung to the small amount of control she'd gained by *choosing* to participate in this ludicrous plan. Even though she'd been bought and paid for like…don't go there.

Too late.

The smell of body odor and urine permeated the air. The other women she'd been arrested with were keeping to themselves on the other side of the holding cell, leaving her only a tattooed gang-banger for company.

"So, Chica, what you in for?"

"Solicitation".

"You a hoe?"

"No. Lil Roxy, I swear it's all a huge misunderstanding."

"Mmhmm, tell it to the judge, Chica. Tell it to the judge."

Her stomach dropped. The difference between that monumental screw up and this one was this one wasn't going to magically disappear. Everyone everywhere knew her name and what she'd done. Well…almost everyone.

When they stepped into the house, Honey's voice greeted them. "I'm tellin' ya, Birdie, I shot right at that fella. If he hadn't jumped out of the way, he'd be pickin' lead out of his behind for a week." She had the cord of the landline phone stretched across the kitchen while she stirred a pot on the stove.

"No, Birdie, I don't think the reporters are here to do an exposé on the scandal down at the senior center. The

American public doesn't care if we use ink dotters or plastic discs to play bingo. I already told you, I think they're here about Scarlett. Though I don't exactly know why. They kept yellin' her name. Until I started shootin'—then they were just yellin'.'"

Honey looked up when the trio ambled into the kitchen, and her eyes went wide as silver dollars. "Birdie, I'm gonna have to call you back. Why? Because the best lookin' man I've ever seen just strolled into my kitchen. What? Lord, no, it's not Wardell Pritchett." Without saying goodbye, she hung up.

"Well, hello handsome." She crossed her chubby arms over her ample breasts. "I'm wonderin' if you're the reason for all those reporters down by our gate."

"Honey, this is Gavin Bain," Scarlett said.

"Well, it's nice to meet you, Gavin Bain." The older woman gave Gavin a coquettish smile. Then the smile turned to a frown. "Hey, don't I know you? You're the fella who got married in *Lass* Vegas. I saw you on TV. There was a picture of you and your wife…"

Her head jerked to Scarlett. "Scarlett Rose Kelly. Tell me you haven't done this thing."

Honey's outburst caught Scarlett off guard. She knew her aunt would be concerned, but she hadn't anticipated this level of censure. "There's no need to be worried. I know it's sudden, but Gavin and I are very happy."

"Worried? I'm not worried. I'm mad as hops. I can't believe you didn't tell me about this as soon as you got home from your trip. Who else knows?" Her frantic expression darted from Scarlett to Floyd.

The two exchanged a look.

Honey held onto a chair for support. "Am I the last to know?"

"I doubt you're the last to know," Floyd said. "I found out about an hour ago, when Sally Pruitt called."

"Sally Pruitt knew before me?"

Scarlett swallowed her laughter at the horror in Honey's voice.

"Gavin and I wanted to tell y'all together. I never anticipated the media would leak the story before we could do that. I'm sorry." She was appalled at how easily the lies flowed from her mouth.

"You do realize you've deprived me of the juiciest piece of gossip this town's heard since 1998." She lowered herself onto a chair and turned to Gavin. "That's when the homecoming queen bribed the football team with cupcakes to win the crown. And when I say cupcakes, I don't mean cupcakes. Capiche?" She gave him a knowing look.

"Molly Jean, stop bein' so dramatic." Floyd went to inspect the contents of the pot on the stove. When he lifted the lid, scents of garlic and basil floated around the kitchen.

"It's not drama, Floyd." She looked at him with wild eyes. "You don't understand. I won't be able to show my face at the beauty shop ever again. This happened in my own family—my own backyard—and I'm the last to know. I'll be ruined." She dropped her head into her hands.

Scarlett looked at Gavin to judge his reaction to this melodrama. He leaned against the counter smiling at Honey, and her stomach did a forward roll. That smile should come with a warning label. *Caution: Panties may drop at the sight.*

She almost passed out when he strolled over to her aunt to crouch down beside her. "Molly Jean, I'm Gavin, and it's very nice to meet you." He took her liver-spotted hand and kissed it.

She let out an honest to goodness titter. "Call me Honey, everybody does. Except for Floyd, he calls me Molly Jean when he's mad at me, which is most of the time." She gave Floyd a withering look.

"Ok. Honey, how about I take you to the beauty shop tomorrow, and you can introduce me to all the ladies? Would that help?"

She lit up like a kid with the key to the Skittles factory. "That would be perfect."

Scarlett stood stunned. Where had this charming man come from? Since they'd met, Gavin had tried to seduce, intimidate and bribe her, all with varying degrees of success. Watching Honey melt into a puddle made her glad he'd never tried to charm her.

***

This soft, round woman in pink velour and enough blue eye shadow to spackle a wall wasn't the sharp-edged, leather-clad, chain-smoking badass Gavin's mind had created. She was about the cutest thing he'd ever seen, and he never used the word "cute." He was surprised when the need to make things right for her propelled him to her side.

Honey looked over her shoulder. "Scarlett, you didn't give the milk away before he bought the cow, did ya darlin'?"

Scarlett fumbled the glass she was retrieving from the cabinet. "Honey."

Gavin coughed.

Floyd made a choking noise.

"It's a perfectly reasonable question." The older woman was all doe-eyed innocence.

Scarlett's face flamed beet red. All she could do was sputter.

"I want to know if you remembered your raisin'." She regarded Gavin. "I used to tell her all the time, men won't buy the cow if they can get the milk for free."

"Sound advice." His somber tone matched hers.

Honey nodded. "It is." She cut a look to Scarlett. "Girls these days give it away too easily. Now, my girl, she's been raised right, but the fact that she hasn't answered me has me worried. Did you lure her to the dark side with those smoky gray eyes?"

Scarlett slammed the glass onto the counter. "Oh, for heaven's sake. No Honey, there was no milk given until the cow was sufficiently purchased. Happy?"

The older woman sat back in her chair supremely satisfied. "Yes, I am."

Gavin laughed out loud. Damn, this woman was funny. Now he knew where Scarlett got her quirky sense of humor.

Floyd cleared his throat. Evidently, he was done with the cow and milk discussion. "Molly Jean, how many times do I have to tell you, your gun is for self-defense? Not for makin' a point. I swear, Scarlett and I are gonna have to spend all our Sundays visiting you at the women's prison if you're not careful."

"And Gavin."

"Huh?" Floyd asked.

"If I get sent to the women's prison, you, Scarlett *and* Gavin will come to visit me. He's family now. Isn't that right, Gavin?"

Gavin glanced at Scarlett. She suppressed a smile and shrugged, letting him know he was on his own. He pulled up the nearest chair and sat facing Honey. "Ah, sure Honey. If you get sent to prison, I promise to visit you every Sunday." Damn, he hoped she never asked him to do anything illegal. He wasn't sure he'd be able to tell her no.

She placed her plump hand on his cheek. "Such a good boy."

Floyd rolled his eyes, and Scarlett said something from behind the refrigerator door that sounded suspiciously like butt-kisser.

"Yoo-hoo, where is everybody?"

A pretty woman, in her late forties, and a teenaged boy came into the kitchen. "What in the world is going on? Brody and I were mobbed at the gate. I thought someone was going to jump into the back of the truck. It was terrifying."

Brody skidded to a stop. "You're Gavin Bain." His back pack slipped off his shoulder and dropped to the floor. "What...how... You're Gavin Bain."

Joyce glanced from Brody to Gavin. "You know him, Brody?"

Scarlett made her way to Gavin and placed her hand on his shoulder. "Joyce—"

"Scarlettmarriedarockstarin*Lass*Vegas!" Honey shouted.

"What?" Joyce looked around the room. As understanding dawned, a look of utter astonishment washed over her face.

Gavin braced himself for the next round of craziness that seemed to accompany the matrimonial announcement.

"Well...this is happy news. Surprising, but happy. Congratulations sweetie, I wish you all the joy in the world." She hugged Scarlett and then reached her hand out to Gavin and gave his hand a good squeeze. "You're a lucky man. Our Scarlett's very special. I'm Joyce by the way, and this is my son Brody."

"I'm Gavin. It's nice to meet you both." Good, Scarlett was watching. Who said he couldn't be polite? Polite was his middle name, damn it.

***

Scarlett placed a glass of iced tea in front of her husband.

Gavin's face lit with surprise. "Thanks."

She didn't know what the big deal was. She'd gotten one for herself, and good manners were just good manners. It didn't mean anything. Aware of her family, she considered what a woman in love would do in this situation. She ran her fingers through his hair, looked longingly into his bottomless eyes, and leaned down to kiss the corner of his mouth. "You're welcome."

His expression warmed as he lifted her hand almost to his mouth, then turned it over and pressed his lips to the center of her palm.

Uh...whoa... Hel-loooo, girly parts!

Really? A kiss to the palm and the tunnel of love was open for business. Geez, she needed to get out more.

Honey put her hand over her heart. "Isn't that the sweetest thing you've ever seen?"

"Adorable," Floyd mocked.

Gavin drained his glass of tea then stood. He draped his arm around Scarlet's shoulder, pulled her to him and squeezed a little too hard. "Well, babe, we better go deal with those reporters."

"What'd you have in mind? Should I get my gun?" She smiled a beauty pageant smile. It was her turn to pour it on way too thick. Lord, if she had to keep this up for long, she was going to get a face cramp.

"Nah, we'll let *Deadeye* handle that." He winked at Honey, who beamed up at him like a sunflower on a summer morning.

Floyd groaned.

Joyce laughed.

"I thought we'd go down to the gate, say hello and let them take a few pictures. Hopefully, they'll leave after they get their pound of flesh."

"Oh, okay." She was glad she'd touched up her makeup earlier. "Should I change?"

"No. You look beautiful."

His intense gaze was so sincere, it confused her. Could he be serious?

No way. It had to be part of the act. But then his calloused finger stroked her jaw, and she wasn't sure what was true anymore. "Alright, if you're sure." She shook out her hands. "I'm nervous."

"It'll be fine." He rubbed his hand up and down her arm.

It would be highly inappropriate if she purred, so she took a small step away from him.

"Before we go, I'm going to step outside and make a phone call." He pulled his phone from his back pocket. "I hope I can get a cell signal out here in the boondocks."

When he left the room, Honey fanned herself. "Scarlett, he is one good-looking man. Darlin', what in heaven's name are you doing?"

As soon as the door thumped shut, Scarlett sprang into action. When Gavin was checking the signal on his phone, she knew exactly what she was going to do. She ran to the pantry and grabbed the aluminum foil, and pulled off a long strip. Her hands worked quickly. She molded and crumpled the foil until her creation resembled a scepter.

She looked up. Three puzzled expressions begged for an answer. "Tell ya in a minute."

She ran out the back door and jumped off of the porch.

She caught up with him at the side of the house. "Hey."

"Yeah?"

"I forgot to give you this." She waved the foil sculpture at him.

"What the hell is that?"

"We don't get very good cell reception out here in the country. This helps. You hold it while you make your call." She placed the foil in her right palm. It extended about ten inches toward the sky. Then she placed the phone in her hand, on top of the foil. The whole thing looked like a prop from a bad sci-fi movie. "See?" She giggled. "You might be a redneck…"

"Are you shittin' me?"

"No. And watch your language."

He stared at her for several long seconds. Seeming to come to some conclusion, he took the phone and foil from her. "Okay. Thanks."

She painted on her *I'm-so-wholesome-I-wouldn't-lie-to-you smile*. "Take your time. See you inside."

When she returned to the kitchen, she saw her family, minus Brody, looking out the kitchen window. She hurried over to watch the show.

"Scarlett, darlin', why is your husband holding a foil wand while talking on the phone?" Joyce said.

"I told him it was the best way to get cell reception out here."

"We have fine cell reception," Joyce said.

"I know, but Gavin's made a few comments about how country we are. He's only kidding," she was quick to add, "but…well…I thought I'd play a tiny practical joke."

She didn't appreciate all his backwoods, hillbilly, boondocks comments, and it was payback time. It was childish, and under normal circumstances, she wouldn't behave this way. But his presence threw her totally off kilter. It was time to level the playing field.

She bit her lip. "Too much?"

"Aww, darlin'," Floyd said. "A little teasing is good in a marriage."

Honey snorted, and then they all busted out laughing.

* * *

Just before the call went through, laughter erupted from inside the house. Gavin saw the whole family duck out of sight. They were weird. Was this normal behavior?

"Hello."

"Hey, Jack. Did you make it to the airport?"

"Yeah, I've got a couple of hours to kill before my flight. How are things there?"

Gavin chuckled and looked back at the house. "They're interesting. Her dad hit me."

"What?"

"I'm fine, but he's got a mean right hook. There's this aunt who's funny as shit, also a housekeeper and her son. Kid's a fan."

"Did you give him your autograph?"

"No. I told him to piss off."

Jack's laughter rang through the phone line. "You're such a punk."

"That's what they say. Can you do me a favor when you get back to L.A.?"

"Sure, what do you need?"

Gavin rattled off a list of things he needed to have done if he wasn't going to be at his condo for a while. Damn he was glad to not be going back to Los Angeles, even if it meant living in Mayberry for the foreseeable future.

"Gav, you still there?"

"Yeah, sorry."

"Have you heard from Mac?" Jack's tone was all business.

"Not since I gave him what information I had about Tara."

"Don't worry. He'll find her."

"And then what?"

"I know how important this is to you, Gav. Don't worry, we'll figure it out together."

The crushing heaviness on his shoulders eased some. "Thanks, man." He drew in a lungful of air and blew it out. "And thanks for your help today. Hopefully, the Storm Side guys will be appeased."

"It's under control. I'll handle the spin. Tell me, where does a rock star learn a word like appease?"

Gavin swatted some kind of flying bug. "I read it on a bathroom wall, *To appease your hard-on, call Mona.*"

Jack laughed. "Anything else you need?"

"Nah, I'm good. If there's a problem, I'll rub some money on it. That seems to work around here." He didn't even try to hide his bitterness. "See ya, man."

Gavin put his phone back in his pocket and looked at the foil antenna. His call to Jack was clear as a bell, so he guessed she'd been telling the truth. He looked at the vastness of the land around the house and wiped the sweat from his brow. Time to feed the beast.

73

Chapter 7

The Ford F-150 bounced into the air. Tools crashed as the bed of the truck slammed back to earth. Gavin gripped the steering wheel until his knuckles turned white. He was going to keep this mother on the road or die trying. It was a matter of pride. Looking like an idiot in front of his wife, even his fake wife, sucked. Another big bump and Scarlett braced her hand on the roof of the cab to keep from smacking her head. *Damn it.*

"Slow down, Gavin. You're going to bust the axle."

"Luanne flew down this drive in a doll-sized convertible. How'd she manage it?" He clutched the wheel even tighter and took his foot off the accelerator. The last thing he needed was to break his father-in-law's truck.

"She knows this drive like the back of her hand. Stay toward the shoulder, and you should be fine."

"Got it."

"Oh, dear Lord," she gasped.

Her panicked intake of air pissed him off. "I'm doing the best I can."

"No. Look." She pointed to the end of the drive. "There have to be fifty reporters."

The sight of the shutterbugs and media made him want to cuss. Once upon a time, he couldn't take a piss without a mob of paparazzi trying to get a shot of it. He didn't want to bring that crap to this family's doorstep. No one deserved to have their privacy violated in such an aggressive way, especially not a family like the Kellys.

Another sharp intake of air came from the passenger side of the vehicle. He'd managed to avoid any more potholes, so he understood that sound. He glanced at her.

She was chewing on her lower lip, and it wouldn't be long until she gnawed right through it.

"Don't be nervous." He spoke to her like she might cut and run. "Let me do the talking, and it will be over before you know it." He eased off the gas and let the truck roll to a stop. She nodded, still riveted to the group at the gate. At least the lip gnawing had stopped.

"Most of the questions will probably center on what happened in Vegas. I'll try to steer them away from that topic, but I doubt it will do any good."

As she sucked her swollen lip back between her teeth, the color drained from her face.

He took her sweaty hand and squeezed. "I've got this, Scarlett. Jack and I came up with a plausible story. We'll tell them we met at the beginning of the week in a hotel elevator. It was love at first sight, blah, blah, blah. By Friday, we couldn't live without each other."

She shot him a look that clearly stated he and Jack were delusional. "I know, it's not great, but it sounds better than we met in a bar, got drunk, and got married. Don't you think?"

She bowed her head. "Yes."

"Scarlett, look at me." Her cornflower eyes brimmed with tears. "We screwed up. Both of us. We can't change that. All we can do is try to walk away with as much dignity as we can."

"Okay."

The truck stopped about fifteen feet from the gate. "If you do have to answer a question, don't panic. Bat those baby blues and turn on your backwoods charm." He studied her for a minute. "Can you do a little Daisy Duke thing? Flip your hair. Put some extra ass-shake in your step?" He tapped the steering wheel as the idea took root. He eyed her conservative peasant top with the drawstring neck. "Loosen the tie on your shirt and let it fall off one shoulder. They won't care what you say if you flash some skin." He emphasized his point with a waggle of his brows.

"Maybe we should go back to the house so I can put on my push-up bra, halter top and denim panties?" She crossed her arms like she was suiting up for battle.

She could cross her arms all she wanted, but it was too late for him. The image of her dressed like that scorched his mind. It was hot. He might burn to ash right there in the cab of the truck.

A push-up bra and denim panties?

Damn.

Double damn.

He drew in a ragged wheeze. It was more difficult than it should be to get the correct amount of air in his system. His brain short-circuited. He didn't even know what denim panties were, but he was wholeheartedly on board with the idea.

Cameras flashed through the windshield. The reporters' squawking was muted, but he could still hear their questions. He needed to get his head out of her panties and onto the circling sharks waiting to eat them alive.

She spoke to him through gritted teeth and a fake smile. "I will not act like some slutty country bumpkin so we can get out of this mess. That is not how I walk away with my dignity. I hope you have another plan because that one's shitty." Her hand flew to her mouth. "Look what you made me do. After only a few hours, I'm as foulmouthed as you are."

He rested one hand on the wheel, and the other stretched along the back of her seat. He laughed. This chick was a hell of a ride. "You've got a temper don't you, Red?" He toyed with a loose curl. "Fine, be yourself. But only answer the questions they ask. Don't elaborate. And for the record, you've got a long way to go before you're as foulmouthed as me." He chucked her under the chin. "But keep practicing. You'll get there."

She gave him a dirty look disguised as an adoring smile.

The minute he exited the truck the ravenous crowd went crazy.

*****

Zings of excitement pinged through Scarlett's body. Not *Yay, we're going on a cruise* excited. More like *I'm about to do something naughty* excited. Totally inappropriate, but she raised her face to the sun and savored the sensations pulsing through her bloodstream.

Gavin gave her a strange look. "Are you alright?"

"Never better." She laughed. If she was the star of this circus, she might as well enjoy it.

"Okay. Here we go. Remember, I'm right beside you." They made their way toward the reporters.

"Gavin, introduce us to your wife!"

"This way Scartlett and Gavin, give us a smile."

"Scarlett, is it true you're pregnant? Was it a shotgun wedding?"

"Congratulations, you two."

"Why'd you run, Scarlett?"

Her bravado failed her when they stopped in front of the crowd. She fought the urge to hide behind Gavin. Instead, she smiled like this was an everyday occurrence. The questions flew at her like mosquitoes on a summer evening.

Gavin whistled loud and shrill. "Quiet down." Scarlett was stunned when they all obeyed. Wow. *You Tarzan. Me Jane.* Oh gosh, she was losing it.

"We'll take a few questions." He wrapped his arm around her shoulder. She welcomed his strong arm and warm man scent. He pointed to a guy in a camo vest and a safari hat. "You first."

"How does it feel to be married, Gav?"

"Great, couldn't be happier." He drew her closer. She leaned into him willingly.

"Scarlett, how do you feel about all of this?" shouted a short man with a bad comb-over. Then again, was there ever a good comb-over?

"Sort of overwhelmed, but very happy." Her arm slid around Gavin's waist. She held onto his shirt for dear life.

A woman with a high bun and white sunglasses yelled, "Tell us how you two met. How long have you known each other?"

"We met last Saturday night in Vegas. We caught an elevator together." He kissed her temple, and tingles exploded from the top of her head down the length of her body. He pointed to a young guy with his baseball cap on backwards. "You're—"

"So basically, you knew each other seven days before you got married?" The woman in the sunglasses interrupted. "You don't think that's kind of fast? Sounds like the same old Gavin, reckless as ever. The Delinquent, in all his glory." All the other reporters laughed.

The muscles in Gavin's back went rigid. Scarlett knew calling him *reckless* was the worst thing the woman could do. The calculating gleam in the reporter's eye let Scarlett know she'd done it on purpose. Hot and raw anger blazed through her. How about some common courtesy?

She peeked up at her husband's handsome face. He'd pulled on his bulletproof rocker mask. The only tell of his distress was a muscle pulsing in his jaw. She got it then. Unreliable and unpredictable, that's how these people saw him. How they would portray him in their rags and TV shows. This was why he'd offered to pay her to stay married. It didn't matter that her acceptance of the money had nothing to do with his problem. He'd paid for her help. She owed him, didn't she?

Her heart rate kicked up while her hands poured sweat. They were maligning him, and she couldn't sit back and let it happen. Unfortunately, there'd be a price to pay. If she redeemed his reputation, she'd put another nail in her own.

But right was right, and it wasn't in her nature to let someone suffer if she could help.

Well, crap. Luanne always said she cared too much about what other people thought.

Well, Luanne, I'm about to make you very happy.

"No. I—"

"Babe," Scarlett cut in. "If you don't mind I'd like to answer this one." She stepped in front of him to shield her husband from the sharks. "I'm the reason we got married so quickly. Gavin wanted to take some time to make sure we were doing the right thing and to involve our family and friends. But...well...I just couldn't wait." She gave Gavin a quick smile over her shoulder. He responded by wrapping both of his arms around her waist and pulling her back to his body.

His body was a live wire sending currents of electricity all the way to her toes. Even her bones buzzed. She rested her arms on top of his, gripping him for support. "When you meet the right person you know it. We knew we were meant to be together the moment those elevator doors closed. Isn't that right, Gavin?" She turned in his arms to look directly into his eyes.

Big mistake.

His gaze cast a sensual net, snaring her. She was willing prey, and her words didn't feel like a lie.

He smiled down at her. "That's right, doll."

"If anyone's reckless it's me, not Gavin."

That, for sure, was a piece of truth.

The reporters hung on every word. She looked back at them and grinned. "Who can blame me? Look at him." Their audience snickered. "He's talented, charismatic and gorgeous. I'm a very lucky woman."

She should step away from him, but she couldn't. It felt too good to be wrapped in his arms. "Do you have anything to add, sweetie?" Her heart faltered. The fire blazing in his gray gaze told her he was as affected by their contact.

"Um…" For a moment he stared at her like he'd forgotten what they were talking about. "No." His voice was like rough sex on satin sheets.

This man lit all her fuses, and he did it with a blow torch. Without her permission, her arms snaked around his neck. A small smile lifted her lips when he moaned at their contact, belly to belly. Rising to the balls of her feet, she sucked on his full bottom lip.

Surprise at her actions registered somewhere in the back of her mind, but she couldn't resist. Didn't want to.

He crushed her to him as his lips parted and he took control. She opened to him. He licked into her mouth. Her knees buckled, but he caught her, tightening his hold around her waist. She moaned and fought the urge to crawl up his body.

The flash of cameras was like a lightning storm, the shout of the photographers a distant thunder. Lost in the sensual kiss, she barely noticed either one.

***

A blow to the head would have been less disorienting than the feel of Scarlett's soft tongue moving against Gavin's body. The sweet invasion jumbled his senses. He couldn't pull her close enough or kiss her hard enough to satisfy his hunger.

She moaned deep in her throat, and when she did, every kiss, every touch, every carnal moment from their night in Vegas came rushing back to him. The memories originated in his brain, but like wild geese fleeing winter, they quickly migrated south.

He'd attributed the passion of that night to the liquor. But standing there, stone-cold sober in the Texas sun, with a mosquito buzzing by his ear, and a trace of manure floating on the breeze, he knew it was more than alcohol. So much more. It was bone deep attraction. Desire and need. There was something else, too. He grasped for the word, but it escaped him.

He reluctantly pulled back from the kiss and looked at Scarlett's swollen lips and flushed cheeks. Desire swirled around them, and she blinked up at him. Neither spoke. They barely breathed. Soft as a feather, she traced her fingers down his face.

His hands were headed down to the promised land of her ass when someone shouted a question. He had to rein it in. Having sex in public had to be as bad as a quickie marriage to a virtual stranger. Right?

Clearing his throat, he stepped back, but only far enough to turn her to face their audience. He kept his arm around her, not ready to let her go. "Alright guys, that's it, thanks for your good wishes."

Disorientation and a raging hard-on made him move slowly. Had a kiss ever felt like that? Not just no, but hell no.

It was amazing. Terrifying.

He didn't know if he wanted to lay her on the ground and finish what they'd started, or jump in Floyd's truck and drive as fast as he could away from Texas.

Thankfully, he got them back to the vehicle. They didn't speak or look at each other.

When he slid behind the wheel, Scarlet scooted across the seat and settled herself next to him. She leaned into him and gave the reporters one last wave. He turned the truck around and headed back to the house. Even though a part of him wanted to bolt, he couldn't help himself. He slid his hand over to her thigh and rested it on her warm, sweet flesh. She felt so damn good.

"Ohmygosh." Her small hands squeezed his arm. "That was unbelievable."

"Yeah." How had this prissy woman knocked him on his ass with one kiss, and made him chase halfway across the country to get to her? He was a rocker, for Christ's sake. Women were a dime a dozen. And they chased him, not the other way around.

"It was insane, petrifying, thrilling, and every other word you could put an exclamation mark after." She fanned her face. "I thought I would faint dead away. I can't believe people have to deal with that every day."

What? I'm about to crash and burn over here and she's all worked up over the reporters?

"It can be pretty bad," His half-hearted response made her look at him.

"Are you alright?" He could feel her studying him. "You're mad because I answered that last question. I should have let you handle it. But I thought it would be better for me to defend you, rather than you defend yourself."

"Yeah. Good thinking." No. He wasn't alright. He was pissed. Performing for the crowd had her flustered. Not that incredible kiss.

"Well, what's the matter?"

He ran his hand across his mouth, trying to wipe away the taste and feel of her. Like that was possible. A snarl of emotions surged through him. This chick had him so tied up in knots, he couldn't think, which put him at a disadvantage.

He only knew one way to level the playing field—attack. "The next time we have to kiss, don't stick your tongue down my throat. You getting off isn't part of this deal." He was a dick. So what else was new?

Scarlett recoiled as if she'd been slapped. "Oh...okay." She looked like a whipped puppy as she slid back to the passenger side of the truck.

His anger calmed his libido, but it didn't improve his driving. He cringed when he hit another pothole. He braced himself for his wife to bitch at him, but she mutely stared out the window.

His conscience twitched. Interesting. He didn't know he still had one. As a welcome back gift to his scruples, he made a small concession. "Listen, Scarlett, I'm tired, and this whole situation has made me jumpy as hell. You're going to have to forget I said that."

***

Embarrassment and indignation swirled around Scarlett's brain like water circling a drain. That had been the best kiss of her whole life.

Not good. Not even great.

Fireworks on the Fourth of July, spectacular.

The kind of kiss that leads to ripped clothes, pulled hair, and hickeys in indiscreet places. But she didn't have any of those things. No. All she had was a gaping hole in her pride and a massive bruise on her heart.

She was the queen of fools. Seriously, if there were an idiot parade she'd be riding on the float. Scooching as far away from him as possible, she wrapped her arms around her middle and stared out the window. What was his problem? She hadn't pinned him down and forced him to kiss her. He'd participated too.

It takes two to tango, bucko.

As apologies went, that one stunk. So what if he was tired and jumpy? That didn't give him the right to speak to her that way. It wasn't like she was at her best, either. Though, unlike him, she'd remained civil. She'd given him iced tea for cryin' out loud. A tiny voice whispered that she'd given him her mouth, her tongue, and her body too. But she shut that hussy up in a hurry.

She desperately searched for her happy place but only found new and inventive ways to maim him. Maybe she and Honey could get adjoining prison cells. Because there was a very good chance she was going to kill Gavin Bain in his sleep.

Chapter 8

Scarlett propped her feet on her coffee table and took a break from writing. She knew bloodthirsty musings over her real life had bled into her creative life when Fiona the Fairy picked up a tree branch and beat the ever living crap out of a tattooed, musical troll. Carousel did want Fiona to be edgier. A homicidal fairy was probably not what they were talking about. But it was satisfying to write.

With the laptop balanced on her lap, she massaged the ache in her temples that radiated to her neck.

That kiss.

She'd initiated it. What was wrong with her? She'd acted like she didn't have a lick of sense.

Just doin' what I was paid to do.

It was a lie. Thankfully, she didn't have to admit the truth because her cell rang.

"Hello, Luanne."

"Can you talk?"

She rolled her eyes at Luanne's conspiratorial whisper. "Yes. Gavin's gone to the barn to help Brody with chores."

"Really?" Incredulity shot through the phone and stabbed her in the ear.

"Yep. He'd rather shovel horse poop than be in the same room as me. And, let me tell ya, the feeling is entirely mutual."

Liar.

"What the hell's going on?" Luanne demanded.

Scarlett considered what to say, but only for a moment. She needed to tell Luanne. "You have to swear you won't say a word about this to anyone."

"Okay."

"Swear."

"Alright, I swear on the collective souls of NSYNC."

A smile spread across Scarlett's face, and her tension ratcheted down somewhat. They'd been swearing on the collective souls of NSYNC since they were twelve years old. She gave Luanne the rundown on her father, Poppy Sims, and Gavin's buy-off.

"Poppy Sims is a manipulative bitch."

"You have no idea." Scarlett had learned that lesson in the absolute worst way.

Scarlett, have you lost weight?

Probably, Poppy, all I've eaten for a month is Ramen Noodles. Being a broke college student sucks.

Hey, I'm going to a party tonight. There'll be tons of food. You can dress up and have a some fun.

Really, Poppy?

Sure. A friend of mine was supposed to go, but she got sick. Here's the address. When you get there, tell them your name is Heaven Leigh.

Why?

Oh, it's just something fun we're all doing.

Okay.

Heaven Leigh? Really? How gullible can one girl be? Heavenly is the last word she'd use to describe that night.

"At least Gavin knows the money's going to a good cause," Luanne said.

"Huh?"

"I said, at least your husband knows you're using the money to help your family."

"No, he doesn't. I didn't tell him. As far as he knows, I'm a greedy gold-digger, and that's the way I want it. This is a family matter. And Gavin's not family." She was counting on the contempt she saw in his glare every time the money was mentioned to serve as a perfect barrier between them. Even so, disappointment kneaded her heart.

"You could have asked me for my help."

"Honestly, it never occurred to me to ask. This is better. Once it's paid to the bank, we won't owe anyone." She was surprised Luanne offered. Her best friend didn't like to draw anyone's attention to her family money. Everyone in Blister County knew the Prices had more money than God. But Scarlett knew that everything Luanne had came at a steep price, thanks to her father.

"How are you gonna explain it to Floyd?"

"He doesn't really have any idea how much I make on my book sales. I'll tell him I've saved up. He doesn't have the cash, and this is my home too. He'll hate it, but he'll take it. Besides I'm going to pay it off then tell him, so even if he wanted to stop me it'll be too late."

"Sounds like you've got it all figured out. I hope it doesn't come back to bite you in the ass."

Me too. "It'll be fine."

"Soooo, *Renegade Bride*, how was the sex?"

Scarlett's headache squeezed tighter. That was the million-dollar question, wasn't it? She wished she had an answer. "Don't call me that."

Luanne laughed. "It's a ridiculous name, but oh so funny. Now quit stalling and give me a play by play of your first time."

Her first time. The sadness and regret she'd held at bay trampled her. She'd held on to her virginity for twenty-five years, guarding it like the Crown Jewels. A giggle bubbled at the thought of her hymen and Queen Elizabeth together. It wasn't like she hadn't had opportunites to lose it. But, anytime she'd been tempted, she remembered a devastated seven-year-old girl watching her foolish, sexually irresponsible mom drive away with a man she'd just met at the Stop-N-Save. Nothing killed desire like childhood mama-trauma.

Her first response was to lie to Luanne. She always told the truth, no matter what the consequence. Now she was about to lie to her best friend. Oh, how the mighty had fallen. "Lou, it was—"

The door opened, and a sweaty rock star stood on the threshold.

"Do not come in here," Scarlett shouted.

"Why the hell not?" He braced his hands on the door jamb and glared at her.

"Luanne, I'll call you back." She pointed at Gavin. "Stop."

"Why?"

"You have horse manure on your jeans."

"What?" He jumped back like he'd been electrocuted.

She vaulted off the sofa and ran from the room.

"Where are you going? A little help here?"

His curses greeted her when she ran outside with a towel. She doubled over laughing when she saw him. He was holding onto the rail while using the edge of the porch to scrape the manure off his jeans. It was on his calves so every time he bent to his task he smeared it up the back of his thigh.

"Stop." She fought for control but lost to another round of giggles.

"What? Why? God, it stinks. Quit laughing." He contorted himself around to try and inspect the damage.

"You've smeared it up your legs."

"This is bullshit." He kicked off his boots.

"Not bull. Horse." The hilarity took her again.

Scarlett's laughter sputtered to a stop when he went for the buttons of his jeans. "Wha...what are you doing?"

"Taking off these shitty pants. What do you think I'm doing?" Buttons undone, he carefully slid them off, revealing a pair of Jockey low-rise trunks and tanned, muscled legs. He should have looked ridiculous standing there in his black underwear, t-shirt, and socks, but he didn't. Not one little bit. Her mouth went as dry as the Mojave Desert.

When he bent to remove his socks, she fought the urge to fall to her knees and worship his incredible backside.

He looked down his body. "I need a shower."

"Yeah." She wished that hadn't sounded so dreamy.

He rested his hands on his hips and shot her a cocky grin. "You like what you see?"

She regained her composure and frowned. "Not exactly."

"Liar." He amped up the wattage on his smile.

"No. Not lying." She bit her lip.

"Then why are you looking at me like that?"

"You have a spot of poop on your…" She pointed to his forehead.

He gagged and grabbed the hem of his shirt.

She looked away. She was a sympathetic puker. If Gavin started barfing, she might follow suit.

There was horse dung all over her porch. His muffled grumbles followed her down the steps as she retrieved the garden hose. The old faucet squeaked when she twisted it on, and cold water poured out. She covered the end of the hose with her thumb to make a more pressurized spray. Geez, he'd made a mess. She ignored his griping and sprayed the steps then turned to wash the porch and froze.

He'd taken his shirt off and was using it to wipe his face. *Oh. My. Lord.* He was standing there in nothing but his underwear. Her fingers itched to stroke the golden skin that provided a perfect canvas for his amazing ink. A tattoo of a lock with a chain wrapped around it peeked above the waistband of his underwear, below his navel and above his… Now, she was drooling.

She yearned to explore the hills and valleys of his abs—with her tongue. Oh, sweet Lord, they *were* incredible abs. The average man didn't have a sculpted six-pack. Then again, he was anything but average.

A tsunami of desire rolled through her senses and crested low in her belly. She wasn't sure how much longer she could stand. The hose hung limp in her hand, cold water pooled on the ground, and blood pounded in her ears. She needed to look away, but her iron-clad willpower failed her.

Suddenly, she was angry, angrier than she'd ever been in her life. No. Not angry. Furious at his hotness, his sexy tattoos, his stupid black trunks, and her incomprehensible reaction to it all.

She snapped.

When she lifted her arm, the water hit him square in the chest. He stumbled backward, and she kept spraying. She couldn't have lowered the hose if she'd wanted to. And, she didn't want to.

"What the fu—?" A mouthful of water shut him up in a hurry.

"Stop saying that!" she shouted.

"What. The. Fuck?" Gavin bellowed.

"Stop it."

"This is for the first drink you bought me." She sprayed him in the face.

"For insisting we get married." The stream moved to his chest.

"Your stupid attorney." Back to his face.

"Comments made in the truck." His chest again.

"And for my lost underwear." She nailed him in the crotch.

There was a distinct possibility she'd turned the bend, never to return. She was appalled at her behavior but helpless to stop. Crazy felt too good.

***

"Have you lost your mind?" Water choked him as he took a shot in the mouth. Righteous indignation glowed in her expressive eyes. She was a Bible-thumping Terminator, and he was her quarry. The image of this lovely avenging angel coming after him with a garden hose was too funny to believe. This would never happen in L.A. Of course, he wouldn't have horse shit from one end of his body to the other in L.A., either. He laughed and a burst of water hit him in the face.

When he stopped sputtering, he gave her a half-hearted glare. "I'm warning you. Stop now, and nobody gets hurt." Her only response was to go for his crotch. Again. She was vicious and seemed to be opposed to him reproducing.

Enough was enough. When she was less than an arm's length away, he pounced. They wrestled for the hose. Impressive. The girl had spunk.

She clung to the hose, but he had some wicked moves of his own and wrenched it from her grip. The water was his. Game on.

A squeal exploded from her when the freakin' cold water poured over the sweet body that'd caused him more hard-ons in the last two days than in the last couple of months.

She screamed. He laughed. "Invigorating, isn't it? Don't worry, you'll get used to it." Her only response was to scream louder. She twisted, turned, bent and bucked. "There's no escape, wild girl. I've got you, and I'm not letting go."

Her shirt rode up, and wet skin rubbed against his bare belly. He could see her pale pink bra through her wet shirt, the thin fabric clinging to her breast. Damn, cold water and a see-through bra—sexy as hell. But it was also hilarious.

When had he had this much fun while fully clothed? Of course, naked and wet was fun, too. It could happen if he could stop laughing long enough to get her undressed.

Her screams turned to laughter as he slipped and they almost went down. His heart did a funny thump thing.

They clung to each other soaking wet, laughing madly and panting hard.

"What the fuck?" he gasped.

She stepped away from him and pushed back the sodden mess of her hair, still giggling. "Could you please refrain from using that word?"

He dropped the hose and bent over with his hands on his knees. It was an effort to catch his breath. He looked up at her from beneath his hair and grinned. "All you had to do was ask."

She shoved him. He caught himself on the porch rail. "You're a terrible person. I'd hoped you weren't. But you totally are."

There wasn't any heat in her words. They were still playing. She took the towel she'd brought for him and her tight round ass disappeared into the house.

Damn. He'd known a lot of outrageous women in his day. But his straight-edged, pillar of society, goody-two-shoes wife was quite possibly the most dangerous woman he'd ever known.

Chapter 9

She'd seen the man in his underwear. And she'd liked it. Honestly, like was too weak of a word for their wet wrestling match.

Best three minutes of her life.

Scarlett stirred the pot of soup on the stove and tried to get her mind right. Gavin Bain was the least appropriate man in the whole world for her. The stories that she'd read and heard about him were legendary. He'd left a trail of bar fights, verbal altercations, trashed hotel rooms, and heartbroken women in his wake. They didn't call him The Delinquent for nothing.

Also, everyone knew how self-absorbed rock stars were, and if there was one thing she couldn't abide, it was selfish, narcissistic people.

Equilibrium returned to her piece by precious piece as she reviewed all the reasons Gavin was not for her and needed to be out of her life as soon as possible.

"Something smells good."

She screamed and flicked the spoon across the room. "Oh, my gosh, you scared me."

"Sorry."

She took in the rock star leaning against the door jamb, grinning like a fool, and knew he wasn't sorry at all.

Lord, had a man ever looked so good?

No, the answer was no.

He wore a faded Seattle Seahawks t-shirt that hugged his pecs and shoulders. It looked so good she wanted to ditch her beloved Dallas Cowboys to become a Seahawks fan. Thin navy sweat pants covered his long legs, legs that she'd seen that afternoon in all their muscled, tan fineness.

Tattooed arms were crossed over his chest. His damp hair looked darker in this light, like polished onyx. It was short but longer on top, and she wanted to spend hours running her fingers through the silky strands.

"Your hair is short." What? Where had that come from?

He chuckled and ran his hand over his head. "Yeah, I've worn it long, but I don't like how it gets in my way. And I'm not really a man-bun kind of guy."

"You should put on some socks. Your feet will get cold." She kept spouting random things, but his bare feet were distracting and somehow incredibly intimate.

He gave her a strange look. "I'm good."

She turned toward the sink and away from him. "Fine, but don't blame me when you catch a chill."

"Got it. What are you making?" He moved to the stove and peeked inside. What small amount of room there was in her galley kitchen was devoured by his presence.

"Joyce brought soup." The words squeezed into the tiny gap between them. He was too close, and he smelled so good. Not cologne good, but Gavin good. She'd noticed this afternoon during their tussle, but now after his shower, it was intoxicating. She wanted to bury her nose in his neck and stay there for a very long time.

"I'm starved. I haven't eaten since this morning. And you gave me quite a workout this afternoon." He chuckled.

"Mm-huh." She retrieved another spoon and gave the pot another stir.

"Can I help?"

"Um..." That was unexpected. "You can get drinks. The glasses are in this cabinet." She pointed to the door just to her left. "I'll get out of your way."

With one step his front was pressed to her back. "No problem," he whispered in her ear. "I can reach."

Holy...wow. The buttery goodness of his voice spread all over her body. Every inch of hard-won ground she'd gained with her little pep talk crumbled under her feet.

"Thanks for your help." While he sounded like warm toffee, her words came out like dehydrated bitterroot.

Thankfully he stepped away, and her blood pressure could regulate. "No problem. What should I put in these?" He held up the glasses.

"I don't have any alcohol."

"Probably best. Know what I mean."

Heat tingled under her cheeks. "Yes...well, there's iced tea and water in the fridge. I'll have tea."

He flipped one of the glasses into the air and caught it. "Coming right up."

When the wild child swooned, she kicked the tramp in the shin, then took the soup to the table.

Once they were seated, she ladled the soup into their bowls. "Be sure to try some of Joyce's beer bread. It's delicious."

He spooned in a bite and groaned. "This is fu—"

She raised her brow.

"Freaking amazing."

"Joyce was a famous chef in San Francisco before she came back to Zachsville."

"What brought her back?" He cut a slice of bread and dunked it in his soup.

"Her husband had an affair with his secretary."

"Original." Disgust trailed behind the word like the tail of a kite. At that moment she liked him very much. "I've got no tolerance for people who cheat. And a man who cheats with his secretary is just lazy."

"I agree." Look at them having a civil conversation. "The worst part is, they ran off together, and he took all of their money."

"He cleaned out their bank account?"

She reached for the knife and cut a piece of bread. "And investments, anywhere they had money. He was some kind of financial guru, so Joyce let him handle all of it. She had a household checking account and a small savings account, nothing more. My understanding is there was a lot of money, and now it's gone. She came back virtually penniless."

Gavin's spoon stopped halfway to his mouth. "Does she need money? Because I've got money."

"I beg your pardon?" She couldn't possibly have heard him correctly.

"If she needs cash I can give her some."

She must've looked like she didn't speak English, because he continued.

"I have money. She doesn't, and she's got a kid, a kid she's obviously nuts about. If she needs assistance, I can help."

His words flailed, flipped, and flopped in her head and she tried to arrange them so that they made sense.

"What? Why are you looking at me like that?"

Her spoon clattered to the table. "Why would you make such an offer? You don't even know her. For heaven's sake, you met her all of three hours ago." She knew she sounded pissy, but she couldn't help it.

"Scarlett, it's not a big deal. I do it all the time." His hair fell over his forehead, and he pushed it out of the way.

"You do it all the time?" Her incredulity spewed from her mouth. "What? You walk up to single moms on the street and throw money at them?"

He scooped up another spoonful of soup. "I donate to an organization in Seattle. It helps get single moms back on their feet. They provide housing, family therapy, educational assistance, financial counseling, and job placement help. I play at their fundraisers." He shrugged like it wasn't a big deal—like he hadn't just pulverized her preconceived notions of him.

She closed her eyes and tried to catch her thoughts running laps around themselves.

"Do you have asthma?"

She glanced over at him. "What? No, why?"

"Because you've done that weird breathing thing a lot this afternoon, and I would have no idea what to do if you had some kind of attack."

"I'm fine." Her hand shook as she picked up her spoon. "No asthma here, so you're safe."

"Alright. If you're sure."

"I'm sure. Eat your soup before it gets cold."

"You don't have to tell me twice. Remind me to thank Joyce the next time I see her."

The grin she gave him was a brittle representation of a genuine smile, but she couldn't help it. She didn't want to think about him having depth and character. She'd placed him in a shallow, entitled, rock god box and that's where she wanted him to stay. Couldn't he simply stay in his box?

He was trouble.

So much trouble.

***

"Dad-gum-it." Scarlett gripped the yarn she knitted with and yanked.

"What's wrong?" His bare feet were propped on the coffee table while he changed the strings on his guitar. Chinese characters were tattooed across the top of one slender foot. She wondered what the symbols meant.

"I dropped a stitch." She'd knitted and ripped out the same row three times. Who wouldn't be distracted? Gavin's agile fingers moved expertly along his guitar. He hummed along to a song from the playlist on her phone. She tried to fight the pull of his dirty whiskey voice, but he was the snake charmer, and she was the snake.

Not to mention the revelation of his philanthropic endeavors still had her reeling. The guy seemed to have a real heart for single moms and didn't that just suck. Well, it was good for the single moms, but bad for her.

The guitar string made a ting when he cut it. "I like your books."

The needles scraped together. "What?"

"I like your books. I couldn't sleep last night and saw them on the bookshelf."

"Oh…well, thank you."

He rested the guitar on his lap and opened a package of strings. "That Fiona is cool. I like that she's kind, but she's not a pushover, you know? She sets those woodsy animals straight. But she's so cool about it that they're all like, *Sure thing, Fiona.*"

All she could do was nod. He got it.

"And she's not all big-headed about being right either. When she's wrong, she straight up says she's wrong. Which makes her alright in my book."

"I wish everyone could see it that way."

"What do mean?" he said around a string he was holding in his mouth.

She uncrossed and recrossed her legs. "It's a long story, but the short version is the Carousel Network told me they wanted to make them into a weekly television show. But when I got to Vegas to meet with them, they said they wanted me to change Fiona and make her more street smart. Basically, take away some of her sweetness. I have a month to get them something new."

"That's bullshit. You should tell 'em to shove it up their asses. You created her. She's yours. Either they like her or they don't. And if they don't, screw 'em."

She could do that. His money was sitting in her bank account, enough to pay off the farm, but then what? She wanted to be able to take care of her family and the contract with Carousel would help her do that. "Not really my style. Honestly, I should be in my office working on my proposal instead of knitting, but at the moment, knitting's more fun."

"What are you making?" He plucked each string, turning the silver knobby things at the top of the guitar while he did.

"A hat, scarf and mitten set for the church bazaar." She wrapped the lavender yarn around her finger then looped it over one needle. "This is the hat."

He paused in his tuning and grinned. "I knew this girl when I was in high school, who wore a knitted swim suit. I never could figure out how it didn't come completely unraveled. Johnny and I spent a whole summer waiting for the strings to come apart. They never did, though."

His mournful tone made her smile. "It was probably manufactured and not hand knitted."

"So the Chinese are responsible for my summer of sexual frustration. I'm glad to know there's someone to blame. Of course, when a guy's sixteen, a cool breeze can cause a boner, so I can't hold too much of a grudge."

"'Fraid so." She shouldn't laugh, but she couldn't help it. He was the most irreverent person she'd ever met, even more brazen than Luanne.

He draped his arms over the guitar, considering. "Do you think that's why I get horny every time I eat an eggroll?"

They both laughed.

She cleared her throat. "Speaking of horny." Smooth move, stupid. She mentally slapped herself. "Did we...I mean..." This was ridiculous. She was a grown woman. Shoulders squared, she plunged forward. "What I mean to say is...have you been tested?"

"Tested for what?"

His bewildered expression would have been comical if the topic weren't so serious. "Tested for HIV?" She bent her head to her work and didn't look up.

Silence.

More silence.

Way too much silence.

Why wasn't he answering her?

She ventured a peek from under her lashes.

"Why are you askin', Red? You got plans for tonight I don't know about?"

His smarmy grin ignited the short fuse she'd been carrying around since she woke up naked in his bed. Every time they carved out a tiny piece of civility, he'd say something crappy and ruin it. "Listen, buddy, this is not easy for me, and you damn well know it. I understand this is a conversation we should have had before we had sex, but at the time, I was a tad bit incapacitated."

He dialed back the slimy smile, but his expression still danced with suppressed humor. Didn't he understand the seriousness of this subject? Anger bubbled up from her toes, scorching her from the inside out. Her muscles coiled, and she actually considered smacking him upside the head.

What was wrong with her? She didn't usually have a hairpin trigger. Ordinarily, she was the picture of self-control.

With a monstrous effort, she smothered her irritation and hoped she could actually speak through gritted teeth. "I would appreciate an answer."

"I got tested a few months ago, and I haven't been with anyone since then."

Her knitting became the most fascinating thing in the world. Prickly heat toasted her neck and cheeks. "It's good to hear you haven't had sex with anyone except me since you were tested. I'm sure we used a condom, but it's still a relief."

"No."

"No, what?"

"No, we didn't use a condom."

"What?"

"We. Did not. Use. A condom."

"Ah…well, that's not good."

"It's fine."

"No. I'm pretty sure it's not fine."

"It's no big deal, Scarlett."

"What in God's name does that mean?"

He fell over laughing.

"Gavin?"

Huge belly laughs came from the sofa. She snagged a pillow and hurled it at him. Screw self-control. "You know what, I don't want to know." She unceremoniously dumped her knitting into its basket. "I'm going to bed."

***

"Wait," he wheezed. "I couldn't get the condom on before you fell asleep." He wiped his eyes with the back of his hand. "You fell asleep Scarlett. We didn't have sex." Shit, she didn't look so good.

"Wha...what?"

"It's true." He sat up and grabbed the guitar before it could slide off the sofa. "You don't have anything to worry about."

"I...we...I'm..." She blinked frantically and started with the deep breathing thing again. "I'm still a virgin?"

"Huh?" She couldn't have said what he thought she said.

"Nothing." With clumsy jerky movements, she grasped her craft basket and tried to flee.

He caught her arm as she dashed past him. "Scarlett, stop."

"No." With a strength that belied her size, she yanked her arm from his grasp and sprinted from the room.

He stared after her. The room tilted, and he had trouble staying upright.

His wife was a virgin? He dropped his head to his hands. An effin' virgin.

What was he supposed to do with that?

Chapter 10

"Why the hell are we up at the butt-crack of dawn?" Gavin rubbed the sleep from his tear ducts and tried to keep up with Scarlett. For some ungodly reason, she was power walking to Floyd's house.

He'd give his left nut for some coffee, but his wife wasn't a coffee drinker. There wasn't a drop of the stuff in her house. Not even instant. Unbelievable.

The episode of *Confessions of a Virgin* she'd treated him to the night before was still looping through his mind. He kept starting and stopping the process of breaking down the intel. Without coffee? Forget about it.

Item number one on the to-do list: Buy a coffee maker. He'd been assured there would be coffee at breakfast. There'd better be, or someone was going to get hurt.

Item number two: Find out why his twenty-five year old wife was a virgin, but, first things first.

"So…no coffee?"

"For the third time, Gavin, I don't drink coffee. I like herbal tea."

"Why?"

"Caffeine is very addictive. The body's a temple and all."

"Interesting." He finally caught up to her.

"Why is that interesting?"

"It's just that several nights ago, in Vegas, you treated your *temple* like a frat house."

She skidded to a stop. "I did not."

He turned to face her and strode backward, amused at the indignant look on her face. "Yea, you pretty much did." Her hands flew to her face, and her shoulders shook. Damn, he hadn't meant to make her cry? He strode back to her. "Scarlett, I'm—"

"Oh, my gosh." She opened her hands so she could peek out and scrunched up her nose like she was too embarrassed to look at him. But she wasn't crying. She was giggling. "I totally did, didn't I?" She fanned her pink cheeks, and continued on her way, still snickering.

That was the last thing he'd expected. She never ceased to amaze him. He followed her laughter, a tether that pulled him along.

"I still can't believe I'm up this early."

"Stop complaining, rock star. It's seven in the morning. Half the county's been up for at least two hours. Besides, you're the one who accepted Honey's invitation to breakfast. It's like you can't tell her no."

He grunted, neither confirming nor denying the allegation. It was absolutely true.

He couldn't say no to the eccentric Honey. There was something about the badly dressed, round, older woman that got to him.

"You're not fooling anyone, Gavin. She's got you wrapped around her pudgy little finger. It's cute." She placed two fingers to her neck and looked at her watch on the opposite wrist. After a few seconds of concentration, she lowered her arms and began to pump them faster, picking up her pace as she did.

Cute. Nobody'd ever called him cute. He smiled. It was ridiculous, of course. He was anything but cute. However, if that's how she saw him, who was he to argue?

Scarlett's firm, delicious butt helped to take his mind off the unfamiliar warm feelings blooming in his chest. She was wearing a snug pink tank top, neon pink cross-trainers and—best of all—black sports leggings with no panty lines. Just her tight ass wrapped in a thin layer of spandex.

Suddenly, he was a lot more awake. He could catch up to her, but he wouldn't do that. The view was fine right where he was.

"Why are you walking so fast?"

"I incorporate exercise into my daily routine whenever I can. I walk three miles every day. It's a fourth of a mile to the big house and back. Later, I will get on my treadmill and finish the rest." Her hair was pulled up in another messy bun, and it bobbed from side to side with every step. It was like a little metronome, clicking off a rhythm.

Watch my ass. Watch my ass. Watch my ass.

So…he watched her ass.

"I know. I saw your schedules around the house. There's one on your dresser, one in the bathroom, and one on the fridge." He didn't mention the old schedules he'd found in her dresser drawers.

She'd set him up in her bedroom while she slept in her office. He'd snooped. Who wouldn't? No startling revelations, though. The most interesting thing he'd found was in her underwear drawer. Behind her sensible panties, of which he was familiar, there was an array of thongs and lacy bikinis in every color under the sun. He'd pawed through garters and sexy bras as well. The drawer was like a mullet, business in the front and party in the back. He chuckled at the analogy.

That bunch of undies was a picture of the woman, herself. On the surface, she was sensible and safe. But under the surface, he'd seen glimpses of the forbidden and naughty. The big question was why did she hide her adventurous side?

"You better hurry up, Gavin. Honey doesn't hold meals for anyone."

Scarlett was standing on the back porch wiping her face with a towel. She brought her right arm over her head and stretched to the left side, exposing the tan skin above her waistband.

The minute he lasered in on her bare stomach, he forgot all about his need for coffee. In fact, he forgot everything because all of the blood drained from his brain and headed straight to his dick. Dammit, she wasn't even trying to be sexy, and still, she lit every cell in his body.

Really? Over a tiny patch of flesh. Come on, Gav. Get it together.

Head down, he marched up the stairs to the porch. She could cool down on her own. The last thing he needed was a hard-on to go with his bacon and eggs.

He was so intent on getting past her without looking at any more enticing tidbits, he ran smack into her delicious body. She was bent forward to stretch her hamstrings, head down, hands touching the ground and butt in the air. Disaster might have been averted if she hadn't been facing away from him. His front rammed directly into her backside. His little head yelled *Score!* His big head concentrated on keeping them upright.

She squeaked and pitched forward.

He wrapped his hands around her small waist and yanked back to stop their forward motion. This only served to intensify the contact between her sweet round butt and his celebratory crotch. "Oh, God." His deep throaty growl hung in the air. For several torturous seconds, they stood immobilized. And then she moved.

"Let go." She wrenched away from him.

"What?" Caught off guard, he tightened his hold on her. She twisted and started to fall.

Gravity. Is. A Bitch.

Worried he would crush her, he clutched her to him and rolled. Like a slow-motion contortionist act, arms and legs pinwheeled and tangled. Her shriek reverberated in his ears. Air wheezed from him when he landed flat on his back with her sprawled on top of him.

She felt damn good. This was a hell of a lot better than his fantasies about her and it sure as hell was better than the alcohol-glazed memories from Vegas. Being a gentleman was overrated. No wonder he'd never tried it before. They were glued together like a preschool project. The fall hurt, but he'd do it a thousand times if this was the payoff.

Her startled indigo eyes were mere inches from his as he struggled to make his lungs work.

Her unruly mane escaped its tie, and his hands slid into her copper curls on their own. "Scarlett."

She quickly put her hands on his chest and scrambled to a seated position, no doubt to minimize the contact between them. But she only made things worse. Now, the woman was sitting astride his hips. The part of her body that was so obviously off limits was nestled snugly against the part of him that was so clearly not. His heart stopped, stuttered, raced and did the one thing it was meant to do—pump copious amounts of blood right where he needed it.

A squeak escaped from her mouth at the evidence of his excellent circulatory system. "Gavin?"

"Don't move. Don't speak. Give me a minute." Even to his own ears, his voice sounded like sandpaper rubbed over raw vocal cords. He drug in a huge amount of air, counted the rafters of the porch and played musical scales in his head to try and kill his hard-on. Another long inhale, an even longer exhale, self-control was within his reach. Just…one…more…minute.

A tiny rock of her hips and a soft moan from her parted lips propelled him beyond caring about restraint, chivalry, or his in-laws on the other side of the door.

His hand went to her neck, and he yanked her mouth to his. Lightning scorched his spine when their lips met. Her immediate response cranked up the urgency of the kiss and his restraint slipped farther from his grasp.

There was nothing elegant about the kiss. He was usually a lot smoother than this, but he couldn't find the reins to slow them down. It didn't start slow and work its way to hot. This thing went from zero to sixty in a nanosecond.

Her hair hung like a curtain around them, a barrier between them and sanity. Cherry blossom and fresh rain surrounded him. It was an accelerant to his already out of control desire.

Hunger for more of her made him go for the strip of exposed skin around her waist, while the other kept her mouth glued to his. Her body was slick and damp from exercise, which conjured his favorite slick damp spot.

He was going to hell. He didn't care.

With a needy whimper, she rocked down on him. He bucked in response. His hands shot down her body to cup her ass, and she deepened the kiss.

A horse neighed, and voices from inside the house drifted through the air. The hard boards of the porch scratched into his back. Slowly, he was dragged back to reality.

Fifty thousand dollars, idiot.

What were they doing? Did she even like him? Or had his fifty thousand dollars bought her attention?

He wanted to believe there was more to Scarlett, but his mother and too many groupies had taught him women were out for themselves. Period. Even the mother of his child betrayed him.

Did she tell him about the pregnancy? No. She took money from Johnny and ran. With more willpower than he thought he possessed, he eased back from the kiss.

***

No, no, no, don't stop.

Flames licked at Scarlett, and she needed more. One taste of him was only a tease. He was a delicacy that was bad for her, but too tempting to resist. She wasn't done, not even close.

Something long, thick, and rock hard pressed against her most intimate place and begged her to squirm closer.

She whined in frustration, not knowing exactly how to get what she wanted.

Her fingers convulsed on his shoulders as her universe narrowed to this man and her body's reaction to him.

To his credit, he didn't hesitate to comply. His warm hand tunneled under her spandex top and found the swell of her breast. His thumb made erotic circles around the tip, setting off a chain reaction of need. She yanked at his T-shirt until she got her hands on his flesh. Oh, that was so good. She was on her way to getting what she wanted.

The screen door creaked, and Floyd cleared his throat.

"Oh, my," Joyce declared.

Honey whooped.

"Dude," Brody added.

This was not the way she wanted to greet her family. Lip-locked and Gavin's hand fused to her breast.

Scarlett jerked upright.

Gavin winced.

"Oh, sorry." Scarlett pushed on his chest to try and stand. But, her legs were like spaghetti. He slowly removed his hand from under her top, disentangled them, and pulled her to her feet.

She straightened her bun and clothes then waited for the self-recrimination…and waited. Nothing. What the heck? She'd been caught lying on top of a man, her tongue down his throat with him firmly at second base. That should have hit all of her humiliation buttons. There'd been some buttons pushed alright, but they had nothing to do with shame and everything to do with the tingling thrill low in her belly.

"What in the world are you two doin' out here?" Floyd crossed his arms, an impressive scowl on his face.

"Floyd, I would think it was perfectly obvious what they were doin'." Honey shook her head like her brother might be mentally incompetent.

"We were just..." Gavin started, but obviously couldn't quite find the words to clarify the situation.

She gave it a try. "You see, we..." Nope, she had nothing.

"For heaven's sake, can we all go into the house?" Floyd shouted. "My breakfast is gettin' cold."

***

Scarlett was the last to enter the kitchen. Her legs were still a bit unstable and her vital signs irregular. The counter was a good place to lean and try to regain her equilibrium. Like that was possible. The undeniable truth was that her life would continue to tilt on its axis as long as Gavin was around. The logical left side of her brain continued calculating the fastest way to get rid of him. However, it appeared the right side of her brain now had a dog in the hunt and wasn't giving up without a fight.

Fabulous.

Thankfully she was with her family, and their steady presence helped strengthen her. She knew who she was around them. She was the good one, the person everyone counted on, and the girl strong enough not to do any more stupid things around her husband.

The rock star in question crossed the kitchen, looking incredibly edible in tight jeans and black studded boots. He fell on the coffee pot like a denim-clad hyena on a dying wildebeest. His light black t-shirt was still rucked up on the side, exposing a wolf's head tattoo. Snarling teeth and red eyes peeked from beneath the fabric, filling her head with salacious images of licking every ink-covered inch of him.

No! She'd never licked another living soul in her life and didn't intend to start with him. Her gaze drifted back to the tan patch of skin and decided to remain open-minded about the licking issue.

"Scarlett?" Gavin waved a hand in her direction.

"Huh? What?"

"Isn't this the tea you drink?" He held up a pink box with white and yellow daisies on it.

"Yes."

"Can I get you a cup?"

"Yes, please." Sexy and thoughtful. How was she supposed to resist that deadly combination?

He hesitated, gave the box a long look and glanced at Joyce with uncertainty clearly written on his face. It was obvious he was out of his depth. Joyce took mercy on him and directed him to the pot of tea she'd already made.

Gavin gave her a grateful smile, and Joyce dropped the cup she was holding. Yep, he had that effect on women. Thankfully her dad was there to catch the mug before it hit the floor. Floyd tactfully turned a slightly discombobulated Joyce away from his son-in-law and led the poor woman to her seat.

"Gavin, you're so sweet," Honey gushed.

"Yes, it's very thoughtful." Joyce agreed, still a little dazzled as she fanned her fuchsia cheeks.

"How do you take your tea?" Gavin held up a pitcher of cream and the sugar bowl.

"Two sugars and a splash of cream, please."

He really is making me tea.

Her heart did a loop-de-loop as he dropped the first cube in. He was careful not to let any splash out and make a mess. His lip was caught between his teeth and his brows were furrowed in deep concentration, like a boy solving a difficult math equation. One more cube was carefully added to the steaming liquid.

"Scarlett, darlin', how did you sleep last night?" Honey rocked on her heels as she asked the question.

"I slept fine." Only half her attention went to her aunt. The other half was totally focused on the man with the teacup.

He stirred her cup one more time after adding the cream, and brought it to her. She gave him a grateful smile and sniffed the sweet aroma that she knew now would always remind her of him. This would be so much easier if he were the classic self-absorbed rock star. But Gavin didn't seem to be that guy. He'd surprised her with humor and kindness. There was also a vulnerability about him that was intriguing and a little heartbreaking.

"Are you suuuure you slept okay?" Her aunt tried again.

"Yes, Honey. Why do you ask?" Scarlett made her way to the table, careful not to spill her tea. She was confused by the question.

"You look kind of worn out. I was concerned something kept you awake last night." The older woman winked at Gavin when he took his seat at the table.

Scarlett stiffened. Uh-oh. This was not good. Now she understood all the geriatric concern about her sleep habits.

"I think she looks lovely." Joyce gave Scarlett's arm a squeeze. She knew as well as Scarlett where this conversation was headed.

"I had a great night's sleep. How about you?" Maybe her aunt would take the bait and change the subject. No such luck.

"You know Joyce, you're right. She does have a certain glow about her, doesn't she?"

Scarlett delicately dabbed her mouth with her napkin. "Thank you. I'm using a new face wash."

The scheming woman shook her head. "No, I don't think it's what you're washing your face with. There's something else goin' on."

"Nope. Not a thing." Scarlett sipped her tea and pretended she didn't have a nosey, inappropriate aunt.

Seeing she wasn't getting the responses she wanted from Scarlett, she zeroed in on another victim. "How about you Gavin, how did you sleep?"

"Molly Jean." The warning in Floyd's voice was undeniable.

Honey was the picture of innocence. "What?"

"You know what. Hush up." Her father gave Honey a *zip it now* look.

His sister rolled her eyes. "I don't know what the big deal is. We're all adults here."

By some unspoken consensus, everyone filled their plates with gusto and disregarded Honey.

Scarlett puffed out a relieved sigh. Hopefully, the family's matriarch would lose interest in the topic and drop it.

But the old girl was made of sterner stuff and would not be thwarted. "All's I'm sayin' is that you get real tired makin'—"

"Biscuits," Scarlett shouted. "I know I get real tired making biscuits." She smiled around the table. "All that kneading and pulling, kneading and pulling, whew, it can be so tiring. My hands ache just thinking about it. Yes, making biscuits can be exhausting and can be nerve racking. I know I was nervous my first time. But Grandma said, 'Girl, get on that horse and ride.'"

Why am I still talking?

"She taught me a secret to making flaky biscuits. In fact, I've never known anyone else who uses this technique. You remember, don't you, Honey? I roll my biscuits out and sprinkle them with a good amount of flour then I roll the dough into a long tubular shape. It takes a lot of coaxing to get the dough to behave. You have to play with it a little."

Shut up, shut up, shut up!

"This can be tricky. If you don't show it the proper encouragement, the whole thing will deflate. The secret is to coat your hands with flour then rub them along the log, back and forth, back and forth. After you see it's going to do what you want, then that's when you put some muscle into it until you're satisfied."

"Then," she exhaled. "You roll it out and cut your biscuits." The last words faded off into nothing.

She squeezed her lids shut and lowered her head. What just happened? Can a brain have diarrhea? Her face and neck were on fire. She briefly thought about running from the room but remembered what her cheer coach, Miss Trish, used to say.

Smile and no one will know how badly you've messed up.

She plastered on a huge smile and slowly looked up. Miss Trish was a damn liar. Her daddy, Honey, and Joyce were staring at her, all in varying degrees of horror and shock. No one said anything. She smiled bigger. Maybe she hadn't had the right amount of wattage to sufficiently convince them she wasn't an idiot. It didn't work.

With all her courage, she turned to Gavin, expecting to see the same expression on his face that the others wore. Instead, his eyes danced with amusement and a spark of heat. Never taking his gaze from hers, he raised a biscuit to his mouth and took a bite.

Oh, my.

Chapter 11

Gavin checked his phone for the billionth time while he rode in the back of Scarlett's fuel-efficient, ultra-safe, mid-sized sedan. The PI hadn't called, texted, or emailed. Damn it. Every minute the man didn't call was another minute he was away from his son.

If it *was* his son. Shit, what a mess.

"Are you okay back there, Gavin?" Honey asked.

"I'm fine. As long as Scarlett gets us there before I die of old age." They were going so slow they were practically going backwards.

Honestly, Honey probably drove faster than his wife.

He inspected a bag marked *Emergency Supplies* on the seat next to him. There was enough stuff in there to survive the apocalypse. "You believe in zombies, Scarlett?"

"Huh?"

"Nothing."

The overly prepared grandma trapped in a delicious twenty-five-year-old's body gave him a dismissive eye roll in the rearview mirror.

"I can't thank you enough for doin' this for me, Gavin." Honey looked into the visor mirror and ran a pink-tipped finger around the outside of her red lips. "The girls are gonna die when they see you." She gave Scarlett a worried look. "I hope Martha Barker can handle it. You know the last time we saw Mickey Gilly in Louisiana she started havin' heart palpitations, and he looks like a shriveled-up ol' raisin. One look at Gavin, here, and she'll probably keel right over."

"Um…thanks, I guess?"

"Don't act like you don't know you're hotter than fire, boy," the geriatric said.

"Okay," he chuckled. Slow molasses filled his chest when the older woman gave him the most adoring smile. The kind of smile a doting grandmother gives to a favorite grandson.

Careful, Bain, that kind of thinking is very dangerous.

Scarlett glanced at him in the mirror again. She sucked in her cheeks, in an obvious effort to stifle a laugh. Not interested in sharing a moment with her, he looked away. The conversation he'd overheard before they left the house still rang in his ears. She'd wasted no time in making sure the money was in her bank account.

Bitterness bit at his insides. It was totally irrational, but he felt he'd been used. Angry resentment of all the times he'd been taken advantage of and exploited by women simmered beneath the surface.

The last year bleeding out on a therapist's couch, to control the eruption of that boiling sewage, had helped, but two days in Scarlett Kelly Bain's company threatened to erode all the ground he'd won.

He was pissed, but why? He'd long ago accepted that people sucked, which meant low expectations for the entire human race. So why was he holding her to a higher standard than he did everyone else?

Because she seemed the most genuine person he'd ever met, devoted to her family and honest to a fault. Then there was the fucking money, which made her…what?

He was so damn confused.

It didn't seem to matter that he was using her too. Or that he'd paid her to get what he wanted. He shouldn't want more from her. This was a business deal like thousands of others in his career. The stupid grudge was because she wasn't who he wanted her to be.

His thoughts and, if he was honest, his feelings about her were like a hamster on a wheel, no matter how fast they moved, they went absolutely nowhere. Until he knew the real Scarlett, he needed to leave her the hell alone.

All this whining made him sick.

The car slowed even more as they entered the city limits of Zachsville. He chuckled when he saw the city limits sign: *Zachsville Texas, population 3500 good people and 3 or 4 grumpy old farts.* He'd missed that yesterday when he and Jack blew through town. Was that just yesterday? It felt like a month ago.

"I can't wait to see Sally Pruitt's face. She thinks she knows everything."

"So is this Sally person your arch enemy or something?" He pulled at the seatbelt that had tightened when Scarlett slammed on the brakes for no apparent reason.

"Oh no, Sally has been Honey's best friend since they were in grade school. But you wouldn't know it by the way they bicker with each other." She cut her aunt a pointed look.

Honey smirked at Gavin. "It's complicated."

Scarlett burst out laughing. "Complicated, huh? You know you'd die for Sally. You're just mad she knew something before you."

"Yes, and whose fault is that?" She turned sideways in her seat and pinned them both with a look. "I have something I want to say to you two. We will have a wedding here in Zachsville." The car swerved violently. "Scarlett, honey, try to keep the car on the road."

"You're the closest thing I have to a daughter, and I love you. I've been planning your wedding since you were a tiny girl. I'm not lettin' a quickie marriage in *Lass* Vegas rob me of giving you the day you deserve." She sat back in her seat. "There, I said my peace."

Scarlett's voice quivered a little, "Um, Honey...I don't—"

"Whatever you want, Honey," Gavin cut in. *That insanity came out of my mouth.* He jerked his gaze to Scarlett's panicked expression.

115

Honey crossed her arms and nodded. "You're darn-tootin'. I'd like to have the wedding at the farm. I'll talk to Brother Randy tomorrow. Do you think he'll have a problem with that, Scarlett?"

"No." Her voice was barely audible.

"Who's Brother Randy?" he asked Honey, but kept a wary eye on his wife, who seemed to be blinking away tears.

"Oh, he's our pastor. You haven't met him yet, Gavin." Honey dug in her purse and pulled out a pen and notepad.

Now he understood. The freaked-out woman behind the wheel might confuse him in many of ways, but God and family meant everything to her. Getting married in front of a Whitney Houston impersonator in Vegas was one thing, but saying vows in front of her pastor and relatives was another thing all together.

Damn, he really screwed this up. He should cut his losses and change the subject. "Honey, how long have you lived in Zachsville?"

"Oh, Lordy, I've been here my whole life." She put her list away. "And I'm not gonna tell ya how long that is," she said, and chuckled.

He laughed as Honey told him a few details about when she was a young girl. Scarlett gave him a small smile in the mirror and mouthed, *thank you.*

"Oooh, we're already causin' a stink." Honey waved at a couple in front of the laundromat. "After we go to the beauty shop we can walk over to the pharmacy and see who's there."

"No. Honey, we'll go to the Dip-n-Do, so you can say hello, and then we're going home. I'm here to keep you from manipulating Gavin into parading all over town."

"You're right dear," Honey said with absolute sincerity.

Gavin didn't believe her for a minute.

Scarlett drove down the main street, which opened onto a town square. Maybe if he got out and pushed the car, they could pick up enough speed to get them there today. Finally, she pulled the car into a parking spot in front of a pink building with a giant wooden pair of scissors above the door.

Gavin exited the vehicle and opened Honey's door. Her hand was soft in his, and the scent of baby powder and gardenias filled his head when she stood next to him. She wore cowboy boots, loose fitting jeans and a purple t-shirt with a pink sequined rearing horse on the front. Below the horse was written *This ain't my first rodeo.*

They walked arm-in-arm up three tall steps. Gavin looked toward the building. "Are they watching?"

Honey smiled up at him, red lipstick on her two front teeth. "Yes, they are." She used her free hand to remove her huge white sunglasses and hooked them in the neck of her shirt.

Scarlett stood with one arm resting on top of the car, and the other draped over the driver's side door. "I'll be back shortly. Gavin, if you need anything text me. You did put my number in your phone, right?"

"Yeah, I've got it. Don't worry, we'll be fine." Did she think he was an idiot? Compared to the rest of his life this trip to town was a piece of cake.

"You two behave yourselves," she called after them.

They ignored her.

A bell tinkled when the salon door opened and two women walked out of the shop. The younger of the two said, "See you next week, Ruby. Remember, don't wash those lovely locks for forty-eight hours or you'll ruin your perm."

"Thank you, Maureen. See you next week," the other woman said, and walked away down the street. Her hair was curled so tight to her head that it looked like a gray helmet.

"Honey Jenkins. I didn't expect to see you here today." Maureen's tone indicated that's exactly what she expected.

"I came for some of that good smellin' shampoo you have," Honey said.

Maureen pulled a cigarette from her smock pocket and lit it. "Who's your friend?"

Honey's mouth parted and she touched her hand to her throat, feigning ignorance to the rock star beside her. She didn't fool anyone. "Oh. This is Scarlett's new husband, Gavin Bain. Gavin, this is Maureen, she owns the Dip-n-Do."

Gavin knew this was his cue. He threw an arm around Honey and smiled his best *People Magazine* smile. "Maureen, it's nice to meet you."

The shop owner plucked a piece of nicotine from her tongue and flicked it away. "I saw it on the news. Sounds like Scarlett went stark ravin' crazy when she was out in Vegas." She exhaled and cigarette smoke engulfed her like a noxious halo. "He's good-lookin' and all, but I don't think he's worth losin' your good name over."

Gavin knew how true the woman's words were, but they still stung.

"Maureen Coulter, you take that back right this minute." Gavin jerked at Honey's outburst. Her soft affable eyes were now hard as granite and shooting anger at Maureen. "I will take my business to Lovely Tresses faster than you can blink. You do not want me as an enemy, Maureen. I know things."

He was glad Honey defended Scarlett. He was frustrated with his wife, but it was unfair for people to talk trash about her. Admittedly, he didn't understand much about families, but what he did know was that they were supposed to stand up for each other.

"You don't talk about my family." Honey jabbed her finger in Maureen's direction. "You know how precious Scarlett is to me, and Gavin is a Kelly now. He will be treated with courtesy and respect, or I promise you, folks will know about that good-for-nothin' son of yours and his interest in—"

"Fine." Maureen held her hands up in surrender. "I take it back. Goodness, Molly Jean, you get so testy." The beautician laughed nervously. "I'm sorry I spoke ill of your family."

"It's not me you need to apologize to." If possible, Honey's glare became more menacing.

"Okaaay." Maureen looked at Gavin. "I'm sorry I was rude, Gavin."

"That's better." Honey took Gavin by the arm and started down the street. He followed obediently.

"What about the shampoo?" Maureen hollered.

"I've decided I don't like the smell as much as I thought I did," Honey snapped.

The bright Texas sun beat down on his head. He barely noticed. He expended all his energy trying to recover from the shock of Honey's words. Never had a woman defended him. Not once. They always blamed him. For everything. Starting with his junkie mom and continuing on to the last woman he briefly dated. According to the opposite sex, he'd been responsible for his mother's addiction, been emotionally unavailable, and everything in between. Hell, even Scarlett blamed him for this screwed-up marriage.

"I'm hungry, how about some lunch at the café?" Honey interrupted his mental ramblings.

"What?"

"I said let's go to the café to get a bite to eat. I've decided to let you treat me to lunch." She was already moving down the sidewalk.

"Scarlett said to wait here for her."

Honey turned to him, fist on her round hips. "Do you always do what people tell you to do?" She raised her precariously drawn-on eyebrows in challenge.

It was a mistake to get attached to this family, but it appeared it was too late. According to Honey, he was now a Kelly. He grinned and ambled toward her. "Nope."

Her hoot of laughter filled the square. "Me either."

***

The faux leather squeaked when Scarlett adjusted her position on the small sofa in the waiting area of the First National Bank of Zachsville. She couldn't sit still. Her legs crossed and uncrossed, she moved from the front of the couch to the back, and the sounds coming from the loveseat were attracting attention. The Harper twins were pointing and laughing until their mother finished her business and dragged them out the door. What was it about eight-year-old boys and potty humor?

The hundred-year-old space hadn't changed much since she was a kid. Something pine-scented pricked her nose but didn't quite cover the smell of mildew and years of cigarette smoke that were as much a part of the old building as the light fixtures. Floor to ceiling windows spanned one side of the room looking out onto the town square. The offices along the other side of the lobby were made entirely of glass. It reminded her of the habitats at the San Antonio Zoo.

She could only see the top of Poppy's head through her glass enclosure because the lower part of her window was frosted. She mentally rehearsed the speech she was going to give the bank president.

Scarlett's sweaty hand ran over the column of her neck, and her fingers found the hammering pulse. The acid in her stomach churned like white-water rapids. She lost track of the laps her heart ran around her chest. Geez, she was a mess.

Who could blame her? Poppy had gotten her thrown in jail for solicitation. Stupid, she'd been so stupid, but how could she have known that *Miss Most Likely to Succeed* ran an escort service?

"When you get to the door, Scarlett, tell them your name is Heaven Leigh."

"Why, Poppy?"

"Oh, it's just a fun thing we're doing."

Scarlett brought her thumbnail to her mouth then stopped. She needed to calm down. Poppy could always smell fear. Any sign of weakness and she'd go for the throat. Scarlett envisioned her peaceful place and tried to find her center. Unfortunately, there was a giant hole where her center should be.

What was she going to say to the woman?

What's up, Poppy. Still turnin' tricks?

No. The best course of action was to ignore the giant pink elephant in the room. No good could come from dredging up the past.

"Ms. Sims will see you now, Scarlett." A petite, older woman in a lavender pantsuit led her to the office and knocked just below the Bank President plate. "Scarlett Kelly to see you, Ma'am."

Scarlett got her first look at Poppy in five years. She was gorgeous as ever. Expertly highlighted blonde locks were swept back in a tasteful chignon, her coral suit set off lovely green eyes. Her skin practically glowed, and the diamond studs in her ears twinkled in the sunlight coming through the window.

"Oh, my Lord! Scarlett." A high pitched squeal was the only warning Scarlett had before Poppy ran around her desk and wrapped her in a death grip. The pretty, pretty princess rocked them from side to side, continuing her incessant squealing. It was like being embraced by the bastard child of an anaconda and a sorority girl.

Scarlett's tear ducts watered from the assault of spicy perfume. Poppy's gravity-defying breasts enveloped Scarlett's head, cutting off all her airways. She would have extricated herself from the death-by-boobs hold, but her old nemesis had pinned her arms to her side so she could only flop her hands.

What the heck?

This was the last thing she'd expected. And if the former *Miss Zachsville* started singing *Kumbaya*, Scarlett was out of there.

Poppy abruptly released her to walk back behind her desk, causing Scarlett to stumble several clumsy steps.

"Sit, Scarlett, sit." The beautiful woman gestured to one of the leather guest chairs.

Scarlett wondered how many eyeballs Poppy had gouged out to get that particular shade of red on her fingernails. "Thanks."

"Sooooo, I heard you got married." Poppy clasped her hands together and leaned onto her desk, like the next words out of Scarlett's mouth would forever change her world.

"Yes." Scarlett's smile was so mechanical she was surprised there wasn't a wind-up key sticking out of her back.

"How deliciously unexpected. You're all the talk this morning. But I'm sure your family's used to that." Poppy gave a shrug and adjusted some papers on her desk.

"I'm sorry? I don't think I understand your meaning." She understood perfectly, but she was going to make the witch say it to her face.

Poppy didn't disappoint. "Well, I mean, your mother caused quite a stir in her day. My mama tells me Mary Kelly was...well...you know that talk." Her smile was sympathetic. Her eyes, though, were malicious and calculating.

It took all the courage Scarlett could muster, but she refused to look away. "Yes, I do know the talk."

I am not my mother, I am not my mother.

Poppy reached her hand toward Scarlett, placing it palm down on the desk. At the same time, she cocked her head, pouted her lip and gave her the *you poor thing* face.

"Yes, well, that's all in the past."

Where it should stay. Didn't these people ever forget anything? "I actually came to talk to you about our farm." She opened her purse, pulled out the check for fifty thousand dollars, and slid it across the desk.

Poppy's big whiskey gaze blinked once. Twice. "What's this?"

"It's the money for the loan on our farm that you called due yesterday." She wanted to do the happy dance as she watched Poppy try to formulate a response.

"Ah…where exactly did you get this money?"

None of your business, witch.

Poppy's lovely tan skin was losing color at an alarming rate. Well, it would be alarming if Scarlett cared. And she didn't.

"This check is from another bank. How do I know the funds are available?" Poppy bit out.

Never comfortable with the folks she went to church with or sat next to at Friday football games knowing her business, she preferred to do her banking in the next town over. "Oh, I assure you the funds are there, but feel free to call and verify." She sat back in her chair and crossed her legs.

Poppy's face readjusted into a professional mask. "Oh, I'm sure that's not necessary."

"Okay, then, I won't take up any more of your time." She stood and slung her purse over her shoulder. "It was good to see you again, Poppy. Have a great day."

Six feet.

Four feet.

A few more steps. She was almost to the door.

Three feet.

One foot. She reached for the handle. The sound of paper ripping and Poppy's icy voice stopped her dead in her tracks.

"Not so fast, Heaven Leigh."

Chapter 12

The cold doorknob in her hand helped keep her upright. Her head fell on the hard wood of the door. "What?"

"You heard me. Now, sit down." The ice in Poppy's words smashed into her like an arctic storm.

She glanced over her shoulder. There was a mound of paper torn to pieces on the desk.

The check.

She made her way back to the chair, where a Chanel-clad nightmare stared back at her.

"I'm afraid your money's no good here, Scarlett." Poppy smiled a sickly sweet smile again.

"What do you mean my money's no good here? I have no idea what this is all about, but you have to take the payment, Poppy."

"It's about the land that your sorry excuse for a farm sits on," Poppy said, in the most reasonable tone imaginable. "It's a beautiful piece of property, perfect for a new housing development. The pond, the creek, all those luscious trees. People will pay top dollar for the illusion of land to sprawl on." She slid open her desk drawer and pulled out a schematic.

Scarlett could only stare. Poppy had lost her mind. She may be the bank president, but she still had to follow bank procedures set by the government.

Poppy pointed a blood-red nail at the drawing. "See? Isn't it gorgeous?" She sounded like a kid showing off a new puppy. "Hiking trails, schools, parks, and million-dollar homes."

"Million-dollar homes? Poppy, who in Zachsville, besides your family and Luanne's, can afford such a thing?"

"No one," she scoffed. "I'll let you in on a super-big secret." She leaned forward. "Crude Co. Industries is going to build its new plant in Holton, only thirty miles away. All those oil execs will need a beautiful place to live. And my new development, located where the Kelly farm currently sits, will be perfect."

"Yeah, it's nice. Too bad you'll have to find somewhere else to build it, because I just paid off the Kelly farm. We own it free and clear." She crossed her arms. "Is your father in on this scam too?"

"Please," she scoffed. "If it were up to the ever-benevolent Hartley Sims, every farmer in this county would have an open line of credit. No, Mom and Dad are on a six-month cruise in Europe. He's happy and clueless."

"So you were going to take our land and leave us with nothing?"

"It sounds so ugly when you put it that way." Poppy tented her fingers and tapped them together. "And now that you've so inconveniently paid off the loan, I'll have to come up with another plan."

Scarlett rose. "Okay. I think we're done here. I'll have my bank draft another check. Any further transactions should be handled through my attorney." But it was clear the bank president wasn't listening to her. Whatever. She'd had enough of this insanity.

Poppy sighed, sat back in her chair and made a *what can you do* gesture with her hands. "I suppose there's only one thing to do, Heaven Leigh."

"You wouldn't."

"In a heartbeat." Her snake's glare confirmed the threat.

"*You* invited me to the party. *You* got me arrested."

The she-devil had the nerve to grin. "True. But I also got you out. So, technically you owe me. It's time to pay up, Heaven."

"I owe you? You're insane. I've always wondered how you managed to escape the arrest and how you got me out."

Poppy adjusted her jacket. "It's not hard when you know people. I have everything I need to destroy you, and I'll use it in a New York minute if you don't give me what I want. That land at pennies on the dollar."

"You want me to betray my father by getting him to sell the land to you?"

"Precisely."

A bark of laughter shot from Scarlett's mouth. "Are you off your meds, Poppy? I would never hurt my family like that."

The dragon-lady behind the desk brushed imaginary lint from her lapel. "Tell me this, Scarlett. How hurt do you think your family will be when they find out their precious girl was arrested for prostitution?" Poppy's hand went over her heart. "What will people say?" she mocked. "And who do you think our friends and neighbors will believe? Zachsville's princess or the town slut's daughter?"

Would she ever outrun her mother's reputation?

"Of course, I'll have to insist you keep this only between us, or things could get really ugly." She winked. "Understand?"

Scarlett gripped the arm of the chair. "Oh, I understand, alright. You're an evil bitch."

"Name-calling, Scarlett? It's so beneath you." Poppy dug in a drawer and tossed a manila envelope on the desk. The edge of a photo peeked out.

Angry tears shoved against Scarlett's eyeballs when she saw the image on the desk. She clamped down her emotions and tried to ignore her mascara stained face in the picture. She would not let Poppy see her lose it. "How can you ask me to do this horrible thing for you?"

Poppy's tone was conciliatory, her expression shocked. "No. No. Not for me, Scarlett. For you." She narrowed her eyes, and all sign of mollification vanished. "Because if you don't, I will release every piece of evidence I have about Heaven Leigh, including her true identity, to the media." She leaned forward, her face as chilling as her next words.

"It'll be a bloodbath."

***

The midday sun scorched Scarlett's retinas when she emerged from the bank. She leaned against the building and dug her sunglasses from her purse. Her arms and legs didn't want to work, the afterburn of too much adrenaline, too fast, in her system.

How had this happened? This problem was supposed to be put to bed. But instead of being resolved it was exponentially worse. She would not give into Poppy's demands.

She. Would. Not.

Yes, she'd been arrested, but she'd never been charged, and it had all gone away. Really, it would only be Poppy's word against hers.

Who do you think people will believe, Zachsville's princess, or the town slut's daughter?

Bile burned her throat. She wanted to hurl, but then she heard the sweetest sound in the world.

"Miss Scarlett, Miss Scarlett." Two five-year-olds barreled down the sidewalk toward her, leaving their mothers in their wake.

"Ginger and Mia, how are you?"

"We're good. We missed you in Sunday school," Ginger said.

"Yeah. Mrs. Ellis was mean. She wouldn't let me turn the storybook, even though I *telled* her you let me do it all the time." The mutinous look on Mia's adorable face was hilarious.

"You *told* her?" Scarlett said.

Mia scrunched her face up for a second and said, "Yes. I *told* her." Her snaggletooth smile melted Scarlett's heart.

"Harry Mosely brought a grasshopper to class, and Mrs. Ellis yelled when he pulled it out of his bag. She has a phe…a pho… What's it called, Mommy?" Ginger asked her mother.

"A phobia. It means Mrs. Ellis is very afraid of something," Ginger's mother answered. "I guess you can tell they really missed you Sunday. But it sounds like you were kind of busy." Ginger's mom, Carol, waggled her eyebrows. Laurie, Mia's mom, gave a throaty mmh-hmm.

Heat exploded across Scarlett's face and neck, and it didn't have anything to do with the Texas sun. She ducked her head. "Yes. I was a little busy."

Both women howled with laughter, and Laurie threw her arms around Scarlett, "Congratulations, girl. I'm so happy for you."

Before Scarlett could respond, Carol jumped into the fray and wrapped them all in a group hug. "I'm happy and jealous. He's hot as fire."

Not to be left out, Mia and Ginger began dancing around singing, "He's hot as fire, he's hot as fire, he's hot as fire."

Thankfully both moms released her and took ahold of their offspring, putting an end to the PG-13 chant.

Ginger pulled on Scarlett's hand. "Is Mr. Scarlett coming to Sunday school with you?"

Scarlett stifled a giggle at the thought of Gavin 'The Delinquent' Bain in a kid's Sunday school class. If Harry Mosley showed him a grasshopper, Gavin would probably drop an "F" bomb then bite the head off the thing. "I doubt it, sweetie."

"Well, we'll let you get on your way. Girls, tell Miss Scarlett goodbye," Laurie said.

"Bye, Miss Scarlett." They both wrapped their skinny arms around Scarlett's legs, making it hard to stand.

"Goodbye girls, see you Sunday." She smiled as she watched them skip down the sidewalk.

"What a touching scene," sneered an older woman with jiggly jowls and hard eyes. Marjorie Stewart, Zachsville's biggest gossip and the mother of her ex-boyfriend, Justin, blocked the sidewalk.

"Hello, Marjorie." The burgeoning bubble of happiness the girls left behind popped at the sight of this spiteful woman.

"I wonder how long you'll be teaching Sunday school after everyone has time to process your spontaneous marriage to a musician." She spat musician like a four letter word.

"Marjorie, I'm not interested in discussing my husband with you. If you'll excuse me?"

"A Las Vegas wedding is so cheap, not to mention tacky. But then again you are your mother's daughter, and if there was ever a tawdry, tacky woman it was Mary Kelly. Hmpf, the apple doesn't fall far from the tree." She pulled her jacket down over her considerable girth. "The best thing to ever happen to my Justin is the day he cut you loose."

"Goodbye, Marjorie." Scarlett stepped past the woman to make her escape. But Marjorie's words rang in her ears. Not the part about Justin, because she'd broken up with him, but the apple not falling far from the tree.

Thoughts of her Sunday school kids floated through her head. She loved them, and they loved her. Their parents loved her. What would they all think when she was exposed?

Her mother's reputation ensured everyone would believe the worst. The truth rarely mattered once gossip started.

Her phone buzzed. With a shaky hand, she fished it from her purse. Five messages from Gavin blinked with insistence.

We're at the café. No worries. Come when you can.
You need to come to the café. ASAP!
Where the hell are you? Hurry!!
Get your ass here. Now!!!

Help!!!!

***

The music reached Scarlett's ears before she got to the diner, and the savory aroma of pot roast met her on the sidewalk. Everything blurred for a second as her vision adjusted to the dim light of the café's interior. Honestly, she didn't need the sense of sight to know what was happening. Honey was at an upright piano in the corner of the restaurant, playing and singing her heart out.

The restaurant's owner let the senior citizens use the diner on Mondays when the restaurant was closed. The piano was there for the Senior Crooners sing-a-long that Honey led. Gavin was sitting next to the piano on an upside down, white, five gallon bucket beating the rhythm of the hymn Honey was belting. He wasn't singing, maybe he didn't know the song, but more likely Honey told him to only accompany her. Her aunt did love the spotlight.

Ronny Lewis, the café's owner, greeted Scarlett at the door. She nodded toward her aunt. "How long has she been at it?"

Ronny chuckled. "This is her third song. Can your husband really sing?"

"Yes. Why?"

"He hasn't sung a note since she sat down. Of course, he could be a bit shell-shocked. She stood him in front of Sally Pruitt's table and told him to raise his shirt to show his tattoos."

Scarlett covered her face with her hands. "No, she didn't."

"Yep." He wiped off a menu with a cloth. "She and Sally seemed to be particularly fascinated with the one right above his jeans…in the front…below his navel."

Scarlett held up her hand to stop him. "I know the one." She couldn't meet Ronny's eyes. "I better go save him." She maneuvered through the tables accepting congratulations as graciously as possible, all the while

131

wanting to crawl in a hole. Honey might love the spotlight, but she hated it.

The upside to the situation with Poppy, if there was an upside, was her marriage to Gavin had been downgraded from *biggest mistake of her life* to just a plain ol' mistake. The biggest mistake of her life had been to trust Poppy Sims.

Relief relaxed Gavin's features when he saw her. A laugh loomed behind her lips, she couldn't help it. His face was so tortured. By the time she made her way to the pair, she'd gotten her laughter under control.

The song ended to polite applause. Honey continued to play a light tune while she decided on her next number. "Gavin, do you know *Love Me Tender?*"

"I do."

Still playing, Honey smiled to the crowd and leaned closer to Gavin. She whispered surreptitiously, "Do you really know it? Because these people expect a certain level of professionalism from me, I don't want you makin' me look bad." She nodded to Peggy Fox and returned her attention to him. "No offense."

"None taken." Gavin's serious face must have conveyed the correct amount of competency because Honey segued into the love song.

When the first strands of the tune began, a low rumble of conversation filled the room. Then Honey and Gavin began to sing. All movement stilled, all chatting ceased. The duo had the entire room's attention, and even the kitchen staff stopped to listen. Honey's sweet soprano, with the perfect amount of vibrato despite her age, blended and melded with Gavin's dry gritty baritone to create something heartbreakingly beautiful.

The melody rose and fell, weaving a spell throughout the room. When they got to the second verse, Gavin took the harmony and deepened the richness of the sound.

Helpless against the pull of his voice, she placed her hand on his shoulder. Zings of pleasure raced up her arm when he wrapped his warm hand around hers.

What was it between them? They'd only known each other a few days, but the moment he whispered in her ear in Vegas, there'd been something linking them together. Was this what it was like for her mother when she met *Mr. Right Now* in the Stop-n-Shop? The instant connection that went beyond allure straight to the bone and blood of her being.

Ridiculous, a bunch of romanticized crap. She needed to get her head out of the clouds. The real world didn't work that way. There were rules to life and when people ignored them everyone got hurt.

"Momma? Where are you goin'?"

"Scarlett, Momma's found the most wonderful man and I'm leaving on a great adventure."

"But what about me?"

Her mother stopped packing and stared at her. "Darlin' don't you want me to be happy?"

"Yes, but can't you be happy here...with me? You're supposed to be with me. It's a rule."

"Oh, my sweet girl, sometimes you have to break the rules for love and happiness. You remember what I'm sayin', you hear me?"

With that priceless piece of advice, Mary Kelly walked out of her daughter's life forever.

She'd remembered, alright. Every step of her life was premeditated, made in the exact opposite direction of her impetuous mother's life. Tightly controlled decisions to ensure respectability and safety ruled her existence. How was it then, she found herself in the precise spot she'd worked so diligently to avoid?

She flinched at the thought and slipped her hand from Gavin's. She bowed her head and averted her teary gaze from the room. Maybe they would think she was moved by the melody.

When the song ended, the place erupted into enthusiastic applause. Some whooped and hollered their approval. Gavin rose and kissed Honey's cheek, then offered her his hand. The two bowed to the audience, accepting their accolades like the seasoned performers they were. One was an international superstar, the other a hometown favorite who'd sung at more weddings and funerals than anyone else in three counties.

The duo made their way to the front door, declining requests for another song. Scarlett followed, a forgotten footnote in the wake of their success. Despite her dark thoughts, a smile tugged at her lips as she witnessed the camaraderie between her husband and aunt.

Once they were outside, Honey grinned up at Gavin. "Good move gettin' us out of there. Always leave 'em wanting more. You remember that when you play your concerts."

He winked and slung a tattooed arm around her aunt's shoulder. "I'll write it down when we get home."

From the corner of her eye, she spied Marjorie Sanders and several of her church cronies scrutinizing the whole scene. A kernel of resentment nudged its way into her heart. How dare they judge her...or Gavin? They didn't know him, and for that matter, they didn't know her.

The accusations of recklessness hurled at Gavin by the reporters yesterday shifted to the front of her mind. His desperation to be seen differently had driven him to offer to pay her, a virtual stranger, to stay married to him. They weren't so different, the two of them, both trying to outrun the ghosts of their past.

Gavin glanced back and extended his hand. "You with me, Red?"

She placed her hand in his. "I'm with ya, rock star."

Chapter 13

He hadn't touched her in three days. She was glad…she was. It was for the best, they needed to keep their distance from each other. And if she said it a few more times she might start to believe it. If he'd never kissed her, held her, touched her, she could think of him as a temporary roommate. But he'd done all of those things and more. She could no more *unremember* them than she could read hieroglyphics.

A slow burn slid down her body. Her pulse tap-danced in her neck. Prickly heat spread across her skin and up her neck. Like a carnal slide show, scenes from their time in Vegas streamed through her mind.

His smoky eyes held her captive as he bit her fingers, every nip like the rev of an engine to her overly sensitive and under-serviced libido. Each kiss up her forearm stole one piece after another of her self-control. When he laved the crook of her elbow with open-mouth kisses, she'd become his creation, a reckless creature ready to beg for what she wanted.

The slam of the screen door brought her back to the present. She drew cleansing air into her body and tried to tamp down the desire swirling inside her. She'd been so easy, ripe for the picking. Embarrassment mixed with the lust and she didn't know whether to run to Gavin or away from him.

She'd lost her mind then and now. But there was something about him.

His rich sexy voice rumbled like thunder on a hot summer day from the next room. She couldn't make out the words, but it didn't matter.

The troublemaker who lived inside her skipped around throwing flowers into the air as she sang, *I'm married, I'm married, I'm married to Gavin Bain.* Scarlett shut her down when the flowers turned to clothes and skipping became pelvic thrusting.

That tramp was seriously inappropriate. And now that she was off her chain, it made it hard for Scarlett to resume her normal routine. Normal. What a joke. She couldn't even spell the word anymore.

Her neatly organized, purposely productive schedule had been obliterated. Instead, she drifted through the day sneaking peeks at Gavin, waiting for the other shoe to drop with Poppy, staring at the blinking cursor on her computer, and wondering how she'd gotten herself into this mess.

Gavin, on the other hand, had been a perfect gentleman.

He helped her dad with chores, did the dishes, or sat on the back porch writing music.

The music was where she saw the true Gavin. The lyrics were still as irreverent as always, but laced with a rawness she'd never heard in his songs before. Nothing was off limits. The songs told stories of his loneliness on the road, of lost love, or love never had. The songs were living photographs of Gavin's heart and it made him all the harder to resist.

That's why she found herself leaning against the wall next to the back door night after night. She'd listen to him weave his tales, always out of sight so she wouldn't disturb him. Or at least that's what she told herself. The truth was she didn't want him to see how his songs, his truth, affected her.

"We're going to Los Angeles." The object of her conflicted thoughts barged into her office and plopped down in the chair next to her desk.

"What?" Geez, he smelled good, woodsy with a touch of spice. She lowered her lids and took a big whiff.

"You alright?" One side of his mouth kicked into a cocky grin.

"Simply resting my eyes."

"Uh-huh." He dragged the word out like he didn't believe her at all.

She bit the inside of her lip and glared at him. "What were you saying?"

"You're so full of it." He laughed. "I said, we're going to L.A. to meet with the Storm Side execs." He beat out a rhythm on his thighs.

That got her attention. She swiveled away from her computer. Might as well, she wasn't making any progress on the new idea for Carousel. "Do I have to go? I have work, and my family needs me here. Plus, the agreement states we will live here for the duration of this marriage."

"The agreement also states we will be seen in public as it benefits one or both of us. Jack thinks it's a good idea for you to go with me to the meeting, and so do I." One black brow hiked up his forehead.

Leaving her comfort zone where she had a modicum of control wasn't appealing. And fear of what Poppy might do hung over her head, but what choice did she have? They had a stupid contract. "Fine. Oh, but not on Sunday."

"Okay, but why?"

His confused expression made her grin. He got a cute wrinkle between his brows when he frowned. It looked like a 'w.' "We have church on Sundays, Gavin."

"Um...alright. Any day but Sunday will work?" He fiddled with some pens lying on her desk and wouldn't meet her eyes.

She chuckled. "Don't worry, Gavin. You're not expected to attend."

"I don't mind." Now he stacked her sticky notes into a pile. He would have sounded more convincing if he'd said he invented cheese.

"Really, Gavin, it's fine. I have to teach Sunday school anyway."

Relief colored his face when he peeked up at her. He gave her his get-out-of-jail-free grin. "Okay, I'll let Jack know."

His discomfort amused her, and the thought of The Delinquent in church...too weird to contemplate.

***

A tremor jolted up Gavin's arms as he jammed the post-hole digger into the ground. The hard Texas soil resisted, then relented. He yanked the sod from the ground with an agitated grunt and flung it aside. When Floyd said he could use some help digging holes for a new fence, he'd jumped at the chance to work off some frustration. His earlier conversation with Scarlett had him tangled up in his feelings. Again.

She knew he'd been uncomfortable with the whole church thing, and, instead of making him sweat, she let him off the hook. He had no idea why it messed with his head or heart so much.

Sweet and funny, every day he liked her more than he should. But she'd taken the money—Stop!

He was sick to death of this emotional Ferris wheel. She was a money grabber, but nothing about her made that true. If it weren't for the damn arrangement, he'd jump on the next plane out of Texas and be gone.

That's what you do, Bain. You run. You're such a coward.

He rammed the ground harder this time. Maybe he could jar loose the self-disgust crusted over his soul. When Johnny died, he ran and hid for almost a year and a half. If it hadn't been for finding Johnny's letter, he'd still be hiding. Strong emotions scared the living shit out of him and one thing he could say about Scarlett, she evoked strong emotions.

"Um…Gavin." Joyce's son, Brody, stood with his hands jammed into his pockets.

"Yeah?" He grabbed the bottom of his shirt and wiped the sweat from his face.

"I was…ah…I was wondering if you…that is if you have time—"

"Spit it out, Brody. What do you want?" Great, now he'd snapped at a kid.

"Could you give me guitar lessons?" Brody's face flamed bright red.

Gavin's throat constricted. The guitar had saved his life. When Johnny taught him to play, he was living on borrowed time. He'd been close to going over the edge, but music pulled him back and gave him a reason to do something other than ruin his life. Johnny told him he could pay it forward one day. But nobody had ever asked him to teach them, until now. It was an honor.

"I know you're busy and probably have more important things to do, so it's cool." The kid pivoted on his boots to retreat.

"Yes." It was all he could manage to say with the elephant sitting on his lungs.

The boy turned back to him and his face transformed. "You mean it?"

He swallowed, trying to get moisture to his voice box. "Sure, I mean it. My best friend taught me to play, and I'm happy to teach you."

"I already know some chords. I need help putting them together. Honey said she'd teach me, but…" Brody's shoulders shook with a shudder.

Gavin laughed, and it felt good. "She makes you uncomfortable?"

"Yes. She says weird stuff sometimes, and I never know if she's kiddin' or not."

139

"She doesn't have much of a filter, it's true." Gavin clapped the kid on the back. "Let me finish this and shower, then we'll get started."

The boy smiled and practically bounced out of his skin. "Do you need any help? I'm pretty good at diggin' holes."

"Nah, I'm good. If you have any homework or chores, go finish them and meet me on Scarlett's back porch in an hour."

"Ok." He turned and then stopped. "Thanks."

"Don't mention it, man. It'll be fun."

***

Gavin didn't know when he'd had less fun. He fought the urge to cover his ears when the boy butchered another chord. Terrible. Yes, he knew most of the chords, but *all thumbs* didn't begin to describe him.

Had he been this bad when he started learning? Probably. He did remember Johnny calling several of their lessons short because he needed to do homework. Thinking back, he should have known that was code for, *Dude, you suck.*

"Remember Brody, don't lift your fingers too far off the fret board when you change chords.

"Like this?"

No, I've seen polar bears with better dexterity.

"Try this." Gavin demonstrated the proper technique.

"Oh, I see." Brody tried again and did the exact same thing he did the first time.

"Yeah. That's great." He was going to hell for lying, but he couldn't bring himself to crush this kid's excitement. "It takes a lot of work, you'll get it. I think I've given you enough to work on for today. What do you say we get back together next week? In the meantime, you should practice. A lot."

Gavin rose and placed Patsy in her case. Scarlett's back porch overlooked a small pond with a dock extending out into the muddy water. A very peaceful spot. He spent time out here writing and hoped the events of the last hour hadn't killed the creative vibe.

Brody put his guitar in its case too. "I'll practice till my fingers bleed, promise."

"Right on." It seemed only fair since his ears were bleeding.

Gavin's phone rang and he pulled it from his pocket along with the piece of foil Scarlett had given him. A little squashed, but it still seemed to work. All his calls to Jack had been crystal clear. He leaned his hip against the railing and noticed the boy's confused expression. What was he staring at?

Whatever. Kids were weird.

"Hey, Jack."

"Hey, Gav. Did you talk to your wife about meeting the Storm Side guys?"

"Yeah, any day but Sunday is good." Why did the boy continue to stare?

"What's happening Sunday?"

"We have church."

Jack laughed. "Are you shitting me?"

Gavin grinned and ran his hands through his hair. "No, man. Evidently, we go to church on Sundays."

"That's priceless. I'll drop a hint to the media. They'll love this, and so will the record execs."

He turned away from Brody's probing gaze and lowered his voice. "You can tell Storm Side but not the media. Church is special to them, and I don't want to do anything to embarrass the family."

Jack snorted. "I'm sorry. I thought I was speaking to The Delinquent."

"Yeah, well. I like the aunt, and I'm pretty sure having a media circus at the church would upset her. So don't do it." He emphasized each word and hoped Jack got the message.

"Ok. How's it going otherwise?"

He considered his roiling emotions related to Scarlett. "Fine." He squinted into the sun. "It's complicated."

"We are not doing complicated. Do you hear me, Gavin? You're supposed to get in and get out. Period."

"I hear ya."

"I'll text you the details about the meeting. Hey, how's Luanne? Has she mentioned me?"

"No, Jaqueline. Would you like me to pass her a note in study hall?"

"Would you?"

Gavin glanced over his shoulder and noticed Brody still staring. "No way, dude, she scares me. Not your type at all, a total badass. She'd have you for lunch and then ask for seconds." Jack went for sweet, docile women, who never had an original thought of their own.

Jack chuckled like a creepy old uncle. "I might change my type for a chance at her."

"Good luck with that." No way in hell Luanne would go there. "Text me later."

He hung up the phone, and put it and the foil in his pocket. Brody followed the movement. "What?"

"Dude, what's with the foil? Is it an L.A. thing?"

Unease tingled at the base of Gavin's spine. "No, it's an *I'm out in the middle of nowhere thing.*" The kid continued to gawk at him. "It helps me get cell reception."

Brody doubled over with laughter. "Who told you that? Man, they got you good. There's a cell tower two miles up the road." His laughter taunted Gavin as he left the porch.

He yanked the foil from his pocket and glared at it. She'd played him. She would pay—big time. He wrenched open the back door. His entire body vibrated with fury as he threw his head back and roared.

"Scarlett Kelly Bain!"

Chapter 14

Scarlett burst into the living room, her expression panicked and wild. "What is it? What happened?"

"Get your as—

Gavin's tirade stalled.

It fell over.

Curled up.

Laid down.

And died, at the sight of her, wet as a water nymph, in nothing but a towel.

Creamy, moist skin wrapped in a tiny bit of fluff tended to do that to a man. Damn. Wet hair cascaded down her back like an amber waterfall, and his thoughts stuttered worse than a preteen boy in a lingerie shop. Clearly, he'd interrupted her shower. Fire raged as lust and anger duked it out for control. He clenched his fist. The foil antenna bit into his palm.

Anger won.

He jammed the offending object in the air and shook it. "What the hell, Scarlett?"

Crimson blossomed across her face. "Um...ah...I don't understand?"

She understood alright. Her guilty eyes searched for the closest escape route.

Oh, no you don't, princess, time to pay the piper.

He stalked toward his prey. "You played me. Did you all have a good laugh?"

She backed up with every step he took in her direction, a predator's tango. "I don't know what the big deal is. It was a little practical joke."

"A joke? You lied to me. You had me traipsing all over this place waving this piece of foil like a majorette. And you call yourself a Sunday school teacher. What would Jesus do, Scarlett?"

When she bit her lip, in an obvious effort to not laugh, he made his move. "Come here."

She screamed and ran to the other side of the sofa, using the piece of furniture as a barrier between them. Her towel slipped half an inch. "It's your own fault. If you hadn't made fun of us hillbillies, I wouldn't have done it."

They bobbed and faked, each trying to be the first to move. "So this," he pointed the piece of foil at her, "is my fault? Because of a few comments I made, you hung me out to dry. You're a vicious, vicious woman." He vaulted over the sofa.

She squealed like a kid on a roller coaster and ran around to the wingback chair. With one hand she tugged her droopy towel back into place and with the other, she pushed her curls from her eyes. She laughed so hard she snorted, which made him laugh.

Where had his anger gone? How did she do that? Completely disarm him.

"I am vicious and ruthless. You better sleep with one eye open, buddy."

Right then, his eyes were glued to where her towel looped together. It was a precarious connection. If she moved too fast, it could fall apart. "Girly, you're the one who needs to watch her back because I'm coming for you."

He dove and grabbed.

She shrieked.

"Gotcha." But only her damp towel hung from his hand. She stood bare-assed naked and…damn.

Holy hell.

She tried to cover herself with her hands. "Close your eyes."

"Not on your life." He didn't know where to look first. It was a buffet of enticing tidbits.

"Turn around."

Her screech hurt his ears, but he could see just fine. Her arms and hands continued their jerky attempts to obscure his view. She seemed to have trouble prioritizing which parts she needed to conceal first.

"Stop looking, please."

Her plaintive whine had zero effect on him. "I would if I could," he lied.

Her hand shot out to snatch an afghan from the couch. She held it in front of herself to shield her nudity. He wished he could kiss the person who had knitted the thing. It had a criminally loose weave, and her best parts were still plainly visible.

"Scarlett." He took a tentative step in her direction.

"Stay right there." Her hand flew up to ward him off.

Yeah, like that would work. "I don't think so." He carefully moved a few more steps toward her, like he'd seen Floyd approach a skittish colt.

She retreated until her back hit the wall. "You're mad at me, remember?"

"Not anymore."

***

Sirens screamed in Scarlett's head. Jolts of panic crackled along her nerves. She was standing naked, with nothing between her and a gorgeous hunk of a man, except for her grandmother's threadbare afghan.

Under any other circumstance and for any other girl, this would be a dream come true. In fact, she may have had this very fantasy as a teenager or even a few days ago. She wanted nothing more than to have Gavin's hands all over her, but given the current mayhem that was her life, she couldn't let him touch her. If he did, there'd be nothing to stop them from consummating this ill-advised marriage. And here's a great idea, let's add ravenous sex hormones and make a complicated situation much worse.

This had to stop. One of them had to be reasonable. So she used the only weapon she had.

"Are you ready to collect on your investment?"

He stood completely still. "What?"

She cinched the afghan tighter around. "You paid a lot of money for me. I suppose you have every right to expect sex."

He scratched the side of his face. "I suppose you're right. But I'm surprised you'd bring it up."

She bit her bottom lip. This was about to get ugly. She could see it in his eyes. Fine with her, she had some pent up emotions that needed to be released. "Why?"

"Because there are several unflattering names they call a woman in your position."

His contempt threatened to bow her spine, but she wouldn't give him the satisfaction. "My position?"

He surveyed her up and down. "Naked women who take large sums of money from men, they're called—"

"You offered me the money, you jackass." Infuriation swirled with the residual desire still pumping through her body. Her emotions collided, exploded, jumbled, and made her simultaneously want to strangle him and climb him like a monkey.

"You didn't have to take it." He stabbed the air with his finger.

"You have no right to judge me, you hypocrite."

He crossed his arms over his chest. "You know what I'd like to know, Scarlett? What happened to the woman who didn't want anything from me?" She opened her mouth to speak, but he continued. "I'll tell you what happened. She deposited my fifty thousand dollars three days ago."

She shoved off the wall and got right in his face. "She sure as hell did." Angry currents of resentment shot through her like radio static. "Because at the first sign of trouble, the spoiled rock star threw money around to get what he wanted."

"You didn't have to take it!"

"Yes, I did!"

"Why?" He jammed his hands on his hips.

The tiny glint of hope in his searching gaze nearly undid her. She had to get out of here, or she'd spill all her secrets. She wanted to tell him and be done with this crap, but Poppy's threat of exposure hung in the air like a noose. "You know what? I don't owe you an explanation."

The last thing she heard as she locked herself in the bathroom was the front door slam shut.

***

Gavin white-knuckled the steering wheel of the old truck, grateful he'd bought the thing. Without a vehicle, he couldn't have escaped the Kelly farm. He barely remembered the drive into town. Damn it, he was furious. It took the fifteen-minute trip to get his breathing under control. His jaw ached from grinding his teeth, and his hands throbbed to hit something.

The speedometer indicated he needed to slow the hell down. Shit. He wouldn't redeem his image if he were hauled away in handcuffs by Zachsville's finest. His foot came off the accelerator. When he entered the town square, he was the picture of a law-abiding citizen.

The truck rolled to a stop in front of the City Café. Stale cigarette smoke and motor oil from the old pickup got stuck in his throat. Suddenly the cab of the truck became too small. He got out and stomped into the restaurant. The locals stared, but he ignored them. Screw 'em.

A pretty young waitress sashayed up to him as soon as he sat down at the counter. "What can I get ya?"

"Coffee. Black."

"Anything else, some dinner or…dessert?"

Dessert meant her, with whipped cream on top. Not tempted, not even a little bit. All his thoughts gravitated to Scarlett's little butt as she'd run from the living room. The sight of his name branded on her milky-white skin made him want to howl with ownership.

"Just coffee."

He raked his hands through his hair. Weariness swept through him, as leftover adrenaline fizzed and dissipated from his bloodstream. How had he gotten himself into this mess? Fu...ah, effin' alcohol.

Not only the alcohol, Bain, and you know it.

No, it hadn't been. Images of chasing Scarlett around the living room and of their combined laughter rolled over him. Had he ever had fun with a woman outside the bedroom before? Not that he could remember. It was pathetic, but he'd laughed more in the last five days than he had in the last five years. He found himself seeking her out during the day to mess with or talk to her, anything to spend time with her.

Even before he got so shit-faced he married a stranger, he knew he wanted to keep her. She was everything he wasn't and like no one else he'd ever known. Her sweetness was a siren's song that hooked him the first moment he'd seen her in that bar, and every day she reeled him closer and closer.

But an out-of-work musician with no social skills, and feral as a cat, had nothing to offer a woman like her. If he could get his career back on track, be at the top again, then maybe...but not now.

Dammit, now he was pissed again. Without even trying, she'd turned his life upside down, and apparently given him amnesia. Because when her towel came off, nothing mattered except getting his hands on her. He hadn't even considered the money until she brought it up.

She was the queen of the mixed message. Why did she keep bringing up the money? The answer danced just out of his reach. Could she be using it as an excuse?"

"Well, well, well, if it isn't Zachsville's newest celebrity." Luanne slid onto the stool next to him.

He glanced at her then back to his clasped hands on the counter. "I'm not in the mood, Luanne."

She bumped her shoulder into his. "Ah come on, I'm just jokin'."

The waitress sat his coffee in front of him, saving him from having to reply. He could feel the attorney studying him.

She laid her hand on his shoulder. "Hey, you're really upset."

Hell, yeah, he was upset.

"What happened? Is Scarlett okay?"

"She's great. Fifty thousand dollars great," he bit out.

"Oh." Luanne made a production of surveying the menu. "Are you eating? You should eat. The food is amazing here."

The tiny terminator, who'd threatened castration for harassing Scarlett, curiously had nothing to say about his insult. Maybe she hadn't caught the offense. "No, I'm not eating. I need to get home to my gold-digger wife."

"Too bad. Today's special is chicken potpie. You haven't lived until you've had Ronny's chicken potpie." She smiled as bright as the Texas sun.

He swiveled on the stool to face her, one arm rested on the counter and the other on the back of her chair. "Cut the crap, Luanne. What the hell is going on?"

She folded the menu, continued her brighter-than-day smile and added in a little twang when she replied, "I have no idea what you're talkin' about."

"Oh, please, I've insulted Scarlett twice in two minutes, and you want to talk about the daily special? No way. You're hiding something."

He gave her his best glare. The attorney stared back. Luanne had mad skills, but his were better. He let The Delinquent bleed into his eyes.

She glanced away first. He had to hand it to her, it took her longer than most.

"Tell me, Luanne."

Now, she wouldn't make eye contact. She pulled ten napkins from the dispenser, one right after the other. "All I'm going to say is that not everything is as it seems." She flagged the waitress down and ordered an iced tea.

"Well, that's as clear as mud." He swigged his coffee. "What does that even mean?"

She shook a yellow packet of sweetener. "If you had to pick ten words to describe Scarlett, where would gold-digger fall on that list?"

The way Scarlett cared for Honey, worried for Joyce, helped Floyd in the barn, tutored Brody, teased him...all of it ran through his mind. "If she hadn't taken the money, I wouldn't put it on at all."

"What does your gut say?" She stirred her iced tea.

"I have no idea."

"Yes, you do—"

Whistling and catcalling came from behind them. They angled their bodies to see the commotion. Every patron's attention was focused on the wall-mounted television behind the counter.

On the TV, his wife danced her heart out on top of a table in the middle of a crowded bar. In the scene, he stood on the ground in front of the makeshift stage undressing her with his hot gaze while the other customers waved dollar bills in the air. With every gyration, her white dress swished and swayed around her butt. The crowd on the screen and the folks in the café went crazy as she performed a spin move, and her *sensible-pantyclad* ass mooned her bar-mates.

All the dancing must have made her thirsty because she sat down on her heels, picked up a shot glass, threw it back, and grabbed him around the neck. After she devoured his mouth, she stood up and continued dancing.

Luanne's quick intake of air jolted him into action. He snatched his cell phone from his pocket and hit a button.

"Oh, my Lord." She seized his arm. "You've got to get her out of town."

"I'm already on it—Jack, I need two tickets to L.A. tonight. I know what I said about Sundays. Just get us out of here. We can be in Houston in…" He looked at Luanne. She held up three fingers. "Three hours. I'll explain later." He threw money on the bar and beat a path to the door, Luanne hot on his tail.

"I'm going with you." Her heels clicked on the sidewalk as she raced to keep up with him.

"Good, I may need some help." He popped the locks on the truck and they climbed in.

"I'll do whatever you need." She braced herself when he took a corner well above the speed limit.

"Warn me if Floyd goes for the shotgun."

Chapter 15

Gavin spotted Floyd coming from the barn and pulled the vehicle to a sliding stop. He and Luanne jumped out of the old truck and made their way to his father-in-law. He knew he'd have a fight on his hand to get Floyd to agree to Scarlett leaving. But he'd heard the way the townspeople laughed and jeered at the TV in the diner. She'd be subjected to the talk that he already knew happened here in Zachsville. And for some ungodly reason, he thought he could protect her from that.

He must be out of his mind to think he could take care of her, or anyone else, but he had to do something.

"Son, you need to slow that thing down." Floyd slipped off his work gloves and stuck them in his back pocket.

"I need to see you all in the house. Are Honey and Joyce inside?"

"They are. What's going on?"

"Where's Brody?"

"At a friend's. Boy, you better tell me what's going on." Floyd crossed his large arms.

Gavin held the screen door open to the house. "Let's go in, and I'll explain."

They found Honey and Joyce in the family room watching the Food Network. "Are we havin' a party?"

"Honey, I need to change the station." Luanne took the remote and flipped channels until she found an entertainment program.

"Someone needs to tell me what's goin' on. Where is Scarlett? Is she alright?" Floyd stepped into the middle of the room.

"Oh, my word," Joyce gasped, and clutched her throat.

"What?" Floyd said.

Joyce pointed to the television.

Floyd stared, transfixed, as Scarlett danced on top of the table. It seemed to take several minutes for his brain to make sense of what he watched. He laced his fingers on top of his head and glanced at the ceiling then back to the television. "Oh, Baby Girl, when you go off the chain, you go all the way."

Honey made a choked sound and Gavin went to her side.

"Gavin, you're going to take care of our girl, aren't you?"

He crouched next to her and placed his hand on her powdered cheek. "Yes. I've already booked us a flight to Los Angeles, leaving tonight. I think it will be better to get her out of town for a while."

He found Floyd's fierce stare. A muscle ticked in the older man's jaw, but he nodded, and the tension flowed out of Gavin.

"Has anyone talked to Scarlett yet?" Joyce dropped down on the sofa next to Honey.

Luanne put her phone in her pocket. "I've been calling her but she hasn't picked up, which probably means she's writing and hasn't seen the story." She put her hand on Gavin's shoulder. "We should go tell her."

Gavin kissed Honey on the forehead. "Don't worry. I've got this."

She closed her eyes and a single tear trickled down her sweet face. "I know."

Floyd stepped in front of him on his way out the door. "Son, that's my daughter on the television. You dragged her into this mess, and I expect you to clean it up. Do I make myself clear?"

He stood motionless, not sure what to do. In the past, if anyone got in his face like Floyd just had, he'd have kicked their ass. But this was Scarlett's father and...he was right. With a gigantic effort, Gavin swallowed his pride. "I know, and I'm sorry. You have my word I'll do everything in my power to make this right."

Floyd nodded again. "Alright then."

Before Gavin made it to the door, Honey's emotion-clogged voice reached him. "And for heaven's sake, Gavin, buy the girl some better underwear."

***

Scarlett hit the delete button on her computer and watched an hour's worth of work disappear. Good riddance. It was crap anyway. She scrubbed her face and glanced at the time on her computer. Gavin had been gone more than an hour and her emotions hadn't settled at all.

She pushed against the memory of standing before him naked and tried to close her mind to the ugly words they'd spewed at each other. But she couldn't forget the hurtful exchange and her body nearly burst into flames when she recalled how he'd devoured every single inch of her with his sizzling stare.

Guilt beat at her conscience for the way she'd treated him. It was cruel to use the money against him. She was a lot of things, but cruel had never been one of them.

She shut down her laptop and went in search of a diversion. Channel surfing and mindless television should do the trick. It was time for Hollywood Entertainer, and though she'd never admit it, she was as much a fangirl of the host, Shay Wallace as Luanne. Yes, a Hollywood hottie and then Wheel of Fortune should do the trick.

She ignored the fact that this was the same evening routine Honey had and what that said about her.

***

Gavin let the truck roll to a stop. "When we get in there you should do the talking."

"Me? You're her husband." Luanne gaped at him.

"Yeah, well, if she's seen the story she'll likely blame me for the whole disaster. If she hasn't seen it, I think it would be better if the information came from you." At her unconvinced stare, he continued, "We...kind of fought before you found me at the diner. Things were said. I doubt she'll believe I have her best interest at heart."

The ferocious elf in the seat next to him gave him a squinty-eyed look. "What did you say to her?"

"Hey, it wasn't only me. She said some crappy things too." He turned off the truck and chuckled. "Trust me, the woman gives as good as she gets."

Luanne's lips twitched, and her expression danced with humor.

"What?" This woman put him on edge, she saw way too much.

"Nothing."

"What is it, dammit?"

"You like her," she teased.

He blew out a breath and glanced away. "Shut up."

"You do. It's written all over your face."

"Jack's been asking about you." It was all he could do not to burst out laughing at the horrified look on her face. Interesting, Luanne at a loss for words. He turned off the truck and exited the vehicle.

She jumped out of the truck and followed him up the walk. "What'd he say? It was probably something crappy, wasn't it? You know what? I don't care."

"Sure you don't."

She played with one of her diamond earrings. "I *don't* care. Really."

He gave her a look that clearly communicated he thought she was full of shit.

She stomped up the porch steps. "Come on. I need to talk to Scarlett."

They pushed open the front door and were greeted by cat-calls coming from the television. Scarlett sat on the sofa, her chin resting on her bent knees and tears streaming down her face. When the clip on the TV got to the end, she rewound it, and the whole thing started over.

"Oh no." Luanne made a choked sound.

"Is she alright? She doesn't look good."

Luanne carefully moved to Scarlett and kneeled in front of her. "Hey, friend. You okay?"

No reply.

"Scarlett?" Luanne rubbed her hands up and down her best friend's arms. "Why don't you turn off the TV?"

Scarlett hit rewind and started the clip again.

Luanne glanced at him over her shoulder, distress etched on her face. "Sweetie, it's going to be alright. Gavin's taking you to Los Angeles. Won't that be fun?"

Scarlett never looked away from the screen. "You know what they're all gonna say, don't you Lou? They're gonna say I'm just like my mother. In fact, I'm pretty sure there's a story about her dancing on a table that gets told anytime her name comes up."

"Oh, sweetie, I know. But you're not your mother," Luanne soothed.

Her mother? What did her mother have to do with any of this? He searched his memory. Had Scarlett ever mentioned the woman before?

"I don't know if that's true anymore, Lou." She hit rewind again. "That," she pointed the remote at the image of her dancing, "looks a whole lot like her."

His wife still hadn't looked at either one of them. She kept watching that damn clip. Her flat, hopeless tone was like thorns scraped along his naked skin. He couldn't wrench his gaze from her. A foreign sensation sliced at his heart and something close to sadness choked him. He'd ruined this poor woman's life.

Luanne whispered something to Scarlett, and without warning his wife vaulted from the sofa and sprinted from the room.

"What did you say to her?" He spat at Luanne.

Luanne rested on her heels. "I told her it wasn't that bad, all anyone really saw was her underwear."

A loud crash and screaming had the two of them bolting toward the back of the house. When they rounded the corner, the sight of Scarlett murdering her *sensible panties* stopped them in their tracks. White material flew into the air, and Scarlett's bawling accompanied the vicious snip of scissors. "Never again. Never again."

Luanne cautiously stepped into the room. "Scarlett, why don't you put the scissors down, and let's talk about this."

Scarlett's head snapped up, and her stormy, bloodshot eyes focused on her best friend. "What do you want to talk about, Luanne, my table-dancing moves, or my shot-shooting skills, maybe what a killer French-kisser I am? I know. Let's talk about how the whole world now knows I wear GRANNY PANTIES."

The pain and humiliation in her voice fastened itself to his feet and drew him into the room. "Scarlett, baby, please don't cry."

Her head jerked around to him. She jumped up and ran at him. Just when he thought she would stab him for getting her into this mess, she dropped the scissors and leapt into his arms. He stumbled back a step but caught her easily.

"Hey, I've got you."

"I'm so sorry," she cried.

"Why are you sorry?"

"I was so mean to you earlier. And your record people must be scandalized by my behavior."

He chuckled. "Scandalized? That was pretty tame compared to most of the people they deal with. Present company included." He inhaled her honeysuckle scent and held her tighter to him. "Don't worry. We'll work this out together, I promise."

He caught sight of Luanne sitting on the floor, a shit-eating grin on her face. Whatever. He wasn't a good person, he knew that, but he wasn't enough of a dick to let this decent woman hang in the wind alone.

Chapter 16

The smell of something delicious lured Scarlett from the safety of the warm shower. The rich, aromatic scent reminded her of home, and the heart-sickness she'd spent twenty minutes scrubbing away thundered over her.

It's over. Move on.

That was easier said than done when the entire free world had seen her behave so badly.

She toweled off, wiped the mirror free of condensation, and nearly fainted. Dark circle ringed eyes, pale, sallow skin, and freckles that stood out like chicken pox on a corpse. She was a hot mess.

No wonder.

She'd cried all the way to the airport the night before, and most of the flight to LAX. They hadn't arrived at Gavin's condo until midnight, when she'd promptly crawled into bed, ready to be done with the whole blessed day.

The ferocious growl that erupted from her stomach reminded her she hadn't eaten since breakfast the day before. Had it only been yesterday that the entire universe had seen...that?

She lowered her head and hid behind the fall of her hair. How had her life gone so far off the rails? Especially when she'd done everything in her power to keep it locked down with tight, focused control, to never give those small-minded, small-town people anything to talk about.

Could she ever show her face in Zachsville again? If it weren't for her family and Luanne, there'd be no going back.

Her family. She'd sent them a few quick texts as they were leaving the farm and hadn't spoken to them since. She dreaded the phone call.

She made her way to her bag, sitting on the bed in the adjoining room. Her favorite yoga pants, a Houston Texan's t-shirt, and fuzzy socks helped her feel human again.

Her phone vibrated, signaling a text. She had thirty-six messages. Most were from Luanne and her family, one from her agent, Marie, and one from an unknown number.

She dropped to the bed and opened the text from Marie.

Call me immediately. Carousel is NOT happy. We need to do damage control, NOW.

No real surprise there, but her heart dropped just the same. She was competitive by nature, and the thought of forfeiting the contest to Sally Bright was more than she could stand. Even though it grated that she had to change what she created to participate in their ridiculous competition. Her books could and should stand on their own merit.

Maybe she didn't want to be associated with them. Maybe she'd tell them to go to hell. Who was she kidding? She wasn't that ballsy. She paged back to her incoming text and made a mental note to call Marie.

Sweat broke out along her hairline, and her heart bucked like a wild mustang when she saw who the owner of the unknown number was. Poppy.

You can run, but you can't hide. Tick-tock, little jailbird. Time's a wastin'. Here's a small sample of what the world will see if you don't convince your father to sell. P.S. Loved your performance yesterday. You've got moves, girl. ☺

That bitch sent her a smiley-face emoji.

Scarlett scrolled down to the picture below the text. An officer was behind her snapping cuffs onto her wrist, as she looked over her shoulder, horror in her eyes, and streaks of black mascara streaming down her face.

The funeral dirge playing in her head swelled to epic proportions. This would be the death of her reputation, the death of everything she'd worked for, the death of her good name. There was still the slim possibility that the Vegas debacle could be written off as a one-time thing. A night of blowing off steam that got out of hand. But this? This would be like catnip for the residents of her fine town. They'd revel in it, be obsessed with it, and spread it like wildfire.

And her family…Poppy's lies would hurt them. Hadn't they endured enough from the judgmental people of Zachsville? She couldn't allow that to happen again.

There really wasn't any other choice. Her family would suffer if she didn't fix this. She grabbed her phone.

"Hey, Lou."

"Hey, dirty dancer, how's it hangin'?"

"Har-har."

"Too soon?"

"Just a tad."

"Sorry. How are you? I've been sick with worry all night." The concern in her bestie's tone gave her the courage to say what needed to be said.

"I'm fine." It wasn't a lie. Physically she was fine. "Listen, I need some help."

"Anything. You know that."

The soft carpet of the bedroom cushioned her steps as she paced. "I need you to listen and don't get mad."

"Hang on." She heard Luanne close her office door. "I'm back, and I promise not to get mad."

"Remember the semester you studied abroad?"

"Yes."

"Right after finals that semester, I ran into Poppy on campus."

"Poppy Sims?"

"Yes. She told me about this party where there'd be food, and I could dress up. I was broke, bored and wanted to have some fun, so I agreed to go. But she said I had to use the name Heaven Leigh to get in. You know Poppy is weird, I thought it was one of her loony ideas to appear superior, so I did it." She stopped pacing and peeked through the blinds. But the only thing she could see was the gray stucco building next door. "It was at this swanky house in the ritzy part of town. As soon as I walked in, I noticed there were a lot of older men at the party. It gave me the creeps watching them with the college girls that were there. To say they had roaming hands is an understatement. I was starting to get uncomfortable and was about to leave when the place was raided. I was arrested and held for twelve hours in the county jail. Then for no apparent reason was released with no charges filed."

"What? Why?"

"She was running an escort service, Luanne. She got away, and somehow got me out. I thought that was the last of it. We never spoke of it again, and thankfully she graduated soon after that. I thought it was a bad dream buried in the past. But when I went to give her the money for the farm she refused to take it and tore up the check."

"That's ridiculous. She can't refuse to take your payment."

"I know, and I told her so, but then she said if I didn't convince Daddy to sell to her she'd release the pictures. They're bad, Lou. She's texted two of them. Hang on, I'll forward the text." She tapped her phone screen and sent the text. When she heard Luanne's gasp, she knew they'd arrived.

"That bitch," Luanne snarled.

"Yep."

"There's a smiley face at the end."

"Apparently, it's her thing."

"She's a sick bitch then."

161

"That's true too."

"What are we going to do?"

Scarlett dropped down onto the bed. Never had six words sounded sweeter to her. "I don't know. I was hoping you would have some ideas."

"I have an appointment in a few minutes, so text me everything you can remember about that night and the people that were there. The other girls, the men, where it was, everything."

"I will. Thank you, Lou. I love you."

"Then start acting like it." The bite in Luanne's words caught her off guard.

Hurt knifed through her heart. "What do you mean? You know I love you."

"This is the second major event in your life that I've found out about after the fact. I gave you a pass on the Gavin thing because it had only been a couple of days. But this thing with Poppy happened years ago, and you're just now telling me about it. That's not how you treat someone you love, Scarlett."

"Excuse me for not wanting anyone to know I was arrested for prostitution."

"Was it true?"

"Was what true?"

"Were you prostituting yourself that night?"

"No! You know I wasn't."

"You're right, I do know. But even if you had been, your family and I would still love you and stand by you. Think about that. I have to go."

The line went dead, leaving Scarlett alone with her guilty conscience. Luanne was right. They would all stand by her. Hadn't they already? She was such an idiot. Still, she'd do anything to protect them.

A pan banged and Gavin cursed downstairs. Knowing she'd have to face him made her gut hurt for a reason, besides the lack of food. One more person she'd let down.

This whole marriage farce was to redeem his reputation, and she didn't think her table dance had done anything to further that endeavor, regardless of what he said.

Another hunger rumble reminded her she'd have to deal with her stomach soon. No more hiding in the comfort of the bedroom. Not that it offered more than the basic required items for a bedroom. A bed, a nightstand, and a lamp adorned the space. That was it. No art, no family mementos, no gold records hung on the walls, just lots and lots of nothing.

She fortified herself, opened the door, and got another whiff of something amazing. As she followed the scent of deliciousness downstairs, she noticed the same sparseness she'd seen in the bedroom. Blank walls, beige carpet, basic furniture. How could a man so full of life and music live in such a hollow space?

In only three short weeks he'd left an impression in her house. Spiral notebooks full of songs, chord charts, picks, and used guitar strings seem to follow in his wake.

He drew beautiful pictures too. She'd hung the first sketch on the fridge, like a proud mom, and marveled at his adorable and unexpected reaction. He'd been embarrassed, and obviously delighted. In fact, she'd gotten up during the night and spied him standing in front of the fridge grinning like a fool at the picture. His drawings now adorned every room of her house.

On the bottom step, her feet faltered, her troubles fled, and sumo-wrestling fireflies filled her empty stomach. Gavin stood shirtless and barefoot, wearing a pair of low-slung Levi's. The guardian angel tattoo on his upper back bunched and moved as he flipped pancakes on the stove.

He was such a contradiction. Not only was he the hot rock star with the ego to go along with it, but he was also kind and unbelievably protective. He'd held her all the way from Zachsville to Houston. When they'd received curious stares at the airport, he arranged for them to wait in the airline's VIP lounge until their flight left. She'd never been so thoroughly cared for.

She took care of her people, and they knew she could take care of herself. But yesterday, when she could barely string three words together, he'd treated her like she was a precious, breakable thing. At the moment when she'd needed him most, he'd been there to save the day.

And she loved him for it.

Her legs turned to rubber, and everything around her blurred and went sideways. She gripped the banister before her butt hit the step.

She loved him.

She loved Gavin.

She loved her husband.

A man who'd paid her to stay married to him. And it didn't seem to matter at all.

This was a complication neither of them needed. How had she let this happen? He'd snuck past her defenses with his tea-making, his sweetness to Honey, and his irreverent sense of humor. And now look at the mess they were in.

A goofy, lovesick grin split her lips when he began to sing along with the music coming from his phone. He and Aretha Franklin sang a duet, and it was awesome. She leaned her shoulder against the banister and watched the show, which included quite a bit of hip action.

She gathered herself, determined to deal with the whole love thing later. The song ended, and she applauded. He swung around, spatula at the ready.

"Oh, hi."

There it was. That boyish grin. And one more brick in the wall she'd erected between them came tumbling down.

"Aretha, huh?" She pulled herself to a standing position and prayed her legs held.

He shrugged. "Guilty pleasure. Besides, that woman can sing."

"That she can." She made her way to the stove to inspect the contents of the skillet. "Those smell great. I'm starving."

"Good. Because they're one of the few things I can cook." He hip-checked her out of the way, then flipped the hotcake. "I have the tea you like."

This man, she just couldn't... Tears stung her throat at his thoughtfulness. She swallowed several times before answering. "Thanks."

"The electric tea kettle is by the sink, the cream is in the fridge, and there's the sugar bowl." He pointed to the island in the middle of the kitchen.

She opened the refrigerator, and it was full of food. "Did you go to the grocery store this morning?"

He peered over his shoulder. "No. I called a service. They deliver."

She rubbed her sleepy eyes. "What time is it?"

"Ten."

"Oh, my gosh. I can't believe I slept so late. I'm kind of embarrassed."

"Why?" He poured more batter into the pan.

"I never sleep this late."

"You had a shit day. I think you're entitled." He nodded to her cup. "Your tea's getting cold."

"Wow."

"What?"

She made her way to the wall of windows that opened to a deck. In the distance, the L.A. skyline shimmered in the California sun. "This view is spectacular."

"Yeah, it's amazing. I hear it's better at night."

She strolled back to the bar and sat facing him. "You don't know?"

"No. Until last night I'd never stayed here. I was so bone tired when we got in, I didn't bother to open the blinds. I rented it sight unseen." She gaped at him like he was speaking Chinese. "I did see pictures of the place. It seemed nice, had good security, and was in the right place. So I rented it." He transferred a pancake to a platter.

That explained a lot. His signature wasn't anywhere in the place. "What about the furniture?"

He wiped up a spot of batter on the counter. "It came furnished. I had Jack call the cleaning service yesterday when I knew we were coming and asked them to get everything ready."

She gaped at him.

"What?"

"I…how…how did you get all of this done so fast?"

He turned the burner off. "In L.A., there's not much you can't have if you throw enough money at it."

A shame bomb exploded inside her and left shrapnel in her conscience. "I'm sorry you had to go to so much trouble for me."

"Hey." He walked around the bar and took her by the shoulders. "We're in this together, remember?"

She rested her forehead against his chest. "Okay."

He stroked her back. "Don't cry anymore, Scarlett. They're not worth it."

For a moment, she savored the feel of his hands on her. Then blinked her dry eyes. There weren't any tears left. She knew he was right, she did. But it was hard to unlearn a lifetime of behavior.

She tilted her head back and peered at him. "At least my family isn't upset with me." She'd texted with them briefly before leaving for the airport the night before.

He curled a stray piece of hair behind her ear. "No, they're not, but they are worried. You should call them."

She leaned into his hand. "I will."

"You're lucky. You know that, right?"

"Yes. I do."

He took his shirt from the back of a chair and pulled it on. The wild child within pouted.

"Okay. Let's eat." He sat down and handed her the platter of pancakes.

The first bite was a religious experience. "Oh, my gosh. These are awesome. Family recipe?"

He snorted. "Not hardly."

She swiped another bite through a puddle of syrup. "Your mom didn't cook?"

He shook his head without looking up from his plate.

"Mine either," she said and stabbed another piece.

"Speaking of your mother, when Luanne and I got to your house you kept talking about her. Why is that?" He loaded two more pancakes onto his plate.

Every bit of doughy goodness she'd eaten coagulated into a nauseating ball in her belly. She did not want to have this conversation with him, but by the same token, she did owe him some explanation for her craziness. He wanted the truth, he probably couldn't handle the truth, but she'd give it to him anyway.

She wrapped her hands around her mug. "My mother was...well, let's just say her reputation wasn't spotless."

He didn't say anything. He sat quietly and waited for her to continue.

She drummed her fingers on the table and refused to meet his gaze. "There are stories that go back before I was born about her outrageous exploits. Running around with other women's husbands, skinny dipping in the local water tower, drunken crying jags. They're ugly and notorious."

He clasped his hands under his chin, still giving her his full attention. "That's rough. But it was a long time ago."

"No one ever forgets, Gavin. Two weeks ago, at the library restoration meeting, Marjorie Stewart reminded me of the time my mother got into a fist fight with a woman in the parking lot of the Dairy Bar. It was humiliating."

"Why did she get into a fight?"

"Some woman confronted her about flirting with her husband, and my mother took offense and went after her with me standing right there. The cops were called, and by the time it was over the whole town was gathered at the Dairy Bar watching my mother get arrested and me get loaded into the back of the squad car with her so my dad could pick me up at the police station. I was six." She couldn't hide the bitterness.

"Shit."

Now that she'd started talking she couldn't seem to stop. "She was absurdly irresponsible too. In the middle of the day, she might decide she wanted to see the sunset over the ocean, and get in her car and drive to the beach three hours away."

"That doesn't sound so reckless."

"It's probably not. Unless you have a five-year-old you forgot about. And that little girl had to sit on the back porch for two hours after school, in the winter, until her father made it home from delivering a horse in the next county." Air puffed in and out of her nose. For a second, she was that scared, cold child waiting for someone to come rescue her.

He set down his fork. "That happened?"

She peered up at him from her half-empty plate. "More than once."

"Damn. They'll let any idiot have a kid."

"After the second time, Daddy asked Honey to come live with us to make sure someone was home to take care of me."

"Why did Floyd stay with her?"

She shrugged. "I don't know. We've never really talked about it. The subject of my mother is very painful for him, so I don't bring it up."

"Where is she now?"

"Dead. One Friday morning, she met a man at the convenience store and by four o'clock that afternoon she was tearing out of our driveway with him. I never saw her

Chapter 17

Scarlett smoothed the skirt of her flouncy yellow polka dot sundress. Not exactly the appropriate attire to wear to a corporate meeting with the executives at Storm Side Records, but Luanne hadn't packed her business casual clothes, so it was the sundress or nothing. For his part, Gavin wore a pair of gray slacks, a black t-shirt, and a black blazer. His motorcycle boots had been replaced by a pair of very expensive loafers. If scruffy-rock-star Gavin was delicious, then polished-and-shined Gavin was downright delectable.

She continued to replay their earlier conversation over in her mind. He'd been left alone for days when he was five. Pity, compassion, empathy, understanding all blended with pride that he'd made something of his life. No wonder she loved him.

The familiar riot of butterflies beating in her stomach when she thought of him made a synchronized loop-de-loop. This had disaster written all over it, and she needed to figure out a way to distance herself from those emotions. It might be a battle she couldn't win.

She made eye contact in the mirrored elevator doors. "Are you nervous?"

"No, why?"

She pointed to his hand beating out a rhythm on his leg.

He looked at it and chuckled. "I didn't even know I was doing it. I'm fine, just excited."

"Why do you think they wanted me to come too?" She blew a loose curl from her eye.

"I have no idea." He reached for her hand. "You look beautiful. At least they won't be able to fault me for my taste in women."

The blush started at her toes and colored her whole body, while contentment slid up her arm from his calloused thumb rubbing little circles on the top of her hand. "Thank you." Oh, sweet baby Jesus, she was a goner.

The shy smile he gave her was just about the last straw. The urge to hit the emergency button and jump his bones was stronger than a California earthquake. But that would be inappropriate, and she knew this meeting was meant to show they both could behave themselves.

The elevator door opened to the waiting room of the office, and they stepped out. The area was…to call it posh would be a gross understatement. It was gorgeous. Thick gray carpet cushioned every step. Silver gilded walls reflected indirect lighting coming from a huge crystal chandelier hung in the middle of the room, over a plush round settee. The whole area screamed *you do not deserve to be here*.

She was raised in the country, but she wasn't a bumpkin. She'd been away to school, gone on vacations, but had never seen anything as opulent as the waiting area of Storm Side Records.

A beautiful Asian woman sat at an antique white desk in the corner of the room. Her almond eyes showed no recognition, nor anticipation of their arrival. She almost looked like a mannequin, so when she spoke it spooked Scarlett a little. "Mr. Bain, Mr. Petty and Mr. Weinberg will see you in a moment. Have a seat. May I get you anything?" she said, as flat as one of Honey's pancakes.

"No, thanks." Gavin pulled them to a pair of black-and-silver wingback chairs.

"Hey. I could use some water. My throat's really dry."

His phone buzzed, and he pulled it from his pocket and checked the screen. "We'll get you a bottle of water when we get back there." His fingers flew across the screen, then he put his phone away. "Jack just pulled into the parking garage. He'll be up in a minute."

"Oh, joy."

"Your throat's not too dry to drip sarcasm there, Red."

She crossed her arms. "He's just not one of my favorite people. In fact, I know you don't suffer fools, so I can't understand why you've hitched your wagon to that idiot."

"First, he's no fool. And second, Jack's about the only person in this town I trust. He worked for the second agency we were with." He played with the gold band on his left hand. She fingered her own band. "We didn't deal with Jack then. He was just starting out, so he was more a glorified gopher than anything else. Anyway, after we'd been with the agency for a couple of years, Jack came to us and told us our manager was working a deal that would be bad for us and that he was dealing under the table. Because of the heads up, we got out of our contract and went somewhere else. Jack lost his job to do the right thing. He has integrity. And in this business, you can count on one hand the number of people who can spell integrity, let alone have it."

"So, you all left, and he started representing Wolfe's Bain?"

"Hell, no." He laughed. "He was a little too green for our taste. But he did help us find an agency that would take care of us. Jack went to work for another group and learned the business, so when I decided to come back, he was the only person I called. He'd just gone out on his own, the timing was right."

"Wow. I can't believe he went out on a limb like that for you guys." Wait until she told Luanne that Jack was one of the good guys. She'd never believe it.

He cracked his knuckles one at a time. "Jack's kind of a vigilante when it comes to his clients. He says what he means and does what he says. You know he's got your back."

"So he's like the Superman of agents?"

He leaned forward in the chair, rested his elbows on his knees, and clasped his hands. "Pretty much."

"Well, if it isn't the happy couple." Jack sauntered into the room.

"You're right, he's a real prince among men," she said from the corner of her mouth.

"Nah, you're right. He's a dick," Gavin whispered.

"Hey, that's Mr. Dick to you, sunshine." Jack shook Gavin's hand.

He bent and kissed Scarlett's cheek. "You're as lovely as ever, Mrs. Bain."

"Thank you, Jack."

"Mr. Petty and Mr. Weinberg will see you now." The receptionist opened the door to the executive office and ushered them into the inner sanctum.

Scarlett's heart started that jitterbug thing it had been doing ever since she'd met Gavin. She smoothed her hair, straightened her dress, and ran her finger across her teeth to make sure she didn't have lipstick on them.

She had no idea what to expect, but the two men sitting in the tricked-out office were not it. One wore buckskin pants, complete with laces down the side, and a dress shirt with turquoise buttons on the front and at the wrist. His straight silver hair was parted in the middle and hung to his waist. He introduced himself as Maury Weinberg. Mr. Wynn Petty, by comparison, was dressed more conservatively, as in, his severe black suit and shirt were topped off with a priest collar...an honest-to-goodness priest collar. He was not a priest. There were photos all over the room of him and his lovely wife and equally lovely daughters. He also sported a man bun.

They all took their seats, and Scarlett finally got her water.

Maury leaned back in his chair and gave her an appraising look. "So, young lady, are you aware you're a viral sensation?"

***

Gavin held his breath. There was a beat of silence that seemed to Gavin to go on forever. Then the two record execs fist bumped and laughed uproariously.

"You just saved us twenty-thousand dollars in promotional money for Gavin's next album," Wynn said.

Beside him, Scarlett stiffened, but somehow found the nerve to say, "Whatever I can do to help."

Maury snickered like a little girl. "Oh, Gavin, you've got yourself a live one there."

Jack put his hand on Gavin's shoulder. "I'm sure you gentlemen remember how it was when you were first in love." He made a *what can you do* gesture.

Wynn steepled his fingers. "Indeed, indeed. What say we get down to business? I'm sure these newlyweds have better things to do today."

Gavin breathed a sigh of relief. Finally. This was it. This would make everything right. Now he could be the kind of role model a kid could look up to.

Maury flipped his hair from his shoulder and opened a binder. "Gavin, Storm Side would love to have you as one of our artists. I'll admit, we were a little concerned by your behavior over the last few days, but after seeing how you looked at your wife in that video, it's obvious you're quite smitten with sweet Scarlett."

Gavin only nodded. What the hell did Maury mean? *He could tell I was smitten?* He was in lust for sure, but Gavin didn't believe in love. So that would never happen.

"Here is our proposal." Maury slid the contract across the table.

He and Jack skimmed it.

Suddenly, he couldn't breathe. "Um...somebody want to explain what this is?" He stabbed his finger to the first paragraph of the contract.

Maury leaned back in his chair and played with the turquoise buttons on his shirt. "We understand that your

175

previous record deal expired before Wolfe's Bain finished recording their last album. After Johnny's death, Gavin, you didn't release that album. We think a perfect way to introduce you to the public as a solo artist is by releasing that record. You sing lead on all of the songs, and we will use CGI to superimpose Johnny into the shot for the music videos and tours.

Both men's snake-oil-salesman smiles struck a match to his anger. He wanted to throw something. Instead, he sat, still as a statue.

Jack was the first to find his voice. "Gentlemen, I'm sure you can understand that Johnny Wolfe's death was and is especially hard on Gavin. I don't think this is the direction he wants to pursue."

Gavin could feel Jack's eyes on him as he stared at the contract. "Have you listened to any of the new songs I sent in the last two days?" He was shocked words could escape his constricted throat.

"We have," Wynn said enthusiastically. "And, believe me, we will use them on the next record, but for the first album this is the direction we would like to go."

"Yes," Maury added. "Your new songs are fantastic, but the public, your fans, expect a certain angst and anger from you, and that's what the Wolfe's Bain album delivers."

"I...um...I'm not sure." Gavin cleared his throat. He hoped to hell he wasn't going to cry. "I don't think I can do that. Wolfe's Bain was Johnny and me, from the start. It was our dream together, and it was awesome, but now he's gone and that time of my life is over. It wouldn't be honoring to him to stick his image on a screen and then turn a profit because we'd done that. I think if you gave the new songs a real chance—"

"I'm afraid the deal on the table, Gavin, is the one where we release the Wolfe's Bain album and promote it." Wynn adjusted his priest collar. "You understand that we are taking a big risk on you, and the WB album is our collateral. It will sell. It's some of your best work to date."

Gavin's mind raced. There had to be a way to salvage this. "How about we use a few of the better cuts from the album and add the new songs in with the old? Also, I don't want to use John's image. That's just creepy."

"No." Maury's genial demeanor dropped off his face quicker than Gavin could blink.

He couldn't believe this. The thing he needed the most was within his grasp, yet he couldn't grab hold of it. "Can I have a couple of days to think about it?"

Wynn rested his clasped hands on the desktop. "I'm afraid not. It's now or never."

"Stop." Scarlett smacked her hand on the desk. "Can't you see how painful this is for him?" She gestured to Gavin. "He doesn't want to do this. I've heard his new songs, and they're amazing. Better than anything he's ever put out. You two vultures, with your ridiculous costumes and make-believe superiority, can take this deal and shove it."

The tension in the room was strung tight as one of his guitar strings. Gavin couldn't believe it. Not even Jack had come to his defense, only the spitfire he'd married.

Wynn was the first to recover. "Young lady, you're jumping into a situation you know nothing about. I suggest you sit quietly and let us do the heavy lifting."

Gavin stood up. The fuse these two idiots lit the minute they gave him their proposal detonated with an explosion of rage. "Actually, she's right. You can take this deal and shove it up your asses." When he got in Wynn's face, the man's eyes widened, and his face turned as white as that asinine collar he wore. "And if you ever speak to my wife like that again, you'll need a priest." He extended his hand to Scarlett. "Come on babe, let's hit the beach."

Chapter 18

Gavin watched in fascination as Scarlett sang Maroon 5's *Sugar* at the top of her lungs while they roared down the highway toward the ocean. She had the worst voice he'd ever heard, but what she lacked in talent she made up for in enthusiasm. No inhibitions at all. So weird, considering in Zachsville she was all closed-up paranoia.

This was the woman he'd married in Las Vegas. Watching her throw her hair around, and sing her heart out, he knew exactly why he'd done it. When she let herself go, Scarlett was more fun than he'd had in his whole life. Both Scarletts were different sides of the same irresistible woman.

She picked up her drink and began to sing into the straw.

He cracked up when she gave him a flirty wink as she sang the word 'shit'. She slapped his arm, then leaned toward him with the cup, and they took the chorus together.

When the song ended, she collapsed into her seat. "I love that song. Have you seen the video? I get goosebumps every time I see it. Can you imagine if Maroon 5 showed up unexpectedly to sing at your wedding?"

"They're cool guys, you'd like them."

She stared at him.

"What?"

"You know Adam Levine?" The reverence in her voice made him laugh.

He shrugged. "Yeah. We played a couple of awards shows together. He's a kick ass guitarist. They're great—"

"Stop talking. I'm trying to get my head around the fact that you know Adam Levine. Whose life am I living?"

"Don't get too excited yet. I just threw away any hope I had of resuming my career."

"Does it help if I tell you that you did the right thing?"

"Yes, it does." He had done the right thing, but that didn't mean it wasn't occupational suicide. In this business, you did not piss off people like Maury Weinberg and Wynn Petty and expect to work again.

He slowed and pulled into the house that used to belong to the best friend he'd ever had—a brother in every way but blood, and the person who'd betrayed him.

"Oh, wow. This was Johnny's house?" She slid her sunglasses onto her head and examined the front of the house.

"Yeah." The pancakes from that morning threatened to make a reappearance. Sweat rolled down his temples and neck, and slid between his shoulders. Shit, he hadn't considered what it would be like to be here again. White knuckles on the steering wheel screamed panic attack, and he tried to make himself relax. Too late, the beast already had him around the throat. "Fuck."

"Gavin?" She shook him. "Hey, look at me." Another hard shake. "I said, look at me."

The command in her voice stopped him. "I'm sorry I said fuck."

She waved away his comment. "Are you alright?"

He wiped his wet brow with the back of his hand. "I haven't been here since he died."

"Oh, Gavin. Why don't we find a hotel and stay there?"

"No." He would face this. One more step to moving on with his life, and he wasn't alone, she was there if it became too much. Selfishly, he was glad she was with him. "I need to see the place. I had all of John's things packed up and moved to storage or shipped to me. There's all new stuff in the house now. My financial guys said I should fix it up to rent, but I couldn't stand the thought of strangers here." He brushed a curl off her forehead. "Besides, the view is killer."

They climbed the steps to the Cape Cod bungalow. When he swung the door open a tiny sound of pleasure whooshed from her mouth. She walked into a large room with pale hardwood floors the same color as the golden shore outside, and a huge floor-to-ceiling window covering the entire back wall. Beyond the window the ocean rolled and foamed on the glowing sands of Malibu Beach. There were infinity pools, but this was an infinity window. The house, the beach, and the surf were connected. The beautiful living room opened onto a large deck that was partly shaded and had steps that lead down to the sand. "Breathtaking," she whispered.

He tossed the keys on the bar and stopped in his tracks. Scarlett silhouetted against the backdrop of the Pacific Ocean *was* the most breathtaking thing he'd ever seen. Emotions he didn't have names for barreled into him one after the other. Being with her was a lot like the water outside the window. Fun and unpredictable, but dangerous if you didn't know what you were doing. And he definitely had no clue what he was doing, but it didn't seem to matter. He was diving in.

"It is." The words barely made it past his constricted vocal chords. He came up beside her, and they stood at the window for a long time watching the surf. Their breaths synced with the flow of the waves, their hands brushed against each other, and there wasn't anywhere else he wanted to be.

She gave him a shy smile and took a half step away from him. "Wanna go for a swim?"

Hmm, let me think about it, her wet and in a bikini? "Absolutely."

He led her to one of the bedrooms and left her to change. The master bedroom was so completely different he had to stand at the entrance and acclimate to his surroundings. It was decorated in blues, grays, and white. Peaceful.

Nothing like it was the last time he'd been here. When Johnny lived here, dirty clothes, alcohol bottles, drug paraphernalia, and sadness covered every inch of the room.

This wasn't the day to remember that. He'd grieved and would continue to grieve his whole life, but today was for the living. He shook off the memory and changed his clothes.

When he made it downstairs, she was standing on the deck looking out at the ocean. Her curls were piled on top of her head, exposing her long neck, and the red bikini they'd bought after leaving Storm Side exposed the rest of her. That caveman sense of ownership ripped through him again when he saw the 'G' of his name peeking above the top edge of her bottoms. He wanted to take them off with his teeth and place open-mouth kisses over his name. Finally, an emotion he could recognize. Good ol' fashioned lust.

But the situation was complicated. Scarlett was complicated. Some might say more trouble than she was worth. Not him. He'd grown to like complicated. He liked her. And even though love was a farce, true friendship wasn't. Next to Johnny, she was becoming the best friend he'd ever had. The reality of his decision to walk out of Storm Side lurked at the door of his mind, but her presence held it at bay.

She understood why he'd done it without him having to explain it to her. He'd never had the feeling of being known before. It was addictive. So no matter what happened with this ridiculous deal they had, they'd stay friends, and he would keep her in his life. Decision made, he went to have fun with the beautiful woman in a bikini.

***

The rough wood of the deck railing scratched Scarlett's hands. The sound of seagulls and surf were better than any massage to relax her muscles and razzed nerves. There'd been two more texts from Poppy when she'd checked her phone, one of a clock and the other of a pair of handcuffs. The woman was psychopathic.

She still had some time to figure out what to do about Poppy. Hopefully, Luanne would have some ideas the next time they spoke.

Marie, on the other hand, had also texted and called several times wanting to discuss strategy.

She wanted more than anything to tell them both to screw off, like Gavin had done to those two idiots at Storm Side.

"Hey."

She glanced over her shoulder and nearly swallowed her tongue. He wore a pair of black board shorts and nothing else. Lordy. He looked like a big, powerful cat stalking toward her. A sexy cat with luscious olive skin and beautiful tattoos.

He carried a cooler, beach chairs, and an umbrella. "Let me help with that." She took the chairs and followed him down to the sand, eating up every motion of the muscles of his back as they flexed from the weight of the cooler.

The call of the water was too much to resist for her overheated mind and body. She dropped the chairs and ran for the waves. The bracing water splashed her skin, and she screamed in delight.

A warm hand snaked around her middle and drew her back against the hard planes of his muscled chest. The swirl of the moving water and the heat of his body turned her bones to mush. She knew she should swim away, but instead, she relaxed into him as he kissed her neck. The world dissappeared, and it was only the two of them at this moment. Her tension slid out to sea when he tightened his hold around her waist.

Then, without warning, he picked her up and dunked her under the water.

She came up spewing and coughing. Her top was pulled to the side, nearly exposing her breast, her bottoms had migrated to places they were never meant to be, and her bun hung off the side of her head. She adjusted the swimsuit, then pulled the rubber band from her wet mop and slid it on her wrist. "You tricked me."

"How?"

"You tricked me with your sexual prowess to get me to drop my guard."

"I have sexual prowess?" His smug smile was a mistake. Scarlett jumped, caught him off guard, and took him under the water. Satisfaction was sweet.

She hollered as he rolled and quickly wrestled back control. "Gavin, behave."

"I don't think so, Red." With a push, she found herself under the tide. The salt burned her nose, but there was something so freeing about letting go with him that she didn't care.

A few more seconds of holding her under the water, then he yanked her up. "Give?"

"Okay, okay. Uncle. I give up."

He set her down and wiped sopping hair from her eyes. "You alright?"

"My ego's bruised, but otherwise I'm fine."

He held her head in his hand and searched her face like she held the answers to every question he'd ever had. For a moment, she thought he would kiss her, but he released her and glanced at the horizon. His tattoos glistened under the water sliding off his tan skin. She wanted to chase each droplet with her tongue.

It was a bad idea.

But here, thousands of miles from her life in Texas, it was hard to remember why that was. And even harder to remember why she cared.

He brushed a finger across her bare shoulder. "You're already burning. We should get out of the sun."

She was burning alright, and it had nothing to do with the sun. His touch ignited a lava pit deep in her body. With him this close, all she could do was nod.

Under the umbrella, she sipped a bottle of water and drew doodles in the sand. He dropped down beside her and dug in the cooler for his own bottle of water. "It's a nice day, but then again, almost every day's a nice day in Southern California. It's the only thing I missed when I moved."

"Why did you move?" When pain slid over his face, she quickly added, "You don't have to answer that."

He picked up sand and let it sift through his fingers. "I don't mind answering. I never talk about it."

He took a deep breath like she'd seen people do before they walked into a haunted house. "After Johnny died I lost my shit. I'd always hated L.A., and after his accident, I hated it even more. The city represented everything that killed him. The booze, the drugs, the money-sucking women, and fake-ass people who tell you what you want to hear because they sure as hell want something from you." He tossed his empty water bottle back in the cooler and snatched another one. "So I got the hell out and moved back to Seattle. That's where we'd grown up." He picked at the label of his drink. "Did you know that Johnny and I grew up in foster care together?"

"I saw it on *Music, Behind the Scenes.*"

He nodded. "I'd been in the system since I was five. Johnny got sucked in when he was twelve after his parents died in a car accident. They had a sickeningly perfect family. You know, where everyone loves each other and they all get along." He looked at her and smiled sheepishly. "Kind of like yours."

She grinned. "Were they off their rockers, too?"

His returning smile was sad. "I don't know. But their deaths haunted him. He never got over it, and he wore the pain like a second skin. That's what *Wrapped in Agony* is about. That was one of the first songs we wrote together."

"It's a great song, but hard to listen to. That line, *Love peels away my skin and eats me from the inside out,* is so raw. It's even sadder now that I know the story."

"Yeah. Johnny said that's how he felt every day."

"I can't imagine living with that much pain. How did he survive?"

"With humor at first. He was one of the funniest people I've ever known. But his humor was dark and bitter, which was fine with me, but most people didn't get him. Then he started self-medicating...until it killed him." He threw a rock into the surf.

Waves continued to crash on the shore, and tiny crabs skittered across the grains of sand. Scarlett drank her water and waited for him to continue.

"I could never understand why he couldn't get over it. I know that sounds harsh and stupid, but I was a throw-away kid. I didn't understand that kind of loss. And by the time I'd figured it out, it was too late."

Throw-away kid. She didn't think she'd ever heard anything sadder. Her heart broke for that little boy all over again. At least Johnny had known what it was like to be loved by two adoring parents. Gavin never had. She wanted to comfort him but knew he'd see it as pity and hate it. She steeled herself to keep her face neutral. "I'm sorry, Gavin."

He flipped a shell off his finger and squinted at the horizon. "I blame myself. If only I'd insisted he go back to rehab, maybe..."

"Did you take him to rehab the first time?"

His head fell back to the top of the beach chair. "The first time, the second time, and every time after that, and every time he'd tell me I was ruining his life. He'd get better, check himself out, do well for a while, and then fall off the wagon again."

"Sounds like you did all you could do. You couldn't be with him twenty-four hours a day, Gavin. The bottom line is, we can want good things for the people in our life, but we can't make them accept it."

"Yeah, I know you're right. But I promised him I'd take care of him when we were kids. It's hard."

Gavin Bain was a brave man. His whole existence was an exercise in courage. Everything had been taken from him, and he'd built a life that he lived on his own terms with brazen boldness.

It was convicting. She'd been given every opportunity in life and made decisions one after another out of fear. She was afraid of her father's reaction, so she never told him how much her mother's death affected her. She was afraid of what people would think of her, so she never told anyone about what happened with Poppy. She was afraid of looking stupid, so she'd agreed to the ridiculous contest Carousel set up.

She was afraid.

She was afraid.

She was afraid.

There was something she could do to change that right now. She grabbed her phone and dialed the familiar number.

Marie picked up on the first ring. "Scarlett. It's about time you returned my call. We have a crisis. Where are you?"

"In Los Angeles."

"What? Why? Never mind. Carousel wants an explanation for that scene on TV. The only explanation I had was that you were on drugs, and that didn't seem the most constructive thing to say."

"I understand. Please convey my deepest apologies to the network."

Marie expelled a sigh. "I will. Now we need to come up with a plausible explanation for that stunt in the bar."

"I'm afraid you misunderstand me, Marie. I have no intention of explaining myself to them. I'm withdrawing from the competition."

"You're what?"

"I'm withdrawing. I should have backed out as soon as they presented it, but I didn't have the guts or the integrity to do it then. I do now."

"What will I tell them?"

"Tell them my work is worth more than this ridiculous game and that it stands on its own merit. Tell them good luck finding anything better than my books."

"Scarlett—"

"I have to go, Marie. I'll be in touch." She jabbed the disconnect button and threw the phone into the bag beside her.

"Right on. 'Bout time you told 'em where to shove their deal, Red."

His approval meant more than one hundred Carousel contracts. "You."

"Me?"

"After watching you today with Maury and Wynn, I was inspired. It took an enormous amount of courage to decline their offer, an offer I know you desperately want. You said no to a lot of money on principle because it would've cheapened your worth and Johnny's memory."

He shrugged. "Yeah, well."

She put her hand on his shoulder. "You stood up for yourself, you didn't compromise, and you didn't let them push you around. It was awesome."

"Yeah. But you stood up to them first, badass."

"And now I've done the same for myself. A little late, but...go us." She held up her bottle of water for a toast.

He tapped his to hers. "Go us."

Chapter 19

The sound of the surf beyond the darkness accompanied the song Gavin played. He and Scarlett were reclining on the patio furniture under the stars. Every strum of the guitar, every crashing wave, every whiff of sea air and Scarlett's perfume melted his muscles until he was boneless.

"Will you play *The One I Never Had*?" Scarlett lay on the deck chair next to him.

"Okay."

"It's my favorite Wolfe's Bain song."

His too, and one of the saddest of all the songs he'd ever written. About a girl he could never have…a life he could never have.

"You wrote the song?"

He continued to strum the guitar. "Yeah."

"Was it about someone or just a great idea?" Her knees were bent, and she'd crossed one leg over the other. A jewel painted onto her pink toenail glinted in the pale light every time she swung her leg.

"Celeste Goldman, my chemistry lab partner, head cheerleader, class president, long blonde hair, big brown eyes, and a Porsche 911, every sixteen-year old's wet dream, and I knew I could never have her or anyone like her. A foster kid with a juvie record didn't date girls like her in real life. It was one of the first songs I ever wrote. I was in some serious lust with that girl, and maybe a little in love too." He played a riff on the neck of the guitar, and didn't add that the song defined his entire life.

"Did she ever know how you felt?"

"Nah. Besides, if she'd been interested it would have only been to piss off her parents. I'm not interested in being anyone's revenge."

She picked an orange from a bowl of fruit on the ground by their lounge chairs. "Don't sell yourself short, rock star. You are mighty fine."

"Am I now?"

"Please." She tossed the orange from hand to hand. "You know you are. You've been one of *People's Sexiest Men of the Year* twice."

He chuckled. "Oh, yeah, I forgot."

"Forgot, my Aunt Fanny."

"Well, Sexiest Man or not, Celeste never gave me more than a courteous smile. I can't say I blame her. I had a perpetual scowl, second-hand clothes, a chip as big as Texas on my shoulder, and zero manners. You don't learn social niceties in the system. You learn to survive."

"Sounds like a lonely way to live."

"It was, but I had Johnny for most of the time I was a ward of the state."

No one knew about Celeste or how shitty his life in the system was, except Johnny, and now she knew too. Maybe this was a test. Maybe if she heard enough, she'd realize what a load of crap she'd picked up in Vegas. He waited for the platitudes to begin. The things people say to make themselves feel better about another person's crappy life.

"Mmm."

Interesting, not one platitude in sight. "Yeah, I left as soon as I could."

"When did you get out?"

"When I was eighteen. I got out about six months before Johnny. I lived on the streets, played for tips, and put my survival skills to the test. When he got out, he inherited some money from his parents' life insurance, so we were able to get a ratty apartment together."

He slid his thumb ring off and slowly rolled it between his fingers. "We'd play on the streets during the day, then any seedy bar we could find at night. One day we're playing, and this guy comes up to us and hands us his card. Tells us to call him if we're interested in a record deal." He laughed and draped his arm over the guitar in his lap. "We didn't let him get three feet away before we chased him down and told him hell yes, we were interested. That was Mike West, our first manager. He got us a demo made, and within six months a record deal with a major label, and the rest is history."

"He didn't do a good job, or what?"

"Mike was a great guy. He looked out for us. Made sure we had food and were safe. But as the money started rolling in our assholery grew exponentially." He rubbed at a nick on the guitar.

"Ah, the classic big-head-rock-star syndrome." Scarlett pushed her fingernail under the skin of the orange and peeled off a long strip.

He loved the sight of her legs in the moonlight, and the crisp smell of orange, and he most definitely loved that she didn't let him get away with anything. "More like dick-head-rock-star syndrome."

She laughed. "You said it, not me."

"Truth is truth. We fired him after the second album because we thought he was holding us back. In truth, he was still trying to protect us from making dumbass business decisions. But you couldn't tell either of us anything. We thought we were gods, and we burned bridges for entertainment back then. It's a wonder either one of us came out with any money."

"Is that why this deal with Storm Side was so important, you need the money?"

"Nah. Thankfully we weren't total idiots and invested well. We kept the rights to our songs, so there are royalties, and I was Johnny's sole beneficiary."

"So why were you willing to do business with those two turds?"

His wife slowly bit down on a juicy wedge of orange, savoring the delicious fruit. The motion of her teeth breaking into the soft flesh, the dribble of juice that ran down her chin, and her soft moan of pleasure turned him on like nothing else ever had. He readjusted himself on the lounge. "I just want to make music again. It's all I know how to do. It's honest work, and I'm good at it." While that was the truth, the bigger issue was he didn't want his son thinking he was a bum and couldn't hold a job.

"Whatever happened to Mike West? Why didn't you contact him when you decided to make a comeback?" She separated the orange and offered him a slice.

He popped it into his mouth. "He's selling insurance in Monroe, Louisiana these days. About six months after Johnny died, I got a card from him. Can you believe it? We treated him like shit, and he tracks me down to give me his condolences. Like I said, a good guy."

"Sounds like it."

"Anyway, he put his phone number on the card, and I gave him a call. He got out of the business about a year after we parted ways, too much stress. Said he wasn't made for the cut-throat nature of the music business. His family has a insurance firm in Monroe, and he runs that with his wife." He held his hand out, and she gave him another slice of orange. "I would've gotten in touch with him eventually, though."

"Why?"

"After I moved back to Seattle I created my own twelve-step program for myself, Asshole's Anonymous. Hello, I'm Gavin, and I'm a bitter, angry asshole. One of the steps is to make amends to people you've wronged, and man did we wrong Mike. We were a couple of stupid pricks."

She snorted.

He set his guitar into the case. "You think I'm bad now, you should've known me then. And Johnny's death made me worse. I couldn't keep living with all of that shit. I would've hurt myself or someone else. So I found a shrink and started therapy."

It was like there was no filter on his mouth, but it felt good to talk about it. He was proud of the work he'd done, proud that he was in a better place. And he wanted her to know he was a better man than he used to be.

"Gavin, that's maybe the bravest thing I've ever heard."

Something sweet and corny spread through his heart, and he liked it. He liked it a bit too much. "I'm sick of talking about myself." He picked up his guitar again. "Want to hear another song?"

He loved hanging out with his wife. She calmed the tilt-a-whirl of bad stuff that spun continuously in his head. Scarlett was the most amazing woman he'd ever known in all ways but one.

What the hell was the deal with the money? It didn't compute. Luanne's words from the day before came back to him.

If you had to pick ten words to describe Scarlett, where would gold-digger fall on that list?

"Scarlett?"

"Mmmh?"

"Why did you change your mind about taking the money?"

Silence.

"Don't get me wrong, I'm glad you did. But I just can't make it fit in my head. You were so against it, almost to the point of doing me bodily harm, and then you weren't."

She threw her legs over the side of the chair, facing him. He thought she would bolt and not answer him, but he was wrong.

"I meant what I said about not wanting your money, and I was royally ticked when you offered it."

He chuckled. "Yeah, I got that. So what changed?"

She played with the hem of her shirt and wouldn't look at him.

He took her chin and tilted her face up so he could see her eyes. "Whatever it is, I won't be mad. I just want to know."

"That day was so insane, and all I wanted to do was run away. But I needed to tell my dad about the marriage. Before I got a chance to talk to him, I overheard a phone conversation between him and Poppy Sims, the new bank president." She wiped a single tear that ran down her cheek and looked back at the ocean. "Poppy called due the loan on the farm. Daddy has to pay fifty thousand dollars or the bank will take our home."

The squeal of feedback from her words reverberating through his head made it hard to compute everything she was saying. This was the last thing he'd expected to hear her say. Not only had she not wanted his money, but she'd compromised herself for her family. His heart damn near burst from his ribs.

"Please understand, the farm's been in our family for three generations. It's all he has, Gavin."

The guitar dropped to the ground, and he was on her before she could finish her sentence. His mouth covered hers and took everything she had to offer, everything he'd wanted since the first time he kissed her in that dark bar in Vegas. She gave as good as she got, and it melted the thin veneer of restraint he tried to keep.

Victory spiked in his bloodstream. He drew back enough to look into her eyes and kissed each side of her delicious mouth. "I knew it."

Her arms went around him and held him tight. "I'm so sorry." She sucked his bottom lip into her mouth and met each thrust of his tongue. Every bone in his jaded, cynical body melted. She was all he'd ever wanted.

Coming up for air, he whispered, "Don't be sorry. Just kiss me like that again."

A sultry smile spread across her face. She slid her hand under his shirt and rested it on his pecs. "I want to touch you. Feel you. See you."

Her breathy words speared him to the spot. Nothing could've made him move while this woman felt her way around his body. Rounded nails trailed and circled his nipple with methodical slowness. "Jesus, you're killing me." Every second that passed, he died a thousand deaths of pleasure. Her fingers explored each muscle. Her delving and probing shot past bone and sinew, straight to the place his desire boiled like molten fire.

He held his breath as her probing hand inched lower. When she got to the band of his shorts, she glanced up at him with glazed, unfocused eyes. "I want to love you, Gavin. Show me how."

Her broken words and trust in him nearly brought him to his knees. "I've got you, baby. Wrap your legs around my waist."

He gripped her ass, welcoming her sweet weight in his arms, and headed for the bedroom. All he wanted to do was throw her down on the bed, yank her legs open and bury himself inside her for days.

But he had to make this right. All the women who'd bounced across his bed had taught him nothing about how to handle a virgin.

He kicked open the door with his foot and welcomed the stabbing pain radiating from his bare foot. If he could focus on that, he might be able to do this without embarrassing himself or hurting her.

Scarlett reclined on the bed. So damn beautiful. Her red hair spread in wild abandon over the pillows, and her hips were encased in jean shorts she wore like a second skin.

She really was going to kill him. "I want to go slow, Scarlett. I've never been someone's first time. I don't want to hurt you."

In response, she undid the snap of her shorts and lowered the zipper.

His mouth went dry when she lifted her hips and pushed the shorts down to kick off the end of the bed, leaving a tiny blue thong in their wake.

Her foot stroked his thigh. "Take off your shirt, Gavin."

It was gone in a second.

"Now your pants." She sat up, crossed her arms and whipped off her top. An indigo lace bra encased her breasts, dusky nipples shadowed behind the fabric.

"Fuck." He studied the wall behind her, anything to stem the raging need pounding through him.

"Is something wrong?"

A strangled laugh nearly choked him. "I could go to jail for the things I want to do to you. I'm hanging on by a thread here, Scarlett."

A warm, low chuckle tumbled from her mouth. "Gavin, look at me. I've waited a long time for this." Her soft fingers clasped his hand. "I've been waiting for you."

Her words gutted him. He'd never been trusted with such a valuable gift before. His hand moved to the top of his shorts and popped the top button. With quick work, his pants joined hers on the ground.

The bed creaked as he lowered his weight onto the mattress, into her open arms. There was no hesitation, no second-guessing. This was where he was meant to be.

Hands, arms, legs, her whole body searched to get closer to him. "I want you inside me."

He licked around the delicate shell of her ear. "I want that too. Patience. We'll get there."

"How can you be patient?"

The secret she was keeping behind the thin strip of lace dipping between her thighs begged to be discovered. He

195

hooked his thumb under the elastic and pulled. The soft, tiny piece of fabric popped and fell away. He swallowed her gasp in a long, drugging kiss.

Moving from her mouth to her neck to her full breast was a journey of discovery and torture. Each cry, each sigh made him desperate for release. He made short work of the barely there, peek-a-boo bra and feasted on one nipple and then the other.

"Gavin…please…it's too much." She dug her nails into his ass and pulled him to her.

"Are you ready for me, baby?" He slipped a finger between her slick folds and circled the tight nub. Her hips bucked and her thighs opened for him to go deeper.

***

"Gavin, I need you." Scarlett didn't care that she was begging. For this man, she'd beg forever.

His finger swirled around the place where her desire built and then pushed inside. Too much. Sensation crashed over her body like the waves outside the bedroom window. Her body acted on an ancient carnal language written deep in her DNA. Her hips pulsed and her thighs fell open.

"That's right, sweetheart. Open for me."

He began to pump with his hand. The slower he went the higher her body ratcheted until thoughts were nothing more than images. Words and logic ceased to exist until the whole world pivoted on what was happening in that bed and deep in her core.

He stroked and circled.

She clawed and whimpered, "Gavin."

"Shhh, don't fight it, Scarlett. Let it happen. It's gonna feel so good, baby. I promise."

The world fell away in pulses of pleasure that blanked her mind. Her body exploded in a kaleidoscope of colors and sounds. His name ripped from her throat in a ragged cry.

He gentled her with a ring of kisses around her neck, then pinned her with the most beautiful gaze she'd ever seen. "You good?"

"Yes, but I want you with me, in me." She could barely pant the words into existence. There was a moment's hesitation when she circled him with her trembling hand. He was big. Maybe too big. "I don't know if this will work."

He choked out a laugh. "Trust me, it's gonna work." He took her mouth and his tongue played with hers until she relaxed again. He broke the kiss and touched his forehead to hers. "I've got to have you, Scarlett."

She hooked one leg over his hip. "I'm all yours."

He reached for the nightstand and grabbed a condom. "I'll go slow."

"Gavin."

"Yeah."

"Don't go slow."

"Okay."

In one long thrust he was deep inside her. It was beyond anything she could've imagined. Her soul flew free only to be caught by him then gifted back to her, only to fly free again. Every move and kiss brought her to the one place she'd waited for her whole life.

He withdrew then plunged back home. Her skin buzzed with delight at every point of contact. Each movement crashed her against the waiting ecstasy.

The soft friction of the sheets, the aroma of the two of them together, and the firestorm in his stare pulled her closer to the edge. When he sucked her nipple into his mouth, she broke into thousands of glittery pieces. The detonation crashed into her with muscle-rippling pleasure. Long, pleading cries of release filled the room. She barely recognized her own voice.

With a hoarse roar, he pounded into her two more times and came.

197

His head rested on her left breast as he rubbed down her waist and over the curve of her hip. "Are you okay?"

A grin she was sure looked as goofy as possible spread across her face. "I'm great." He rolled to the side. "I'll be right back." Once the condom was dealt with he returned and lay facing her.

She trailed a thumb down his cheek. "You were great."

Warm lips covered hers with a sweet, easy kiss. "Thanks, but you don't have anything to compare it to," he said with a groggy slur.

"You're tired. Sleep." She snuggled into his side. "And by the way, that just means nobody compares to you."

His arms tightened around her as a light snore blew against her hair, and she thought how true those words were.

Chapter 20

Scarlett squinted against the California sunshine streaming through the bedroom window.

Déjà vu.

She'd been here before, waking up with his hand on her breast—but this time she welcomed his warm body wrapped around hers. This time she never wanted to leave.

Zings of sensation still fired through her body from last night's lovemaking. She wanted to hold them inside her, so she never forgot this feeling. His hands, his lips, his tongue had sent her over the edge more than once. She'd won the sexual lottery with this god. It was everything she'd hoped it would be and so much more. When a girl waits as long as she had, there were certain expectations, and Gavin didn't disappoint. In fact, he hadn't disappointed twice.

This changed everything. She would get hurt because she'd given into love and desire. She'd worry about that another day. Right now, with the heat and smell of him all around her, it seemed like the best possible decision she could've made.

But what about tomorrow and the day after that? She didn't have a plan for anything beyond this moment in bed with her husband.

"I can hear you thinking," said the sleepy man behind her.

"Sorry to wake you." His voice chased away her confused and worried thoughts. She snuggled back into his hard body.

"Don't let your body write a check you're not willing to cash, little girl." He flipped her over and began to explore her body with his mouth.

"I—ahhh."

199

He delved and played, pulling her further under with each lick and kiss. The wild child inside her chanted more, more, more, and for once they were in complete agreement.

His phone rang. They ignored it. It rang again.

She almost ignored it a second time for the promise his talented mouth offered. "You better get that. My phone is downstairs. It might be my family."

With a curse, he rolled to grab his phone. He glanced at the screen then fumbled with the phone. "Hello. Yeah. No, it's fine, I'm up." He adjusted the pillow behind his back. "Las Vegas? Are you shitting me?" He plowed his fingers through his hair.

What in the world had him so upset?

"And they're still living there?" He kicked off the blanket and sat on the edge of the bed with his head in his hand.

"Yeah. Yeah. Email it to me. Thanks."

He let the phone slip through his fingers and stared out the window.

"Gavin? Are you alright?"

"No." He shot the word at her like a bullet.

Wanting to give him space but hating that he was so obviously upset, she crawled across the bed to kneel beside him. "Can you tell me what's wrong?"

He didn't answer. Instead he grabbed his jeans and yanked them on, exiting the room without a sound.

She gathered the sheet to her breast. Her mind raced. What had happened? A tiny sliver of her heart hurt that Gavin had shut her out. But a bigger part, the part he owned, ached for him because something serious was going on with him.

He came striding back into the room with his laptop, his face sober and determined. He motioned for her to scoot over, then propped himself against the headboard and pulled her to sit beside him. She didn't understand what was going on, but if he wanted her close, then that's where she would be.

She put her hand on his face and turned him toward her. "Tell me what's wrong, you're scaring me. Is it my family, more media attention...*me?*"

He took her hand and kissed her palm. "That was a private investigator I hired to find..."

"To find what?" She searched his face for some explanation.

"My son."

***

Her face went white as bone. Maybe he should've broken it to her more gently. "Scarlett—"

"Your son?" She sat up and put some distance between them. He didn't blame her.

"Well, I think he's my son."

"You think? I don't understand." She wrestled the sheet to cover her nudity.

"After Johnny's accident, all of his things were boxed up and sent to me. At the time the thought of picking through his belongings seemed obscene. But a few months ago I finally got the courage to go through some of the boxes, and I found this letter." He took his wallet from the nightstand and showed her the note.

While Scarlett read, he tried to wrap his brain around the fact that his son was in Las Vegas. He'd just been in Las Vegas. How close had he been to him? Had he passed him on the street?

The paper shook as she read. He watched and tried to judge her reaction. Her small hand went to her mouth, and then she gasped and looked at him. "He paid her off?"

"Yes." There it was again. The gut shot that broke his heart.

She turned back to the letter and read more. "Johnny never told you about this?"

"No. I think he was coming to my house when he had his accident. It's dated the same day. But who knows. His behavior had become so erratic he could've written it that morning and forgotten about it by that evening."

"I'm so sorry, Gavin. Has the private investigator found Tara and the baby?"

He scrubbed his face. "Yeah. He found the birth certificate. But he's not living with Tara. He's with an aunt. Doug, the PI, is emailing me the info."

"Then what?"

His computer dinged, and his answer clogged in his throat. With an unsteady hand, he opened the email. There was an address, and the aunt's name—Kristy Phillips. There were two attachments. He opened the first, and a birth certificate came on the screen. The name Aiden Bradley Bain burned his retinas. He couldn't look away from it. Tara was listed as the mother, but the place for the father was blank.

"Aiden Bain. It's a good name." She stroked her hand up and down his arm.

He opened the other attachment. The smiling face of a blond-haired boy with serious gray eyes stared back at him. "Oh, my..." He gripped the computer so tightly he thought it would crack. If there was any doubt this child was his son, it vanished the moment he saw those eyes. They were his eyes. He looked at them every morning in the mirror.

"He's beautiful," she whispered.

"Two years old. Two fucking years." He shook his head. "Johnny, I'd kick your ass if you were here right now." His voice broke on the last word. Shit, he couldn't see the screen for all the moisture in his eyes. With several deliberate blinks and years of practiced apathy, he managed not to cry like a baby.

Scarlett didn't try to tell him it would be alright. She just held him, and with her head resting on his shoulder they stared into the perfect face of his son.

"So, what are we gonna do?" Her voice was soft.

"We?" He wished his voice was stronger, but he was using all his air to keep his lungs moving.

"Yes. We." Her smiled knitted some of his wounds together.

"I don't know." He set the computer aside. "I want to go talk to the aunt. I want to meet my son."

"Okay." She threw the sheet back and got out of bed.

"Yeah? You're not going to tell me to wait for a paternity test or let the lawyers hash it out?"

She pulled his shirt over her naked body. "Nope."

"Really?"

"Would it do any good if I did?"

"Not one bit." He laughed.

She nodded. "Also, I can't imagine what you're feeling, but if it were me, I'd want to know immediately if he was well taken care of and safe. So no, I won't try to stop you."

He jumped off the bed and kissed her sweetly. "Thank you."

"I'm with you, rock star." Her warm fingers caressed his face. "I've got your back."

***

The drive back to L.A. to retrieve the rest of their belongings took half the time it had yesterday. Scarlett understood the urgency. She'd meant what she said. Wild horses wouldn't keep her away from her child. Pity was something he would hate, but she couldn't help it. To be betrayed by his best friend, the man who'd been closer than a brother, must be a terrible burden to bear.

"How much money did Johnny give her?"

"I have no idea. It must've been a lot for her to have never come to me for more. Then again, she wouldn't have been able to find me without a lot of effort."

"What do you mean?"

"After John died I was drowning. I got the hell out of L.A. and moved back to Washington State. For about eight months I lived in Neah Bay, on the Olympic Peninsula, population eight hundred sixty-five. Have you ever heard of it?"

"No."

"Exactly. It's incredibly beautiful. But more importantly, remote. It sits at the very tip of the peninsula, about as far away from people and Los Angeles as I could get. No one knew me, or if they did, they left me alone. I needed that time to grieve, time to get my shit together, time to come to terms with my life without my best friend, my brother."

"Did it work?"

"Yes and no. I grieved. But I don't know if I'll ever be able to come to terms with Johnny's death. I made some peace, though. The real work came with my shrink when I got back to Seattle. I really felt like I'd put it all in its place. You know?" He tapped his thumb ring against the gear shift. "Then this happened."

"I can't imagine how you feel." She turned in her seat and took his hand. "You obviously still love him, but you're also furious with him. And rightfully so. It must eat at you—the unfinished business."

He glanced at her. "Yeah. That's exactly it. If he were alive, we'd fight hard about this, like bloodshed hard, then make up, and figure out how to get my son back. Even though he did this stupid thing with Tara, he would've been on my side. That's how we were. In his own twisted way, he was trying to protect me."

She clasped his hand.

His thumb brushed back and forth over her knuckles. "You must feel the same way about your mom, huh?"

"What?"

"Your mom. You probably feel the same way about her."

She withdrew her hand and flipped down the visor mirror. "That was a long time ago, and it's really not the same." Her fingers wove through her unmanageable mane as she picked up one piece then the other to braid it.

"Isn't it? You still love her, but you also have to be hurt and angry she left you. You never got to resolve things with her either."

The love, pain, and longing her mother left in her irresponsible wake pushed against Scarlett's eyes. "My mother chose to leave me. Johnny didn't choose to leave you. It is different."

He shrugged. "I don't think it matters if they chose it or not. People we loved still left us. And I'd think it's harder for you. You were a kid."

The pop of the visor being flipped up filled the car. "It's not the same, Gavin. And being a kid has nothing to do with it. I'm just glad I didn't have to suffer a lifetime of her antics."

He scratched the side of his face. "But you kind of have suffered because of her. Haven't you? I mean, you told me you felt like everyone compared you to her. Plus, she's your mother. Every kid loves their mom. Mine was crap, and I still loved her."

"Can we not talk about this?"

"Fine. But I don't think life happens to us in a vacuum, Scarlett. One thing connects to another, like a screwed-up puzzle."

She started to argue. But with the clarity of a lightning bolt, she realized he was right. She did carry around an ugly ball of love, fury, and hurt because of her mother. She mostly focused on the fury—it was safer—but the love and hurt were huge pieces of that *screwed-up puzzle* too.

Things began to click into place, and she could see all the ways her unresolved feelings about her mother had influenced her whole life. Her inability to truly trust people. How did she know they wouldn't leave her if they knew the real her? The way she kept secrets to protect those she loved. That was a lie. She kept secrets to protect herself.

And her compulsion to be perfect and never step the slightest bit out of line. All the things she knew were holding her back in her life, but were so much a part of her that she found safety and comfort in them.

He was right. But it was too much to unravel while trapped in a vehicle with a man who saw too much. Who needed a therapist when she had her own rock-n-roll shrink?

And she didn't like it one bit.

Chapter 21

Music dragged Scarlett back to semi-consciousness. She cracked her lids open enough to watch Gavin, but not enough to let him know she was awake. His gritty moonshine voice filled the car as he sang along with the radio.

Disheveled black locks fell in all directions around his head like he'd raked his hand through it repeatedly. Scarlett knew if she looked, there'd be the little w between his brows. Thinking, probably worrying. She understood. She'd do the same thing.

He'd shaved this morning, and put on nice jeans, and a long-sleeve shirt. He'd done that to cover his tattoos. He wanted to make a good impression on his son.

The love pounding in her heart was a dangerous thing, but she couldn't seem to help it and was tired of fighting it.

The hum of the seat motor caught his attention. He smiled at her. Unable to resist, she stroked his cheek, and he leaned into her hand. She loved it when he did that. It was such an affectionate move from such a strong man. She didn't think he was aware of doing it. "How much farther?"

"Thirty minutes. Are you okay, do you need a bathroom break?"

"I'm fine. The question is, how are you?"

He ran his hand along the top of the steering wheel. "I'm not sure. I'd be lying if I hadn't considered this might not be a good idea. Maybe I should let Jack handle it."

"Lord, no." She retrieved lip balm from her purse.

He laughed. "I keep telling you he's not that bad. But, yeah, I feel like I need to try and speak with the aunt and let her know I didn't know about Aiden until a few months ago. You know?"

"I do. You know how I feel on the subject. No one could keep me from my child. Then again, I may not be the best person to listen to on this subject. I'm a teeny bit sensitive when it comes to parents and their children."

"You're the perfect person. You tell me exactly what I want to hear." He flashed her a killer grin.

"Whatever, rock star."

He took the wheel with his left hand and slipped his right hand around her neck, stroking her jaw with his thumb. "Are you sure you're alright? Was last night…"

"I'm great. Never better." Fire crawled up her neck and shot down to her belly at the mention of last night.

"Yeah?" The self-satisfied smile he gave her was way too cute for one guy.

She pursed her lips to keep from laughing. "You don't have to look so smug."

He pulled her to him, keeping one eye on the road. She went willingly. There was no denying him. "And just so you know, I've never been better, either." His mouth found hers. He kissed her until she was crazed, until all she wanted was him, and gravel crunched under the tires.

He'd drifted to the shoulder of the road. He eased the car back into their lane. "Damn, woman, you make me lose my head."

She knew exactly how he felt.

***

Gavin knew there were beautiful, upscale areas of Las Vegas, with huge, gorgeous homes, and lots of money. Unfortunately, Kristy Phillips and Aiden didn't live in one of those areas. The grubby streets he drove down, past clusters of homeless people, were as depressing as the rundown buildings surrounding the sad duplex that held his child and the boy's aunt.

"Oh, my," Scarlett whispered when they pulled to a stop in front of the house.

He rested both arms on the steering wheel and dropped his chin to his folded hands. "You've got to be shittin' me." He glanced at the address on the mailbox again, hoping they had the wrong place. Nope, right address. "What the hell did Tara do with the money Johnny gave to her?"

"She obviously didn't invest it into a decent place to live."

The xeriscape lawn consisted of a handful of white rocks, several stubby bushes, and a cactus leaning against the chain-link fence that surrounded the house. He'd seen prison yards with more cheer. The only bright spot was the door on the right, which was freshly painted a soft powder blue with a pot of colorful flowers next to it.

"What am I doin'?" He couldn't peel his gaze from the run-down house.

"We can leave. I'll support you no matter what you decide." The warmth of her hand rubbing his back did little to calm the torrent of conflicting emotions. Leaving here and letting her help him forget this whole damn mess wasn't an option—he had to know. After the joke of his childhood, there was no way he could let his flesh and blood grow up without being taken care of, without being loved. The idea of it had haunted him since he first found that damn letter.

He seized the door handle and was out of the car before he could talk himself out of it. Scarlett's door closed behind him. His hand shook so bad, he had trouble lifting the gate handle.

Scarlett wrapped her hand over his and squeezed. The woman was better than any drug. His heart stopped racing, and his pulse evened out.

"Do you want me to knock?" Her sweet voice washed over him like honey.

"No. I'll do it." He hooked his aviators in the collar of his t-shirt and nearly lost it when he heard children's songs coming from the other side of the blue door.

"You've got this." She squeezed his shoulder.

He rapped three times on the door.

Several locks slid open, then it opened only as far as the chain would allow. A blonde woman with two pigtails and a weary expression assessed him. There was a small flash of recognition in her eyes.

"What are you doing here?" She angled her body so he couldn't see into the front room.

"Kr—" He had to clear his throat, which had gone as dry as her sad, non-existent yard. "Kristy Phillips?"

She didn't say anything, just stared at him with an expression way too old for her young face. However, she hadn't slammed the door in their faces, so that was a good sign. Right? "I'm Gavin—"

"I know who you are. What. Are. You. Doing. Here? I have paperwork saying you'll never bother us."

She didn't take her gaze from his. It was disturbing. Like she'd evaluated him and found him at the bottom of the shit heap. "Can we come—wait, what?"

"I have a legal document saying you will never bother us or try to take Aiden."

"Kristy, I don't know what you're talking about, but I can assure you I never signed anything like that. In fact, I didn't even know about Aiden until a few months ago." What in the hell had Johnny done?

She didn't say anything, but her unimpressed glare never left his face.

"Can we please come in?"

"She's not gonna start dancing on my table, is she?" Kristy asked, without cracking the slightest smile.

Scarlett leaned in. "No. That was just a misunderstanding. I'm not really like that."

"Sure you're not." The blonde gatekeeper had the best poker face he'd ever seen. Not one flicker of emotion crossed her face.

She closed the door. He looked at Scarlett, who shrugged. Then he heard the jangle of the chain, and relief flooded him.

The door swung open, and a blond-haired toddler stood behind some kind of kid-friendly fence that had been set up in the middle of the pristine, if worn, living room. Kristy quickly went to the boy, picked him up and snuggled him in her arms.

Gavin was transfixed. The house could've fallen down around them, and he wouldn't have been able to rip his gaze from Aiden Bradley Bain.

Scarlett cleared her throat. "May we sit down?"

"I'd rather you didn't." Kristy adjusted the child on her hip.

For the first time, he noticed her clothes. She wore a t-shirt intentionally ripped in strategic places to show skin and cleavage, but she was otherwise covered up. The fuzzy socks on her feet were a drastic contrast to the fishnet hose and short schoolgirl skirt. A hooker? God, he hoped not.

"What do you want? I'm about to go to work." She smoothed her hand over Aiden's hair.

"I…uh…" He looked at Scarlett for help.

"I think what Gavin's trying to say is, he wanted to meet Aiden and talk to you for a bit."

She tightened her grip around the baby. "Why now?"

"Like I said, I only found out about him a couple of months ago. I've had a private investigator looking for him since that day."

Disbelief colored every inch of her face.

"I swear it's true. Where's Tara? Is she…"

"Dead? Ha." Kristy sat on the arm of the sofa and handed Aiden a stuffed animal. "Last time I heard anything from her she was in Miami with some band."

The contents of Gavin's stomach were on a countdown. "When was the last time she saw Aiden?"

211

"When he was six weeks old. She lost the baby weight and took off. Her last words to me were, *I've gotten what I wanted out of him, you can have him, see what you can get.*"

"Are you shi—"

"No cussing around the baby," Kristy ground out.

Scarlett took his hand again. The gentle pressure helped him haul in his temper. "You're right. I'm sorry." He would have continued, but the boy started to jabber, and it sounded a lot like, *"Who's that?"*

The girl kissed Aiden's fat cheek. "These are some old friends, but they're leaving soon." She turned her attention back to Gavin. "Isn't that right?"

"Kristy, have you had him since he was six weeks old?" Scarlett said.

"Do you see anybody else around here?" The stupid was implied.

He had to give it to his wife. She wasn't deterred by the kid's punky attitude. "Who does he stay with while you work? Where do you work?"

"That's none of your business. Aiden's mine. I take care of him. End of story."

"Technically—"

"Technically, legally, and in every other way, he's mine. I got Tara to sign a paper making me his legal guardian. I had to. I couldn't get medical care for him. I have the document you signed."

"And she did that? Just signed away her rights?" he spit out. He was shocked the woman would give up her gravy train so easily.

"She did it because some really bad people were looking for her, and I told her I would tell them where to find her if she didn't. She knew I would too, so she signed."

Too much shitty information at once had his brain spinning. He massaged his forehead. "If Tara was only trying to use him for money, why didn't she try to get more? It doesn't make sense."

"Um, it was made perfectly clear in the signed agreement that there would be no more money. Tara had to agree to that before that other guy would give her the cash."

"I want to see that document."

"It's not here. It's in a safety deposit box at the bank. I don't have time to get it because I have to go to work." She checked her watch. "You need to go now."

"No." He couldn't go yet. Not yet.

Kristy stood and took a menacing step toward him. "You get out of my house, or I'll call the cops. You have no right to him. He. Is. Mine."

"I'm his father."

"Prove it."

"Hey, let's all calm down," Scarlett coaxed. "Kristy, you've obviously taken excellent care of Aiden, and no one's trying to take him from you." The girl glared at her. "He's not. He only wants to get to know him. You can imagine it's all a huge shock."

Kristy's stance became less hostile, and Gavin took that as a good sign.

"Do you think we can see you tomorrow? Maybe take ya'll to lunch?" Scarlett spoke to her like a negotiator in a hostage situation.

"I don't know." The fear and distrust in this young girl's eyes gutted him. He couldn't even be mad at her. He understood it. He'd lived it.

Scarlett wouldn't be deterred. "Surely a quick meal—"

"It's okay." He put his arm around his wife's waist. To Kristy, he said, "I know we're freaking you out, Kristy. I get it. I'm going to leave my cell number." He pulled out a fast food receipt and a pen and wrote his number on it. "Call if you change your mind."

Kristy visibly relaxed. He knew she would. She now had the power back. He understood that too.

"Come on, babe."

Kristy cleared her throat. "Wait."

"Yeah?"

"There's that chicken place at the intersection up the road. They have a playground. We can meet there at eleven."

He nodded. "Okay."

"Okay."

"Can I touch him before I go?" He had a compulsive need to stroke the kid's blond head.

"No. That's weird."

He chuckled. "You're right. It is. But you'll meet with us tomorrow?"

Scarlett opened the door.

"I said I would." Kristy walked toward them. "Here." She leaned Aiden toward Gavin but kept a firm grip on the boy. "Don't touch his face. I don't know where your hands have been."

The feel of Aiden's soft hair shot straight to his soul. "Hey, bud."

Gavin's life narrowed down to one thing.

The sweet toothy grin of his son.

***

Scarlett couldn't believe how well Gavin had managed the situation with the aunt. "Did you see her shirt?"

He glanced over his shoulder then pulled onto the street. "What there was of it, yeah."

"No. I mean the logo on it."

"No."

"It was the name of a casino. She must be a waitress or something. I'm going to google it." She tapped away on her phone.

"That's a relief. At first, I thought she might be a hooker."

"Me too. You handled her beautifully."

"She's scared, desperate, and pissed off. I get that."

Scarlett guessed he probably did, and that broke her heart. "What document was she talking about?"

"I have no idea. I guess we'll find out tomorrow. Did you see that face?"

The goofy grin he wore told her exactly who he was talking about. "I sure did. He's adorable."

"He has intelligent eyes, too. Don't you think?" The pride in his voice sang through the car.

"Absolutely."

He slid her a sheepish grin. "I sound like every other stupid parent in the world talking about their kid. Don't I?"

"Yes, and it's sweet." She played with the hair at his temple.

"I'm not sweet, Scarlett. You should know that."

"I know no such thing. I can name a number of sweet things you've done in the short time I've known you."

"Really? Name 'em."

"You took Honey to town so she could show you off, and you offered to help Joyce financially. You helped my dad with chores and Brody with guitar lessons. Oh, and there's the little matter of getting me out of Zachsville before the whole town could ridicule me, just to name a few."

The pink stain under his tan skin told her he was completely embarrassed. But the truth was the truth.

"Where do you want to stay while we're here?" he asked.

The change in subject caught her off guard. She let him do it because he was so thoroughly uncomfortable. "Not the Bellagio."

He laughed. "Not the Bellagio."

Her insides went sideways at the sound of his laughter, even though everything about this trip to Las Vegas was surreal. She was happy to be here with him. So much so that it'd take wild horses to drag her away from him.

Chapter 22

"You what?"

Gavin held the phone away from his ear as Jack railed.

"I can't believe you, Gavin. We specifically talked about this."

"Jack, calm the hell down. What did you expect me to do? Sit around and wait for a bunch of lawyers to tell me when I could meet my son?"

"That's exactly what I expected you to do. Damn it to hell, Gavin. What if you spooked her and she runs?"

Gavin could hear the clicking of computer keys on the other end of the line. "She's not going anywhere. She doesn't have two nickels to rub together. No way can she afford to run anywhere."

"Desperate people do desperate things."

Didn't he know it? His whole life had been a series of desperate events.

"Besides, we don't even know if the kid is yours."

"He's mine." There wasn't a doubt in Gavin's mind that Aiden Bradley Bain was his flesh and blood. A jolt of euphoria and terror lit him up at the thought.

"How exactly do you know that? Did you perform a DNA spot check?"

"No. But he's mine." Aiden's gray stare was burned into his brain. "Speaking of DNA, Scarlett got online and found out that we can get results of a DNA test back in one to three days at a private lab. Can you set that up?"

"Scarlett did, huh?" There was a sneer in Jack's tone.

"What's that supposed to mean?"

"Nothing. I wonder how much of this sentimental trip was your wife's idea?"

"It was all my idea. She's been supportive, but that's it. Now get off my ass and tell me if you can set up the test, or do I need to handle that?"

"No. I'll do it. Sorry. I don't really blame you for seeing him. I'd probably have done the same thing, but not without consulting my attorney first."

Gavin chuckled. "Noted. Any other news?" Meaning any news about a record deal.

"No. I'm still working it. Something will come up. Have you thought about doing it yourself?"

"What?"

"Starting your own label, and doing it yourself. Several big-name artists have gone indie, and it would give you the control you obviously want."

"I don't know, man. Seems kind of desperate to me. No one else wants me, so I'll DIY it."

"It's not like that. Just think about it."

"Alright."

"Back to the kid."

"Aiden."

"Okay, Aiden. You said that Tara signed over legal guardianship to the sister?"

"According to Kristy, yes. That's good, right? Tara's out of the picture, so I should be able to get custody?"

"I don't know. We'll have to run it by Rutledge, the attorney I hired to deal with this. Keep your shit together and stay out of trouble. Your image will be an issue if this comes down to a custody battle. And keep your wife from dancing on any more tables."

"Are you kidding me? You sound like those idiots in her small town. You worry about my career, I'll worry about Scarlett."

"I am worrying about your career, your kid, and your livelihood. I'm your friend, Gav, I worry. And an out-of-work rock star with anger management issues and a bad reputation is going to be a hard sell to a judge."

"Got it. I gotta go." He hung up before Jack could say another word. The ones he'd already said had found their mark.

***

Scarlett rode the elevator to the top floor of Caesars Palace. After they'd checked in, she'd gone down to the hotel gift shop to purchase a few forgotten toiletries. Unless she was willing to sell a kidney to pay for hair de-frizzer and shower gel for sensitive skin, she'd need to venture outside the hotel to find a drugstore.

The elevator opened into the foyer of the suite Gavin had rented. It was too much room for the two of them, but she knew he hoped Kristy would let Aiden come and stay with them at the hotel.

The suite was quiet and dark except for the faint sound of a guitar coming from beyond the open balcony door. The music drew her to the terrace, where she found Gavin reclining on a lounge chair strumming his guitar, an open bottle of Jack Daniels next to him on the ground.

She knocked on the door frame. "Hey, rock star. Can I join you?"

He didn't say anything, only motioned with his hand to the chair next to him, then continued playing.

A dark sadness rolled off him like fog on a desolate island, the force of it so strong that she had to fight her way through it. She sat, propped her feet up, and tried to appear as casual as possible. Something was terribly wrong.

The silence between them drowned out the melody of the guitar. He paused in playing to take a swig straight from the bottle of whiskey.

His body language clearly said back off, but she knew he needed her to push him beyond whatever this was. "So, what's up?"

"Nothin'." Another strum, another swig.

"Really?" She picked up the half-empty bottle from the ground. "Cause it looks like you've been pretty busy here."

A grunt was his only reply.

She'd already learned that he wouldn't talk until he was ready, and sometimes not at all. So she lay there looking at the stars and listened to him play. There was no conversation for twenty minutes and thankfully no more drinking either.

This appeared to be a *not at all* kind of night, and her heart broke at that. She wanted to be there for him, to be his comfort. But she was learning that you can't make people want you or see your value, no matter how hard you try. She reached for her shoes and stood up. "Good night, Gavin." A kiss to the temple, then she would leave him to brood alone.

"Wait." His voice was like rocks in a grinder. He took her hand. "Please, don't go."

"Okay." She resumed her place on the chair. "Do you want to talk?"

"Not really."

"Alright." So what if he didn't want to talk. He wanted her there, and a small zip of hope buzzed in her heart.

"I spoke to Jack while you were out."

"No wonder you're in a foul mood."

The ghost of a smile shuffled across his face. "Yeah, well." He continued to play softly. Still, he didn't look at her. "There was this foster family I lived with for a short while when I was six. They were the only really great people I was ever assigned to. The mom stayed at home, and the dad worked in a factory. They had a son of their own and me. Sam and I shared a room. But it was good, you know?"

"It sounds nice." She had no idea where he was going with this.

"It was. Shirley, the mom, always had a snack ready for us when we got home from school, and I remember my clothes always smelled like her perfume." The song he was playing changed. "I loved that smell. Sometimes I'll walk down the street or be in a crowded room and get a whiff of it. It always makes me smile."

"Mmm." It was all she could manage without crying, and if she cried he'd stop talking. It was the saddest, sweetest thing she'd ever heard.

"And Bill, the dad, he was a big guy. I remember thinking his arms were like the Hulk's. He came home every day at six o'clock. Sam and I would wait on the front porch for him. Seeing him walk up the drive was the best part of my whole day. He had to be tired, but he'd toss the ball with us, or chase us around until Shirley called us in for dinner. While we ate, he'd talk about his work, what they were making, how those things would be used to make other's people's lives better. At night, he'd read to us before bed or tell ridiculous stories until we were laughing our asses off. Then he'd turn off the light, and say, 'Sleep well, men.'" A chord changed punctuated the sweet night-time blessing.

"That sounds nice. How long were you with them?" The words slipped around the tears in her throat.

"About nine months. Looking back, I think they were probably going to adopt me, or at least make me a permanent placement, but her sister and brother-in-law were killed in a motorcycle accident, and they had to take in their two kids. There wasn't enough room or money for me to stay."

Sorrow flooded her tear ducts and a sob fought to escape her mouth, but she battled them back.

"When they broke it to me, I was devastated. Bill told me I had to be brave, and to always remember to work hard and be a man." He cleared his throat. "It's probably the only reason I've never completely self-destructed."

"Where did you go from there?"

"After that, the homes they put me in were not stellar. Most of the dads didn't work, or if they did, they'd come home and drink all evening, or not come home at all. I don't know if I was ever truly clean after that. Nobody cared enough to make sure we bathed or did homework, or whatever. It wasn't until I started living in the group home and they required us to shower, keep our beds made, and keep our shit picked up that I felt clean again. Weird, huh?"

"Not so weird," she whispered.

"When I was twelve, Johnny moved into the group home, and he had all these great memories of his mom and dad. He worshiped his dad. He taught him to play guitar, then he taught me."

"And now you've taught Brody." This was an easier topic to talk about.

He huffed a laugh. "I tried to teach Brody. He's a little...challenged. Anyway, the point is, real men, good men, good father type men, work, and they teach their kids to work. I mean, look at Floyd, he's one of the hardest working men I've ever met."

"I don't understand—"

"I'm a thirty-year-old, unemployed musician, Scarlett. Except for about a year when I was sixteen, I've never done what most people would call an honest day's work in my life. After that, I stood on street corners and played music for money, and stole if I had to. Once Johnny and I got a record deal, we busted our asses to make our music the best it could be. That was my work. Real men work, Scarlett. Men who have things to offer their children work. And I..."

She got it now. Since he didn't have a record deal and couldn't make music, he didn't think he could be a father to Aiden. It didn't matter that he didn't need to play another show or make another record to provide for the boy. Work equaled a good useful man.

Standing, she took the guitar from him and straddled his lap. Her fingers threaded through his hair, and she lifted his face to meet her gaze. The desolate pain punctured through her hard-won composure. "I'm not going to tell you how messed up your thinking is, or how hard you've worked to accomplish all that you have. And I'm not going to tell you you're wrong because it's how you feel and I respect that. I'm only going to say that you deserve to have someone look at you the way I look at my father, and to love you like there's nobody else in the whole world better than you."

He started to protest, but she silenced him with a kiss, then another, then another until she felt his taut muscles relax. His hands flattened on her back, the heat from them burning through the fabric of her thin cotton dress. The fire between them scorched her from the inside out.

This good man needed to know he was worth loving. She couldn't say the words *I love you*. That wasn't the arrangement. But she could show him. She felt for the bottom of his t-shirt and pulled it over his head. His penetrating look simmered with enough intensity to steal her hammering heart. She kissed his eyes, his cheeks, his lips, and trailed kisses down his neck to the cross over his heart.

He grabbed the bottom of her dress and yanked it over her head. She sat straddling him, naked except for bra and panties, totally unashamed. The approval in his eyes was all she needed to own this moment.

"God, you're beautiful." The desperation in his words was like kerosene, volatile and combustible. He strung kisses down her neck, and his calloused fingers stroked sensitive places that ignited her own desperate want. Reality existed somewhere beyond the here and now with him.

"Take me to bed, Gavin." It was a plea, not a request or a command.

In one swift movement, he stood with her in his arms. They didn't break the kiss, her legs clasped around his body. Every step he took caused his jeans to rub against the most intimate part of her, while his fingers dug into the soft flesh of her backside. A moan ripped from both of them when he pulled her closer. Every part of her touched every part of him. The erotic electricity that coursed between them was a drug she craved.

She needed him. He needed her. She would communicate her love for him in the only language she could.

The one he spoke fluently.

Chapter 23

Gavin's uneaten chicken sandwich sat in front of him, while he and Kristy watched Scarlett play with Aiden on the restaurant's playground. Two weeks ago, he hadn't known any of them. The enormity of it all made his head hurt. Well, that and the half bottle of whiskey he'd swallowed last night.

Scarlett picked Aiden up and twirled him around. He could hear his son's happy giggles through the glass of the restaurant. She had that effect on people. He'd been in a dark place when she'd returned from her errands last night, and she'd loved him back toward the light.

Another twirl, another giggle, and his damn heart barely fit in his ribcage.

"You gonna eat those?" Kristy pointed to his untouched fries.

"They're all yours." She looked like she needed every available calorie on the table and then some.

"Thanks." She snatched the fries and wasted no time devouring them. In a t-shirt and shorts, beat-up tennis shoes and no make-up, she looked about sixteen years old. He threw pain relievers back with a slug of soda.

"How old are you?"

"Your private detective didn't tell you?" There was venom in the words, tempered, but they definitely had a bite to them.

"I didn't ask, and if he did, I don't remember."

"Twenty-one," she said, but wouldn't meet his eyes.

He knocked his knuckles on the table once to get her attention. "Really?"

"Fine. I'm nineteen."

Aiden was almost two, so she'd been solely responsible for him since she was seventeen. His gut twisted around the anger that had lived there since he found out about Johnny's deception. All the things that could've gone wrong raced through his head. "How did you support yourself and Aiden?"

She shrugged and dragged three fries through a river of ketchup. "Tara left me some money."

"How much did Johnny give her?"

"Half a mil."

"Five hundred thousand dollars?"

"Yeah." She wiped her hands on a napkin and reached into Aiden's diaper bag, withdrew a manila envelope, and slid it across the table.

The crinkle of the envelope opening and Kristy slurping the last of her drink were the only sounds in the nearly empty fast-food joint. He set the packet down and wiped his sweaty hands on his jeans, then pulled out a stack of legal-looking papers.

It was a contract stating that Tara would receive half a million dollars in exchange for her silence about the baby. It also stated that she couldn't come after him for more money and that he would never try to gain custody of the child. Johnny had forged his signature.

He fisted his hands and counted to ten...then twenty...then thirty.

Johnny, I'm going to kick your ass in the afterlife.

Guilt slapped him. It was clear by the contract language that his best friend and brother had, in a really screwed-up way, been trying to protect him. Even so, the anger was bitter to swallow.

He pointed to the last paper in the stack. "That's not my signature. I've never seen this before in my life."

Kristy threw her wadded up napkin onto the table, then crossed her arms defiantly. "That's not my problem. I'm the one who takes care of him, who takes him to the doctor and stays up with him when he's sick. Me. Not you. Not Tara."

She was right, she'd done it all and done it by herself. "How did you get medical care for him without Tara around?"

"Can I have your sandwich too?" She reached out and nabbed it without permission.

Changing the subject, like that would work, such a rookie mistake. "Kristy?" He gave her his Delinquent glare.

"Tara used some of the money to buy a new identity."

"Why?"

She rolled her eyes with all the force of her nineteen-year-old self. "Bad people were after her. I told you this."

He'd forgotten. A horrible thought crashed into his head. "Are you and Aiden in danger?"

"No." She began to tear the napkin to pieces.

"But you were?"

She shrugged. "I gave them what money I had left, and they stopped harassing me. That was two years ago, and I haven't heard from them since." She seemed to realize how vulnerable her admission made her. His back went ramrod straight. "We're fine. I handled it. Just like I've handled everything else that pertains to Aiden and me."

The small amount of food he'd eaten threatened to make a reappearance. She must've been scared shitless. He was scared shitless for them. The first thing that had to be done was to get them out of that hole they lived in and into someplace safe.

Kristy seemed to be unaware of the bomb blast she'd ignited. "Anyway, I used her old driver's license and social security card to get the things I need for Aiden," she mumbled into her soda.

"And you haven't been caught?"

"No. We look enough alike for me to pass as her."

Did she have any idea how much trouble she could get into? Probably not. There'd be time to deal with her fraud later, but he would need to get someone on it ASAP. The second item on the list, keep Kristy's ass out of jail.

He wanted her protected in case this ever came back on her. It wasn't her fault, she was just trying to survive and keep his son alive. He understood and respected the hell out of her for it.

"Anyway, Tara is now Sasha Strong. Doesn't matter, good riddance is what I say. I want an ice cream cone now."

She might say she didn't care, but he could read the hurt in her eyes. He'd let her off the hook for now and pass the name, Sasha Strong, to Jack. He shoved the sleeves of his Henley up his arms. "Do you know where she is?"

"After the bad guy, there was a rapper, then another bad guy, and now she's livin' with some professional football player in Florida. Supposedly they're getting married."

He looked at her, then out the window to Aiden, and shook his head.

She let out a sigh as big as Nevada. "Yeah. I know."

They were silent for a long moment. Tara had screwed them both over and not given one damn about it either.

Kristy squared her shoulders. "So what do you want?"

"You have to ask?"

"Yes."

"I want my son. I know you're attached to him, and I'd never cut you out of his life, but he's my son, and he belongs with me."

Wrong thing to say. Gavin knew it the minute he saw fire flash in Kristy's eyes.

"You're his father, huh? Where exactly were you when I was sitting in the ER all night while he ran a raging fever? Or when I was getting two hours of sleep at a stretch for the first six months of his life? And when I was trying to decide which was more crucial—food or medicine? You arrogant ass." She yanked her purse and Aiden's baby backpack from the seat beside her.

He gripped the backpack and held on. "I shouldn't have said that. I was out of line. Please don't leave."

If looks could kill, he'd have been cut to ribbons. She sat slowly. "I. Am. His. Mother. The only one he's ever known, and I will not just hand him over to you. We don't even know if he's really yours. I *know* he's mine. So get your fancy lawyers, I'm not scared of you."

The set of her jaw and her rigid posture told him she absolutely wasn't afraid of him. "I want a DNA test." She crossed her arms over her chest. Her gaze held a calculating glint.

"Fine." He wasn't afraid of her either.

"I've heard those things can take a couple of months to get the results. A lot can happen in a couple of months."

"It can, but if you go to a private lab, you can get them back in one to three days."

She choked on her drink. "One to three days?"

"We're not enemies, Kristy. We both want what's best for Aiden. Can we at least agree on that?"

"I can agree that I want what's best for him."

They weren't getting anywhere this way. "What about you?"

"What about me?"

"What did you want to do with your life before you unexpectedly became Aiden's mother?"

She picked at her nail. "It doesn't matter. I have Aiden, nothing else matters."

"But what if it did matter? What would you want?"

She fiddled with the group of bracelets on her wrist. "I wanted to study marketing. I'd already been accepted to UNLV. I was considered a junior because of dual credit classes I'd taken in high school. But then Tara had the baby…and now I have Aiden. Dreams change."

"Tell me about it." He watched his wife and his son chase after each other. Who could have predicted he'd be sitting here wondering about the safety of playground equipment, and how fast he could get his wife back into bed. Life was weird and a little awesome.

"You can't seriously be thinking you're going to raise Aiden with your lifestyle. I mean, what? You'll have a kid-sized room set up for him on the tour bus?" She threw the obliterated napkin on the table. "You have no idea what you're asking for. It's hard as hell. You worry all the time. You have to watch him all the time. You're responsible for him all the time. How are you going to do that?"

"We'll figure it out."

"You and her?" She jerked her head toward the window. "From what I saw on TV, this relationship seems sketchy at best."

Their relationship might have been sketchy in the beginning, but not now. He and Scarlett were solid. She got him, and he got her. A smile split his face when he saw Aiden gave Scarlett a kiss on the cheek. This would work. He knew it. "We'll handle it."

***

Scarlett wanted this little boy worse than she'd wanted anything in her whole life. From the moment he'd taken her hand, she'd fallen completely in love.

It made no sense. Absolutely no sense at all, but love was funny that way.

She loved Gavin. The epitome of the kind of man she'd avoided her whole life, the kind of man that sang the same song as her soul. He and this towheaded child, with his cupid's bow mouth, dimples, and a face that could go from serious to joyful in a heartbeat, had crashed through her defenses, and she was head over heels. Neither of them was on her meticulous life list. But they'd both barreled in and shredded that list to pieces. And she couldn't be happier.

"Play." Aiden pulled her hand toward the slide.

She laughed at his order. "Okay, little man. I'll play with you."

229

He climbed the small ladder of the playscape while she stood behind him. When he positioned himself in the right place, he pointed to the bottom of the slide. "Catch."

"Alright." She snatched him up to keep him from hitting the ground. If happiness had a sound, it was the way his giggles rang off the walls of the enclosed playground.

"Again, again." His short legs worked double time to get back to the ladder.

They spent the better part of half an hour this way, and every time she caught him and swung him into the air he squealed with glee.

It amazed her how many of Gavin's mannerisms the kid had, the way he lifted one side of his mouth when he was about to slide like he was about to do the most amazing thing possible. Or how he cocked his head when she talked to him, and how his little brow wrinkled when she told him they needed to rest and drink some water. Except for the dimples and the white-blond hair, he was the spitting image of his father. She knew Gavin was talking to Kristy about a DNA test, but it was only a formality.

"Hey, hey. I got a *mushtush*." His grin was too much.

"What, Aiden? What do you have?" He was speaking English, but she didn't speak toddler.

He pointed to his upper lip where there was a thin line of milk. "I got a *muchtush*."

"Oh, a mustache." She laughed, and he beamed. "It's a very nice mustache."

"Yeah." He nodded, then jumped down and ran for the tiny house in the middle of the play area.

"Hey."

"My name is Scarlett, Aiden. Can you say that?"

"No."

"Can you try?"

He huffed like she'd asked him to clean the toilet. Clearly, he had some of his aunt's mannerisms too. "Scawit."

She ruffled his hair. "Close enough."

He shrieked and ran into the maze, then poked his head out. "Where is the boy?"

"The boy?"

"The biiiiig boy." He puffed his chest out and spread his arms as wide as possible.

Gavin. "He's inside."

"With Kiki?"

"Yes, he's with your Aunt Kristy."

He spun plastic blocks attached to the metal rods. "Can he play?"

Her heart almost burst. Gavin would love it so much if Aiden asked him to play. "Why don't you go ask?"

She opened the door and watched through the window as Gavin's mini-me ran up to the table and asked his question. The two reactions to that request couldn't have been farther apart. Kristy turned as white as a sheet, and Gavin's face lit up like the sky on the Fourth of July.

He got up and turned to Kristy and said something. She shook her head. With a shrug, he turned to Aiden, who held out a pudgy little hand. The *Fourth of July* look turned into something completely different. Like he'd hit the game-winning homerun in the World Series, on his birthday, while receiving a Grammy and opening the best Christmas present he'd ever been given.

Her husband and his son. Happiness, fear, devotion, anxiety, and love slipped over her heart in a waterfall of tenderness.

Tears she hadn't expected blurred the scene. When they came through the door, she gave Gavin a thumbs up. The matching grins on both boys were cuter than anything she'd ever seen.

"Come play, Scawit."

"I will in a minute. You play with Gavin for a bit. I need to rest." No way would she take this moment from her husband. She sat at a table on the perimeter of the play area. At first, Gavin was tentative and overly careful, but Aiden quickly put an end to that. Soon they were both laughing and running around like crazy men. Unlike her, Gavin crawled up the bigger slides and went down with Aiden between his legs.

It could be this way. She saw it all play out in her imagination. Their life. The three of them, together for always.

Her phone signaled an incoming text. Without looking at the sender, she opened the message and gasped.

Another picture.

In it, she sat on a metal bench bolted to the wall, with a gang banger named Lil Roxy on one side and a homeless woman named Wanda on the other. Both rested their heads on Scarlett's shoulders, sound asleep. It was hard to see all the details because of the cell bars, but her black pantyhose were ripped, her red curls were a riotous tangled mess, and her mascara-ringed eyes still held the same horror as in the previous picture.

Below the picture was another message from her tormentor. *You meet the most interesting people in jail – Poppy.* ☺

That effin' smiley face emoji must be the new sign of the devil.

She was doomed. There'd be no coming back from these pictures. She looked at the boy who'd stolen her heart and the man who owned it and knew she'd never be more than an acquaintance to one and a memory for the other.

Chapter 24

"Sit here and close your eyes." Gavin let Scarlett lead him to the sofa in the middle of the hotel suite.

He clutched her around the waist, pulled her to him, and began an assault on one of his favorite places, the spot below her ear. "What do you have in mind, wife?"

"I should've known you wouldn't follow orders." She removed his hands and stepped out of his reach. "Behave."

"Never." Kissing that bottom lip caught between her teeth became his prime objective.

"Come here."

A quick push and he landed on the cushions. "No. Close your eyes."

"Fine." He threw his hands over his eyes. "Satisfied?" As he relaxed into the sofa, the lab results crinkled in his pocket. Tremors of joy raced through his body. That was all the proof he needed.

It was official.

He was Aiden Bradley Bain's father.

There was that feeling again. The one he'd had since the moment he'd seen Aiden. Like the first drop of a rollercoaster coated in melted caramel. He had no word for it, but it was now part of his DNA and he knew the ride would be more than he could've ever dreamed.

A loud squeak and a muttered curse came from one of the bedrooms. What was Scarlett planning? He hoped it didn't have anything to do with hot wax. Been there, done that, had the scars to prove it. Although, with her, he'd be willing to try again.

"Keep 'em closed." She was back in the room, and it sounded like she was rearranging furniture. This time the squeak was louder. "Shit."

He wanted to peek, but he kept his eyes covered and chuckled. "Ugly talk from such a pretty mouth. Do you kiss your daddy with that mouth, missy?"

The fragrance of honeysuckle and vanilla surrounded him. He drank it in and hot fantasies raced through his brain in living color. He wasn't a patient man. He took what he wanted, when he wanted it, and if she didn't get on with the program, she could forget about him following her rules and being a good boy.

Impatience evaporated in a heartbeat as long fingers ran through his hair, nails scraped his scalp and down his neck. The couch cushion on his right then his left sank as a delicious, heated weight straddled his hips. He groaned as she nestled closer to his engorged cock. Damn, this was better than any fucking fantasy.

Warm breath licked against his ear. "The only man I want to kiss with this potty mouth is you." Air rushed from his lungs and blood thrummed in his ears. She kissed him senseless. He had to have more.

Gavin ran his hands under her shirt to find the skin he craved, but she broke away from him. "What the—?"

"I love kissing you."

"Then get back over here and finish what you started."

She laughed. The warm sound spilled around him, doing funny things to his heart. He was hard as a brick and all he wanted was to make her happy. "Okay, woman, since kissing isn't what you have in mind, what now?"

She leaned in to rub her breast against his chest. Urgent kisses went up his neck, and just when he thought he'd happily die on this couch, she bit his earlobe.

"You're so easy, Gavin. I never said kissing wasn't on my mind. But there's something else that needs to be done first." She patted his pecs. "Keep your eyes closed. Good things come to those who wait."

"If I wait too much longer, I might be damaged goods forever."

"I promise I'll make it worth your while," she whispered in his ear. "Now close 'em."

Wound up as he was, he happily obeyed. He may have to sit there with his eyes shut, but she couldn't stop him from thinking about her in the lace teddy or the other silky things he'd bought her.

More shuffling, and the occasional grunt.

"I hope all this noise means you're naked and you're setting up some kind of sexual obstacle course." Now that would be fun.

"Okay. Open your eyes."

The excitement in her voice was contagious and he was curious.

He raised his lids.

Aaannnd his eyeballs nearly fell out of his head.

Desire came to a screeching halt into a big-ass wall *of what the hell*?

Balloons were everywhere. Blue ones, silver ones, and one giant *It's a Boy!* A car seat sat atop the loaded-down service cart. Some kind of folded-up contraption with a picture of a playpen on the side rested on the bottom shelf. Gifts, large and small, all wrapped in blue and silver paper with huge bows, covered the rest of the trolley.

She threw her arms above her head. "Happy Daddy Day!" she yelled, clapped her hands, and ended with blowing an obnoxious noisemaker.

His world made a sharp shift, and it took the rest of him a minute to catch up. The synapses in his brain were firing too fast to form words. All he could do was sit bug-eyed and mute.

"Oh, no. Do you hate it? I shouldn't have surprised you. It's a shock. You're in shock."

Nobody in his life had ever done anything like this for him. Nobody had ever given a shit. Nobody but this crazy little redhead from Texas who'd completely rocked his world.

"Gavin, say something."

Without taking his eye off his bounty, he took her wrist and pulled. She landed across his lap with a squeak. This was where she belonged. He cupped her face in his hand. She needed, no, he needed her to understand what this meant to him. "Not one person in my life has ever done anything like this for me. I'm blown away. I love it. Thank you."

"You're welcome." Her warm hand brushed down his cheek. "I want you to have all the stuff for your new life with Aiden."

What he needed for his new life with Aiden was her. She got him. He'd never understood the intoxicating power of that until now. He was drunk on it. Smashed out of his mind on the happiness and contentment she brought to his life.

For someone who lived by his words, he couldn't express what he wanted, but he could show her. With a slight adjustment, he laid her on the sofa. The leather conformed around her with a groan. Her gorgeous hair fanned out like a crown of fire. He stroked her full bottom lip with his thumb and died just a little when she sucked it into her mouth. Not to be distracted from the message he had to make her understand, he continued with his exploration. Fingers glided along her throat, pausing to feel her run-away pulse.

"You're so damn beautiful. Las Vegas was the best decision I've ever made." He shifted his weight on top of her. "Never doubt it."

"Gavin, please." Her unfocused expression and restless hands across his shoulders told him what she wanted.

His response was lips to lips, tongue to tongue. She was open, wanting, waiting.

"I want you, Scarlett. Can I have you, baby?"

She wrapped one leg around his hip and tilted her pelvis up to meet his. "Yes."

Being with her was the best thing he'd ever done, better than making music, better than playing concerts, better than adoring fans. Her sighs of pleasure were the only applause he needed to hear.

"Lift up, sweetheart."

She sat up and skimmed her thin cotton top over her head. Pale pink lace with pebbled nipples underneath sent hot blood to all parts south. His hands trembled as he unhooked the front clasp of her bra and pulled the cups away from her spectacular breasts.

"Take your shirt off, Gavin." She lay back to watch.

He was happy to comply, it was gone in a heartbeat.

She sighed and lowered her lashes. "I want to see all of you." A saucy smile tilted her lips. "Strip."

He wasn't sure when he'd lost the lead, but he wasn't about to argue. He stood and started to unbutton his jeans. "You too."

A slow blush stained her creamy cheeks, and she raised her hips off the sofa, and pushed her clothes down. Soft curves ended where he most wanted to be. She was perfect. She was his.

He ditched his pants and paused when he heard her sharp intake of air.

"Your body should be immortalized in marble and worshiped." She reached out and touched his hip.

"I don't care a thing about being immortalized, but feel free to worship all you want."

She laughed. "Come here."

He lay down on the sofa to circle her nipple with deliberate slowness. The velvety touch of her soft skin under his calloused fingers was a jolt of electricity through his body. It scalded away the bad shit from his past and left nothing but sweetness in its path.

He cupped her breasts and laved open-mouthed kisses on the tips.

"So, good, Gavin. So, good." Breathless pants filled the air. Her lids lowered and she arched toward him.

Each movement, each breathy whisper, let him know how lost she was in his arms. *Be here with me.* He had to make sure. He wasn't just the bad-boy rocker. He was Gavin. And he needed to know she saw him. "Look at me." Gravel lined the harshness of his command.

Surprise and worry reflected in her puzzled gaze.

"I...I didn't mean to sound..." What the hell was he trying to say?

Scarlett smiled and his heart grew ten sizes. Everything was in her eyes. That unnamed emotion he'd been grasping for all his life. "Hey." She traced his clenched jaw. "I'm here. I'm with you."

Passion shot through him like a rocket blast and his mouth crashed down on hers. She opened for him and urged him further. Her hips restlessly pulsed under him. The smell of sex swirled around them. He had to have her soon or he would explode.

"Open for me."

She let her legs fall apart and he slipped into her wet entrance with one finger then two. She gripped his shoulder and cried out.

"Easy, baby, easy. I've got you."

He trailed kisses down her body, swirled his tongue in her navel and paid homage from one hipbone to the other. The erotic exploration continued to the inside of her luscious thighs. He glanced up at her. "Do you trust me?"

Her fingers threaded through his hair. "Yes."

It was all the permission he needed. He claimed her with his mouth. Every movement and lick took her to where he wanted her to be. Her pleas ricocheted off his heart. Every desperate moan was a victory cry for him and he didn't stop until she screamed his name.

He gathered her in his arms while she trembled in the aftermath. She pressed small kisses in the crook of his neck and sighed.

He pulled back to see her face. "You like that?"

"Mmmm, soooo much."

Her half-drunk smile made him grin. "Yeah?"

"Yeah. But I want all of you, Gavin."

He ripped a foil package open. "You can have whatever you want."

With a quick slide, he was inside her. Her soft heat around his hardness nearly robbed what reason he had left. "Scarlett, you feel—"

Her nails scored his back. "Stop talking, rock star, and move." Desperation coated her words.

"Like this." He rocked his hips.

"Yes...ah, yes."

They moved as one, climbing and searching together. They each took. They each gave. Being with her, inside her, was like nothing else he'd ever experienced. This was making love. This was real. What he'd known since Vegas, but was too stupid to realize, crystallized with each thrust.

Fuck. I'm in love.

Afraid she would run, he kept the words locked away. So, with each stroke, each sigh, each kiss, he communicated what he couldn't say out loud.

Stroke.

I love you.

Sigh.

So much.

Kiss.

I'm scared shitless, but I don't care.

He poured love into her until they lay spent and satisfied.

When it was over, she owned him, body and soul. She freed the brokenness in him. Baptized and resurrected him with her sweetness, and made him a new man.

***

Scarlett moved to the music, while people pressed in all around them. Perfume, body odor and lust rose around them. The deep bass of the song pulsed through her body, like musical foreplay.

After her surprise baby shower and their afternoon of sex, they decided to go out and celebrate. They'd ended up at this crowded, dark club with go-go dancers behind glass walls above the bar and in cages around the room. It was the perfect place to blend in and go unnoticed.

Their love-making had been different this afternoon, stronger, deeper, almost sacred. It changed things, and it almost certainly meant she'd walk away from this relationship with a broken heart.

Gavin moved in behind her, and all thought of protecting herself fled. The music wove around them and tied them together. One of his hands burned a path down her side to rest low on her hip. Calloused fingers played with the hem of her skirt and rucked the fabric up to find the sensitive skin of her thigh. There were people all around, and she could have cared less. He was all that mattered.

His other arm wound around her waist and drew her to him. She arched back to press her bottom into him. They fit together perfectly. Goosebumps fanned over her skin when he trailed warm kisses up the column of her damp throat. In this moment she could forget this was pretend and let her love for him lead her. She flung her arm up and around his neck and tangled her fingers in the smooth strands of his hair.

Her head lolled on his shoulder to encourage his sultry exploration. The music beat a tribal rhythm and a rainbow of laser lights strobed across the room. All of it heightened the insistent pulse between her thighs. She moaned and slid her free hand down and around to grab his butt.

In one smooth move, he spun her to face him. The bass vibrated through her bones as his lips tasted and teased the corner of her mouth. It became difficult to distinguish between the bedlam around them and the chaos this man created inside of her.

The same madness must have affected him too. Tentative exploration changed to a direct onslaught of her lips. It was like when he played guitar on stage—no holds barred and demanding a response. The room fell away, and they became their own creation of want and need.

"You're mine tonight." He nipped then licked the lobe of her ear.

His stubble only added to the hormonal frenzy going on in her body. "You sure about that?" When had she become such a flirty vixen? It was a newly acquired skill, and she was just getting the hang of it. She had a lot of sexual exploration to make up for. Good thing she had the perfect teacher.

A pink-tipped hand slid over Gavin's shoulder. Then another. A buxom brunette with red pouty lips whispered something into her husband's ear. The way the harlot's mouth slid into a seductive smile left no doubt as to what she'd offered. Gavin tried to shake her off, but the woman glued herself to his back.

A veil of crimson washed over Scarlett's vision. "Take your hands off him."

"And who are you?" the hussy slurred.

"His wife." A torrent of rage rushed through Scarlett's desire-soaked brain. What the hell did this woman think she was doing?

The tramp ran the fingers of one hand through Gavin's hair while still holding on with the other. "That's okay. We can share."

Scarlett snatched the offending hand out of Gavin's hair. "Get your fucking hands off my husband." The graveled tone of her voice had no effect on the leech. In fact, the interloper's other hand was making its way down his body to what was hers.

Gavin jerked out of the woman's clutches. "You need to leave. Now." He was all Delinquent and scary as hell.

Unfortunately, party girl missed the signal and came in for a kiss. Scarlett didn't think, didn't weigh the consequences, didn't try to logic it out, she only reacted. She pushed Gavin out of the way, took hold of the woman's ponytail and yanked, pulling the woman eye to eye with her. "If you touch him again, I promise I will knock the ever-lovin' shit out of you." She jerked on the ponytail again. The woman tried to free herself, but Scarlett held on. "I am half redneck, sister. I will put my high-heeled shoe up your skinny butt before you know what hit you."

The brunette threw her hands in the air. "Fine. Some people are no fun."

The fury inside her refused to dissipate, and she had to force herself not to go after the bitch. On second thought, that skinny-assed, fake-boobed, cheap-perfumed whore needed to be taught a lesson. But Gavin secured her to his body, stopping her from going after the slut.

"Whoa, wildcat," he whispered into her ear.

She turned into his arms and breathed him in. *Mine, mine, mine.*

He took her face in his hands. "It turns me on when rule-breaker Scarlett comes out to play."

Her mother's words echoed from the past.

"Oh, my sweet girl, sometimes you have to break the rules for love and happiness. You remember what I'm sayin', you hear me?"

Something about that connection was bad, but then Gavin kissed her and she lost the ability to think.

Chapter 25

Was there anything better than a happy kid laughing? Scarlett didn't think so. Aiden's giggles, while Gavin pushed him on the swing, were almost enough to calm the brewing storm inside her. Almost, but not quite.

How could she be so deliriously happy and totally miserable at the same time?

Her mother's words…it was only a coincidence. Wasn't it? She kept telling herself it was. But deep down she was afraid it wasn't.

She'd nearly gotten into a fight last night. Fire-hot rage still charred her senses when she thought of that woman's hands on her husband. She did not do things like that. She taught Sunday school for heaven's sake. And yanking a woman bald-headed in a jealous fit didn't seem very Christian.

The wild child had broken her tethers and taken over. If she was honest, that girl had been running the show for a while now. If that little monster was in the driver's seat, it could only mean trouble for her and anyone she loved.

"Scaawit." The sing-songy voice cut through her misery.

"Yes, Aiden."

"Come pway."

"Yeah. Scarlett, come play." The growl in Gavin's voice latched onto her ovaries and caused gooseflesh to bloom up her arm. That coupled with his sexy smiles was all the convincing she needed.

"Okay." Lord, she was easy.

She got behind Aiden's swing since Gavin was in front of him. It was a beautiful day, unseasonably cool for a Nevada spring day. Luckily, they had the whole park to

243

themselves. After last night, she couldn't be trusted if any other woman ogled her husband, and she'd hate to whip a bunch of soccer moms.

"Boy?" Aiden addressed Gavin. It was what he'd been calling him ever since they met, and it was adorable.

"Yes?"

"I wike you."

Gavin stopped the swing. His Adam's apple bobbed several times. "You do, huh? Well, I like you too, Aiden."

"Slide, now?"

"Sure." The word came forced through Gavin's beautiful lips.

Her husband needed a moment, so she lifted Aiden from the swing and set him on the ground. "Run, be free, little boy." She chased him for a second until he ran to the safety of the slide.

Gavin's muscles were tight as she looped her arm through his and leaned her head on his shoulder. "Pretty awesome, huh?"

"I never thought…" He untangled his arm from her embrace, then slipped it over her shoulder.

Her arms went around his waist. Love saturated every cell of her being, and she snuggled into his side. "I know."

Aiden poked his head over the plastic wall of the slide and made a face, which made them laugh.

His grip on her shoulder tightened. "I was wondering. How would you feel about making this relationship between us more permanent?"

What? Had he really said that? She examined his rugged profile and saw the muscle ticking in his jaw. "More permanent than marriage?"

"Yeah." He looked at her then, sober intent latched onto her like a tracker beam. The thrill of it curled her toes. Warm fingers brushed a hair that had gotten stuck in her lip gloss.

"We're good together, really good. And I know you already love Aiden."

Two choices lay before her—the carefully controlled life she'd dedicated herself to, safe but lonely, or the riotous chaotic life with him, so full of color, drama, and love. Did she dare?

A flash of light over Gavin's shoulder caught her attention. A guy in a hat and sunglasses stood across the playground with a camera pointed at Aiden.

She felt every ounce of blood drain from her face.

"What is it?"

"Paparazzi. Get Aiden." She shoved him toward where the boy was still playing. The tiny pebbles of the playground crunched under her feet as she ran to where the reporter stood snapping pictures of her boy. The mama bear rose in her and with a cry, she launched herself at the guy.

"Hey. Get off me," the coward squealed.

Distantly, she heard Gavin calling her name and Aiden crying, but she was way past reason. "Give me that camera, you cock-sucker."

"I'm calling the cops." He shoved at her, but he was scrawny, and she had righteous indignation on her side. No contest, really.

She yanked the camera from around his neck and rolled to her feet. Gavin reached her side and took the camera from her, while the reporter scrambled to pull his phone from his pocket.

Scarlett seized it and chucked it as far as she could. "Oh, no you don't."

"What the hell? You crazy bitch."

Gavin got in the guy's face, but never touched him. "Be quiet."

"I sure as hell won't."

The death stare Gavin gave the guy shut him up fast. "Yes. You will."

"Scarlett," Gavin said without taking his eyes from the man. "Go to the car. Aiden is there in his car seat."

"But—"

"Go. Please. I'll handle this." There wasn't any anger in his appearance when he looked at her, but there was steel in his voice.

"Okay."

He turned back to the paparazzi. "What will it take to make the photos and this situation go away?"

The guy's answer was lost in the wind. Who cared anyway. The damage had been done and done by her. By the time she got to the car, Aiden had fallen asleep in his seat.

Her erratic pants mixing with Aiden's sweet baby snores sounded obscene. Her vulgarity and his innocence should never be in the same place at the same time. This was where she'd never wanted to find herself.

She stared out the window and grasped for the reins of her out-of-control life. It was useless. They were gone. Flapping in the wind along with her self-respect.

The man at the center of her whole chaotic life pulled his wallet from his pocket and handed the reporter a wad of cash. The two men shook hands, so civilized. Who would've guessed The Delinquent would be the voice of reason in this situation. If that wasn't a sad commentary on the state of her life, she didn't know what was.

She'd acted like an insane person, in front of his kid no less, and now he had to clean up the mess.

All the times her father had apologized for her mother's behavior, or carried her home drunk and crying, clicked through Scarlett's brain like a warped slide show. Her stomach danced out of time with her spasming throat. Tears brimmed and hung like dead fruit on her lashes, then dropped lifelessly to her cheek.

She flipped down the visor mirror to wipe them away and clean up any damage from the brawl. Her worst fears had come to life. The mantra that got her through the days and nights of her life was no longer true. The awful proof stared her in the face.

She was her mother.

***

The cool air-conditioned air blew over Scarlett's sweaty skin as she waited in the car while Gavin took Aiden back to Kristy. She'd chosen to hide in the car rather than face the retelling of the story, or Aiden's over-protective aunt's reaction. Plus, they probably wanted to discuss what effect the incident would have on their child.

She was the outsider and an unstable one at that. Loneliness fell over her like a heavy, wet blanket. She grabbed her phone and dialed the only person who would understand her despair.

Luanne answered on the first ring. "Hey, it's about time you called me."

Scarlett could hear Luanne moving around, opening and closing drawers. "What are you doing?"

"My father called and wants to have dinner tonight, and I don't have anything to wear."

"Please, your closet looks like the petite section at Neiman's. Wear the bronze sleeveless dress with the high collar. It makes your eyes and shoulders look amazing."

"Mmmm, do you think so? He likes brighter colors on me. I don't know."

She hated the hesitancy in her friend's voice. The strongest woman she'd ever known was reduced to a crumbling mess of insecurity and indecision whenever her father could be bothered to give her some attention. Luanne could stand toe-to-toe with anyone and tell them to go to hell without blinking an eye…everyone except her father.

"So what's up?"

For some reason, she couldn't bring herself to tell the story. "Nothing." She swallowed the tears clogging her throat. "I wanted to check in."

"How's L.A.?"

"Gavin and I are in Las Vegas."

"What? Why?"

"I'll tell ya later. It's a long story."

"Okay. Well, if you're not in L.A. you don't have to endure that asshat, Jack. That's got to make you happy. Kill me now if I have to spend more than a few minutes in his company again."

She laughed. "I think you protest too much, Ms. Price. He's a handsome guy."

"I don't date anyone who spends more on hair care products than me."

"Words to live by."

"Exactly. Oh, hang on, someone rang the doorbell."

Scarlett adjusted the air vent.

"What the hell?" Luanne said.

"What's going on?"

"There's a manila envelope on my doorstep."

"Who's it from?"

"Poppy Sims."

Ice coated Scarlett's arteries. "What's in it?" She knew. She just knew.

"Give me a minute. I'm gonna put you on speaker." The crackle of paper being ripped open filled the line. "Oh, no, Scarlett." The shock in her friend's voice was almost her undoing.

"They're the pictures, right?"

"Yes." Paper rustled through the phone. "Wait, there's a note. I thought your BFF might need legal representation when I release these to the public. Poppy." There's a smiley face at the end."

"Apparently, it's her thing."

"Sick."

"Yes."

Scarlett chewed on her nail. This was bad. Poppy was seriously going to release those pictures. She'd hoped that she'd been bluffing, but she wasn't. And combined with everything else...

"What are you going to do?"

She glanced at the three people who'd just emerged from Kristy's house. Gavin leaned in to kiss Aiden on the head. The thought of humiliating either of them was a knife shot to the kidneys. "I don't know. I can't betray my father and ask him to sell to her. So I'll have to deal with the fallout of the pictures being made public."

Obviously misunderstanding Scarlett's meaning, Luanne said, "About time you learn to deal with the ignorant people of Zachsville. Tell 'em to stick it up their collective ass."

"Hang on, got a text." Scarlett checked her phone and knew the end was near.

I've been patient. I've been kind. But I still don't have my property. Remember, you brought this on yourself. 24 hours and counting.

"Shit, damn, hell." She hit the door with the side of her fist to punctuate each word.

"Scarlett? What's happened?"

"She's going to do it, the text said twenty-four hours and counting." Angry tears blurred her vision and obscured her view of the two people who'd become everything to her. "I've got to go."

"Wait, I'm coming out there. Let me deal with my dad, I'll get the first flight out tomorrow. I'm waiting on some information that could make this all go away. Scarlett, did you hear me?"

She didn't even respond. She couldn't. What do you say when the last straw drops?

Chapter 26

Gavin peered at Scarlett from the corner of his eye. As long as he lived, he'd never forget the sight of her flying through the air at that weasel. His avenging angel. The one that would always stand with him.

"Was Kristy upset when you told her what happened?"

He shrugged. "You know Kristy."

"So, yes?"

"She'll get over it. She was glad you stopped the guy."

"I'm sorry."

"I'm not." He took her hand and kissed her scraped knuckles. "I'm only sorry you got banged up. Are you okay?"

"I'm fine."

She was lying. He knew she was still upset. Who could blame her? Hell, he was upset. That asshole should've never been taking pictures of Aiden. True, she'd gone a little crazy, but she was protecting his son, so she got a pass. They would talk about it, but not until they were back in their room.

The cool hotel parking garage provided a respite from the Las Vegas sun. She clung to his hand as they made their way to the elevators. "Jack's coming tonight."

The finger she'd been chewing on came out of her mouth. "Why?"

"He's going to start coordinating the custody agreement with a family attorney here."

"That's good."

Scarlett's sad expression wrecked him. He crowded her into the corner and took her face in his hands. "Look at me," he demanded.

Her shocked blue eyes quickly softened, and her lips parted. It was an invitation that he gladly accepted. He licked the corner of her mouth. That was all it took. The fierceness of her kiss drew something savage from him.

Her hands went to his ass and pulled him close. They fit together perfectly. The warmth of her skin under her shirt shot lust straight to his bloodstream.

The doors swooshed open, and a couple walked in. He reluctantly let go of her with a final nip of her lip. The cool metal of the elevator wall as he leaned against it helped to lower his temperature. Scarlett plastered herself to his side. The desperation of her grip on his arm confused him. If she thought he was going anywhere without her, she was wrong.

The woman made a huffing noise and wrinkled her nose at them like she smelled something bad.

Silence filled the car as they made their ascent. When the bell dinged, the woman looked back at them with another huff.

"What's your problem, lady?" Scarlett sneered.

The old biddy's mouth dropped open, and she scurried through the doors.

Scarlett stepped to the opening and shouted, "You don't know me." She yanked a hair tie from her wrist and pulled her hair into a ponytail. "People like that make me so mad."

The elevator opened into their suite. "I know they do," he said. "You've got to learn to ignore 'em. What they think has no bearing on how I live my life."

"You don't understand." She didn't stop but headed straight for the bedroom.

He knew he should let her work it out, but that wasn't his style. He snagged two water bottles from the fridge and went to find her. "Are you thirst—"

"I have to leave."

"What?" She couldn't have said what he thought she said. But the open suitcase on the bed confirmed it.

251

"I have to go. Leave. Right now." She threw handfuls of clothes into her bag.

"Is this about what happened today?" This couldn't be happening. He could fix it. Shit, he had no idea how to fix it. "Scarlett, I don't understand."

"Did you see me at the park? I attacked that man, Gavin. I physically took him to the ground. Who am I?" She pointed in the direction of the elevator with a handful of shirts. "And that woman? My hands itched to slap that superior look off her face." She paced like an animal that had been caged way too long.

"Scarlett—"

"Last night I went off in a jealous rage because I don't want anyone to look at you. Tell me, Gavin, how is that sustainable? You're a freakin' rock star. People look at you all the time. How am I supposed to handle myself with women pawing at you? I'll lose my mind...I'm not fit. Just talking about it makes me nuts. I have no control. I'm exactly like my mother, Gavin. I'll hurt you." Her hair stuck to her sweaty face, and her miserable eyes filled with tears. "And what about Aiden?"

"What about him?"

"What happens when I hurt him too?"

"You would never do that. Never. You're not that person." He tried to take the clothes from her hand.

She wrenched away and screamed, "I've been that person since the night I met you! You've done this to me. My life was normal until I met you. My reputation was spotless until I met you." Her trembling hand covered her mouth.

The garments fell from his numb fingers. This was his fucking fault? Sure it was, one more person's life he'd ruined. And she was about to be another person to leave him.

Pink blotches stained her pale cheeks. "Oh, Gavin. I...I'm so—"

"Stop talking. Just shut the hell up." He backed away from her. The helpless look on her face almost broke through his hurt and fury. Almost. She clutched his arm, but he shook her off.

"Please let me explain?"

"And then you'll leave?" She refused to meet his eyes. "Answer me," he yelled and hit the door with the flat of his hand.

"Yes."

"Well, fuck that. I'll save you the trouble." He slammed her suitcase shut and shoved it at her. "Get the hell out of here. I've got no room in my life for cowards." The accusation shot across the room and found its mark.

She stumbled a step. "I'm not a coward. I'm trying to protect you and Aiden. Can't you see that?" Her gutted expression only made him angrier. Why wouldn't she fight for them?

"Protect me? Ha! What I see is you trying to protect yourself. You want your boring, respectable, fake life back, and you've made it perfectly clear that I'm standing in the way of you having that. So go. Go!"

She nodded. "Okay." With her bag in hand, she walked to the elevator and pushed the call button, never looking back.

He followed her into the living room. This was a nightmare. The shattering of his broken dreams opened the place where his meanness lived. The agony that slashed through him demanded she bleed too. "I'm glad you're leaving. I don't want you anywhere near me, or my son." She physically jerked like she'd taken a blow. Bullseye.

"I understand," she said without turning around. The doors slipped open, and she entered the car. When she turned to face him, the tracks of her tears were like a road map to nowhere. "Goodbye, Gavin."

The doors slid shut on his future.

Son of a bitch.

Chapter 27

The full bottle of whiskey taunted Gavin from the coffee table, the oblivion it offered a dirty temptation. It sat untouched. What was the point?

She'd still be gone.

One thing was for sure, he couldn't raise Aiden without her. What did he know about raising a kid? She'd been the heart of him, and without her, he had nothing to give. He wasn't even sure he had the right wiring for love and affection.

No, Aiden didn't need him around to screw up his life too. He'd never forgive himself if that happened. No. It was best to let Kristy raise him.

Only thing to do now was to set them up with a nanny and a nice house where she and Aiden could live.

Pain oozed from every pore, and the cavern in his chest ripped wider. He hugged his guitar to his chest. He hadn't played a note, but he didn't want to be alone, and he needed the comfort Patsy provided.

The elevator indicated a visitor, and Jack strolled in. "Geez, turn on some damn lights."

"Turn 'em on yourself if it bothers you," he mumbled.

"Are you drunk?"

"No. I just like sitting in the dark."

Jack flipped on lights. "You look like shit."

He placed the guitar back in the case. "Yeah, well I feel like shit."

"Where's your wife?"

"Gone."

"Gone?"

"She took off. She ran out on me."

Jack took the chair opposite him. "Whoa. Slow down and start from the beginning."

Gavin ran his hands down his face. "She left me, man."

"Why? Did you two get into a fight?"

"No. She left to *protect* Aiden and me."

"From what? Sunday school overload?" Jack unbuttoned his jacket and reclined into the chair.

"Turns out I've made her into someone who could hurt us, or some shit like that." He picked up the bottle of whiskey and examined the label. It wasn't too late to get hammered. Bile filled his throat. The thought of mixing alcohol with his misery made him nauseous. He tossed the closed bottle onto the cushion beside him.

Jack pressed his fingers into his closed eyes. "You're going to have to give me a minute to catch up."

"Once you've caught up, we need to talk about the divorce and setting Aiden and his aunt up with a house, and college funds for both. And a nanny."

"Aiden and his aunt? What are you saying?"

"I'm not going to fight Kristy for custody. I don't know what I was thinking before. Honestly, the thought of me raising a kid is laughable. And to try to do it without Scarlett would be dangerous. What do I know about the care and welfare of a child? I don't have a clue what to do."

Jack sat forward in the chair. "Are you sure that's what you want?"

"Yeah. It is." It was the very last thing he wanted, but he hadn't been lying to Jack. He didn't know the first thing about raising a kid.

Jack rubbed his chin, then waved his hand in the air, as if to say *what can you do?* "We always knew the marriage had an expiration date, and since you rejected Storm Side's offer, we don't really need her anymore. Frankly, she's turning out to be more trouble than she's worth." He loosened his tie, slipped it off and stuck it in his pocket. "But it's too bad about the kid. We could've gotten a lot of miles out of him. 'Gavin Bain the dad' plays well, but hey, screw 'em both. Who needs 'em, right? They were both dead weight anyway."

Fury hurtled Gavin from his seat, and he took Jack by the shoulders and pinned him to the chair. "Shut your mouth, you son of a bitch. That's my family you're talking about."

"Really?" Jack gritted out. "Then why aren't you fighting for them, you idiot."

He released Jack like the man was on fire. "What?"

His friend sat up and straightened his jacket. "If they're your family, then why are you throwing them away?"

"You heard the part where Scarlett left me, right?" Gavin's legs wouldn't hold him anymore, and he dropped down on the ottoman.

"Yes, but that doesn't explain why you're going to walk away from your son."

"I… What if I can't do it? What if I screw him up?" That was the real issue. A weight that had hung around his neck since the first time he read Johnny's letter and knew he might have a kid in the world. The thought of turning Aiden from the happy, loving boy he was into something bitter and sad kept him awake at night.

Jack rested his arms on his thighs, his hands clasped. "Do you know why I decided to represent you?"

"No."

"You're loyal to a fault, and you have more heart in those golden hands of yours than most people in this business have in their whole bodies. You stood by Johnny for years—even when he relapsed and did stupid shit, you never gave up on him. I don't care what you say, there's no way you can walk away from your people like this. That's not who you are, Gav. You're a good man, and you'll be a great dad. Now can you get your shit together before we have to hug or something?"

Gavin's lips twitched. "Piss off."

"Gladly." Jack slapped his leg and sat back. "Seriously, you can raise this boy. I believe in you."

"Thanks, man." His people. Jack was right. Aiden, Scarlett, Kristy, Scarlett's family, even his lawyer were his people. Strange how a man who'd lived most of his life alone could accumulate so many individuals he cared about in such a short period of time.

"Is the thing with Scarlett really over?"

Gavin exhaled and let his head fall to the back of the sofa. "I don't know, man."

Then the elevator dinged again, and Kristy stumbled in carrying a screaming Aiden.

He was up and at their side before they crossed the threshold. Aiden fell into his arms, burying his face in Gavin's neck. Fear rattled his bones as he tried to check the boy for injuries. "What's wrong?" He put his palm on Aiden's forehead. "Is he sick?"

"No. He hasn't stopped crying since you dropped him off, and he keeps asking for the boy. He got so upset when I tried to leave him at Maxine's he threw up all over the place." Now she was crying too. "I couldn't leave him, so I called work to tell them, and they fired me. Just like that. What am I supposed to do now? I didn't know where else to go."

He wrapped his arm around her shoulder, and she fell completely apart. A fierce protectiveness rushed through him. "Hey, I've got you. You're not alone anymore."

He ignored Jack, who was grinning like a fool.

He rocked his son and Kristy, and let the knowledge that none of them would ever be alone again cradle his heart.

***

It was late by the time Scarlett got back to Zachsville. Lucky for her, there were flights out of Las Vegas to Houston every hour. She maneuvered the rental car through the streets of her hometown until she came to a quaint yellow house on Austin Street.

She'd called Luanne as soon as she got to the airport and asked if she could stay at her house tonight. She couldn't bear to go home yet.

The door to the house flew open the minute she knocked. Her best friend didn't look like her normal pulled-together self, but then again, it was late.

"Get in here. You look like hell."

"You don't look much better."

Luanne dismissed her comment with two words. "My father."

"Do you want to talk about it?" Please say yes.

"He says he wants to be more involved in my life."

"Why do you look—"

"I really don't want to talk about it."

Case closed. When Luanne made up her mind about something, there was no changing it. It didn't matter how normal or outrageous the decision, it was set in stone until she decided it wasn't.

"Sit down, before you fall down. When's the last time you ate?" Luanne moved a pile of papers off the sofa.

"I don't know. Gavin and I split fries at lunch." The words collided with the tears stuck in her throat.

"Why did you leave?"

"I'm in love with him."

"Well, duh. I knew that the minute you didn't call the cops on them at the farm."

"I wasn't—"

"You may not have known it then, but it was written all over your face." She crossed her legs and nestled into the corner of the sofa.

Was Luanne right? Had she been in love with him from the beginning? Probably. Why else would she have agreed to marry him? "It doesn't matter anymore."

"Those tears and your red nose say different. I don't understand why you left if you care this much about him?"

"Because I don't only love him, I love Aiden as well. I won't let a child grow up the way I did," Scarlett said.

Luanne's brow creased. "You lost me. Who's Aiden?"

Scarlett yanked a tissue from the box on the side table and wiped her face. "He's Gavin's two-year-old son."

"What?"

"Gavin has a son he just found out about, and his name is Aiden." When she saw the baffled look on Luanne's face, she said, "It's a long story."

"I don't care. Spill."

"Gavin was with a woman and she got pregnant. She tried to tell him, but Johnny got to her first and paid her to keep her quiet. He never told Gavin about the baby. Gavin only found out a few months ago, when he was going through some of Johnny's things. He's had a PI looking for them. He got a call last week that the boy and his aunt were living in Vegas."

Luanne wrapped a throw around her legs. "Where's the mom?"

"Gone."

"Shit."

"Yes. She left when Aiden was six weeks old. Aiden's nineteen-year-old aunt has been raising him for the last two years."

Luanne shook her head. "I think my brain exploded."

"I know." She hugged a pillow to her chest. "Jack arranged a DNA test at a private lab and Aiden is definitely Gavin's son. You should see him, Lou. He's adorable and so sweet. I love him, and that's why I can't be in his life."

"I still don't get it." Luanne grabbed a forgotten glass of wine from the coffee table and threw it back.

"Over the last week, I've all but cussed out a room full of record execs, all but had sex in the wide open for anyone to see, nearly fought two women over Gavin, and took a reporter out. Now the Poppy thing is about to explode, not to mention the original Vegas event. I'm a walking embarrassment."

"You're not, Scarlett. That's—"

Scarlett leapt from the sofa. "Yes. I am." Her hands went to either side of her head. Her voice rising with every word. "Why doesn't anybody get this? I won't humiliate my husband and my child like…"

"Like your mother."

"Yes."

The silence squeezed in around them.

Luanne held her hand out to Scarlett. "Come sit down."

It was either sit or collapse on the floor. She sat.

"Scarlett, look at me."

She met her best friend's eyes.

"I'm about to tell you some truths, and you're not going to like them, but you need to listen."

"There's nothing—"

"Stop talking. Listen. Your mother was a selfish, manipulative, narcissist who didn't care about anyone or anything but herself. The things she did to your father, to you, and to herself were cruel, dangerous, and eventually got her killed. You're nothing like her. Nothing."

She wiped the tears from her face. "I look like her, and have her mannerisms. Everyone says so."

"So what? I look like my dad, but would you say I'm an unscrupulous asshole who shirks her responsibilities?"

"Of course not."

"Are you sure? I'm as stubborn and as driven as him."

"I don't care. You're not like Marcus Price at all. Just because you share his DNA, doesn't mean you could ever be as horrible as he's been. I don't ever want to hear you compare yourself to him ever again. Do you hear me?"

Luanne's perfect black eyebrow arched in challenge.

Scarlett couldn't meet her eyes. "It's different."

"Oh, is it?"

"Yes." She clutched her middle. "There's this wild thing that lives inside me, Lou. It's constantly trying to get out. And when I'm with Gavin, it runs stark ravin' crazy."

"Okay, so?"

"So, I can't control it. I see him and I want to strip naked and beat the crap out of anyone who dares to look his way. I'm a menace."

Luanne laughed. "You're not a menace."

"It's not funny. It scares the crap out of me. And now Poppy. She's going to release those pictures and you know I'll never convince everyone that I wasn't a call girl. I would never put Aiden through that. Once those photos hit the Internet, they'll always be there. And, Gavin." Tears choked her. "He was so hurt and angry. He told me to leave and that he didn't want me around him and Aiden."

"Oh, for God's sake, it's because he's an idiot."

"Because he knows I'm bad for him and Aiden."

"Listen, I'll admit Poppy is a loose cannon. But honestly, Scarlett, who cares? There weren't any charges filed, and you were released within twelve hours. It was a misunderstanding. The only people who will give a damn are the people in this town, and don't you think it's time you stopped living your life for a bunch of people you don't care about?"

"You don't understand."

Luanne shook her head. "I never thought I'd say this, but I'm really disappointed in you."

The words speared through her heart. "Luanne."

"No, really. I guess you are like your mother. She ran out on the people who loved her, crushed the ones who loved her, threw her family away because she was a weak, selfish woman. I never thought you'd do the same thing, but you are." She rose to grab something from her briefcase. The slap of the large envelope on the coffee table rang through the silence. "This is everything you need to bury Poppy. What you choose to do with it is up to you.

But you don't need it to get your life back. You only need to stop being such a coward and stand up for yourself and the people who love you. And stop being so damn selfish."

"Luanne, I—"

"I'm going to bed. I won't be here in the morning. I have a meeting."

Scarlett stared at her friend as she left the room. A huge stone sat on her chest. Was she throwing her family away?

No. She was protecting them.

Wasn't she?

Chapter 28

"Slow down, bud. There are more pancakes." Gavin laughed when Aiden gave him a syrupy smile.

"Panie-cakes," the toddler said around a mouth full of food.

He, Aiden, Kristy, and Jack sat around the breakfast table in the suite. They made a weird sort of family.

There was only one person missing.

Kristy cleared her throat. "So, I…um…I was hoping we could work something out. A custody thing or…maybe…visitation?" She bit her lip and tears glinted in her eyes. "Don't get me wrong, I love him like mad. But he has a father, maybe I can just be his aunt." The liquid rolling down her face spoke of her devotion to his son. "I mean, I can't believe we've made it as long as we have."

"You made it because you're a fighter. I know you love him. You don't have to worry about that, and you can see him anytime you want. I want you to be part of his life."

She wiped a tear from her cheek. "That might be hard if you live far away."

"Hey. I'll always get you to us. In fact, why don't you come with us?" Gavin warmed to the idea as soon as it popped into his head. "We'll get you an apartment close by."

Her face lit up and she looked younger than her nineteen years. "Where are we going to live?"

He laughed. "I haven't quite decided that yet."

"I'll get the papers drawn up and we'll get them signed," Jack said, and got up to answer the room phone.

"Boy! More panie-cakes," Aiden yelled.

Kristy smoothed the hair from his forehead. "Aiden, can you say daddy?"

"Daddy." His triumphant smile squeezed Gavin's heart. She pointed to Gavin. "This is Daddy, not boy."

Aiden looked between the two of them, then shouted, "More panie-cakes, Daddy!"

And his world made a one-hundred-eighty-degree turn. His focus, his mission, became being the best damn dad in the whole freakin' world. "You can have all the pancakes you want, dude."

"Okay, send her up." Jack hung up the phone. "Prepare yourselves for Hurricane Luanne."

"What?" Gavin's fork clattered to his plate.

Jack rubbed his hands together in anticipation. "She's here and on her way up."

"Who's Luanne?" Kristy asked.

"Scarlett's BFF." Jack pressed his tie against his chest and sat down at the table.

Dread slammed Gavin's heart into a wall. Why was she here? Surely not to serve him with divorce papers yet. He wasn't ready for that. He'd lain awake all night trying to come up with a plan to fix things with his wife. No fucking way was he signing anything until he'd spoken to Scarlett face to face.

"Where is Scarlett?" Kristy looked around like she'd just realized the woman wasn't around.

"Yes, Gavin, where is your wife?" Luanne stormed into the room.

Jack started singing *Maneater*.

"Put a sock in it, Counselor. I didn't come to see you. In fact, why are you here? In broad daylight, no less. Blood suckers are nocturnal, aren't they?"

"Oooh, good one, Luanne. That really stung."

"Bite me, Jack."

Jack stood and towered over her. "Ask me nicely."

"I'll tell you what. You hold your breath and wait for me to ask you for anything."

He chuckled. "Nah, I'd probably die a slow, agonizing death."

"You got that right, Jacka—"

"No cussing in front of Aiden," Gavin cut in.

"Yeah, Luanne, no cussing in front of Aiden," Jack taunted.

"Stop it, you two. You're scaring the baby." Kristy picked Aiden up and sat him on her lap, his lips trembling as he ogled the adults.

"I'm sorry. You're right." Luanne moved to the boy. "Hey, little guy, I'm your Aunt Luanne." She smoothed her hand over his hair.

He hid his face and giggled.

Jack snorted. "Aunt Luanne?"

She shot him a death glare, then turned her attention back to the child. "Your Aunt Honey is going to eat you up, you precious thing."

"Who's Aunt Honey?" Kristy searched the faces of the adults.

"Scarlett's aunt. She's a bit eccentric, but sweet as sugar. I'm Luanne Price, Scarlett's best friend."

"And rottweiler."

"Ignore Jack. He has unrequited feelings for me and can't get over it."

"Right. Because I've lost the last shred of my sanity." Jack went back to his seat at the table.

A tiny ray of hope pried its way into Gavin's heart, maybe all was not lost. "What are you doing here, Luanne? And why did you say that Honey would love Aiden?"

"Because she will. And I'm here to drag your sorry a-double-s back to Texas."

Gavin threw his napkin on the table. "Scarlett left. She doesn't want me."

"Oh, boo-hoo." Her fist went to her hips. "Is that why she's at my house crying her eyes out? And I heard you told her to leave, that you didn't want her around you or Aiden."

The words he'd thrown at Scarlett still burned his throat. He regretted saying them more than anything. He ran his fingers along the edge of the table and wouldn't look at Luanne. "I did." With more courage than he knew he had, he met her eyes. "And it was the stupidest thing I've ever done."

Luanne placed both hands on the table and leaned toward him. "So, are you going to keep being stupid, or are you going to wise up and realize she left because she loves you and Aiden."

She loved him? A giant ball of joy smacked him in the head and he couldn't help the goofy grin that spread across his face. "She does?"

"Yes, you idiot. But she's freaking out. There's stuff you don't know about that has her acting the way she is."

"I know about her mom."

"It's not that, it's something else."

He pushed his plate out of the way. "What else?" He didn't like that Luanne had more information than him.

"Poppy Sims, the new bank president, owned and operated an escort service while we were all in school at UT. Nobody knew. It was a complete shock to me."

He rested his elbows on the table and clasped his hands. "I don't see what this has to do with Scarlett."

"She tricked Scarlett into attending one of her *parties*, and the place was raided. Scarlett was arrested for p-r-o-s-t-i-t-u-t-i-o-n."

"What?" Kristy yelled.

"You've got to be kidding," Jack said.

"Are you fu—" He glanced at Aiden playing happily with the spoon. "Are you *freaking* kidding me?"

Luanne dropped into one of the dining room chairs. "No. Poppy got away and wasn't arrested, but she managed to get pictures of Scarlett being cuffed and in a jail cell.

She's threatening to release the photos to the media unless Scarlett convinces Floyd to sell Poppy the farm. She wants it for some multi-million-dollar housing development. Your wife found out yesterday that Poppy's going to release them this evening, because there's no way Scarlett will ever do what that *B* told her to do."

"That's awful." Kristy pushed the butter knife out of Aiden's reach.

"You're handling it, right, Luanne?" Jack was in total lawyer mode.

"Absolutely," she replied. "She has what she needs to shut this down forever. I hired a private investigator, and apparently Poppy wasn't very careful and burned a lot of bridges when she left Austin. He had no problem finding people to talk."

Jack nodded. "Good job."

If Gavin hadn't been so furious he'd have been curious about the pink tint on Luanne's cheeks at Jack's compliment. But rage seethed beneath his skin. Someone was trying to hurt his woman. "When did she find out?"

"After you left the park, while she was waiting for you in the car."

He dropped his head into his hands. "Kristy, cover Aiden's ears."

"Done," Kristy said.

"Fuuuuuck. I said all that shit to her." He ran both hands over his head. "She must hate me."

"Ha. She's too busy hating herself to hate you. Me, on the other hand…"

Jack chuckled.

"Hey. Don't talk to him like that," Kristy said.

"It's fine. I deserve it."

"Yes, you do, but what are you going to do about it?"

Aiden wiggled out of Kristy's hold and ran around the table to Gavin. "Daddy."

Would he ever get tired of hearing that word? Hell no. He picked Aiden up and studied his smiling face, and knew no one else could raise him better than he could, like he knew no one could love Scarlett more than he did. She belonged with him, and he'd spend the rest of his life proving it to her.

"Kristy, have you ever been to Zachsville, Texas?"

"Um…no."

"Pack your bags. You're going to love it."

***

Scarlett strode past Poppy's secretary without stopping. She had no idea how to save her marriage, or even if she could, after walking out on Gavin. But this was one thing she could do. Luanne was right. She needed to stand up for herself and stop caring what people she didn't care about thought of her.

The manila envelope in her purse was only there as a backup plan. Poppy was batshit crazy and she might not back down without it.

A braid of fury, fear, and indignation wound through her and spurred her forward. She was on a mission for herself, for Gavin, and for Aiden. If she had any hope of repairing the damage she'd done, she had to be willing to do whatever it took to get them back. And it started with Poppy Sims.

"Scarlett, if you'll wait I'll see if Ms. Sims is available." The assistant jumped up from her desk and trotted after her.

"That's okay. I've got it." She flung Poppy's office door open.

Shock skated across her enemy's face for the briefest of seconds, then her mask of superiority slid back into place. "It's fine Elaine. I'll see Ms. Kelly."

Scarlett closed the door in Elaine's face.

"Scarlett, you really should work on your manners. I guess that's to be expected from someone raised the way you were." Poppy stacked papers into a pile.

"I was raised just fine, Poppy. However, I question the way you were raised. But that's not why I came to see you."

"Are you here to tell me what I want to hear?" Poppy purred.

"Nope." She flung her arms wide. "I came to tell you to do your worst. I'm not afraid of you."

Poppy's brows crawled up her forehead. "You should be."

Scarlett shrugged. "Maybe, but I'm not. In fact, I think you should be afraid of me."

The most unladylike snort shot from Poppy's lips. "Oh, and why is that?"

Scarlett examined her nails, then slid her own snake look at Poppy. "Because I spoke to your father this morning. He and your mother are having a lovely time, by the way. Or they were until they heard about the nastiness going on here in Zachsville."

Every ounce of color drained from Poppy's face. "You're lying."

"No. I'm not." Scarlett scrunched her nose up and drew air through her teeth. "I have to say, they were as shocked as I was to find out you were running an escort service in college. For different reasons, of course."

"How would you even get in touch with him?" The woman's voice sounded like she'd drained a canister of helium.

"Your father is one of my father's oldest friends. He had his number." She rested her hands on Poppy's desk. "So release your photos and tell your story. I don't give a damn because once the town finds out you were Madame Millicent, an innocent case of mistaken identity won't matter to them at all." She doubted that were true. This

269

town's life blood was gossip, but in light of all she had to lose it simply didn't matter anymore.

Poppy's bloodless face filled with rage. "I'll get you for this."

Scarlett stopped at the door and glanced back at her nemesis. "No. You won't. And if you ever threaten my family again, you'll regret it. I was raised to protect family no matter what. Which means, if you come near my family or me again, I'll put a boot so far up your ass, you'll need a surgeon to remove it. Have a nice day."

Chapter 29

"She what?" Floyd exploded.

Scarlett looked into the shocked faces of Honey, Joyce, and her father. "Poppy blackmailed me so I would convince you to sell the farm."

"That's ridiculous. What on earth could she have to blackmail you with?" Honey said.

Scarlett tore a paper napkin into tiny pieces. Her newfound courage didn't quite help with confessing all to her family. It had taken every ounce of the stuff she could muster to march into the kitchen and tell her story. "My junior year in college Poppy invited me to a party. Shortly after I arrived the cops raided the place. I was arrested for prostitution."

"What?" they all said in unison.

"Turns out Poppy had an escort service providing the company of young women to older men." She shrugged. "Wrong place, wrong time."

Joyce's hand flew to her mouth. "Oh, my word."

"I always knew that girl was twisted." Honey crossed her arms over her chest.

Floyd wrapped Scarlett into a fierce hug. "Oh, my poor girl. You must've been terrified. Why didn't you tell us?"

As tempting as it was to hide in her father's embrace, everything needed to be brought into the open. She untangled herself and sat up to tell the truth. "I was afraid of what you'd think of me."

"Scarlett, I could—"

"Let me finish. I was afraid you'd think I was like mama, and I didn't want to hurt you like that." She didn't stop the tear that rolled down her cheek.

Honey took her hand. "Oh, darlin'. You could never disappoint us."

"We love you," Joyce said.

Her father stared at the tabletop and didn't say a word. The knot in her stomach cinched tighter as all of her fears hung in the air between them. She could let it lie. Take Honey and Joyce's words and move on with her life. She'd never hold her father's silence against him. This was painful for him, too. But she'd spent too much of her life hiding her feelings and she wasn't doing it anymore. "Daddy?"

The wrecked look on his face nearly had her backtracking and telling him he didn't have to say anything. But she didn't. She only waited for him to speak.

"This is my fault." His words sounded like glass crushed underfoot.

She wrapped her fingers around his folded hands. "What? How is any of this your fault? I'm the one who trusted Poppy. Then I complicated it by not trusting you enough to tell you what happened."

"If I could've gotten past my own pain and embarrassment when your mother left we could've talked about it. You would've known that you are nothing like your mother. Yes, you look like her, but that's where the similarity ends." His chest expanded then deflated, as he gazed out the window. "I loved that woman, but it wasn't healthy, she wasn't healthy. I thought my love and our family could heal her. But I was wrong. So wrong." He turned back to Scarlett and cupped her cheek. "And you've paid the price, darlin'. Can you ever forgive me?"

She started to tell him there was nothing to forgive, but realized he needed forgiveness like she needed transparency. "Of course I forgive you." She leaned in, wiped his tears, and kissed his cheek. "I love you, Daddy."

"And I love you, sweet girl."

"I want to know how you got out of jail." Honey pulled a plate of cookies toward her, like she was settling in for a story.

Scarlett smoothed her hair from her face. "I honestly don't know. The next day they let me go with no explanation. When I got outside, Poppy was there. I walked right past her, got a cab, went home, and never spoke of it again. Luanne didn't even know. But I've had a lot of time to think about it, and I definitely saw a county judge at the party. Maybe she got him to pull some strings and get me out. Who knows? She's not stable."

"And wicked," Joyce said.

"She has pictures of me being arrested and in jail that she's threatened to send to the media, and considering the whole Gavin thing..."

"Oh, no she's not." Floyd dug his phone from his pocket. "I'll call Hartley right this minute and tell him everything his daughter's done."

Scarlett took the phone from his shaking hands. "No need. I already did." She'd forgive herself for the pride and self-satisfaction in her voice.

Honey's eyes got as big as saucers. "You did?"

"Yep. He was none too pleased, and neither was she when I went to the bank and told her."

"Did you also kick her ass?" Floyd asked.

"No, but it was made clear that it was the next step if she messed with the Kellys again."

Honey slapped the table. "I like this new Scarlett. Now, darlin'...tell us the rest." She arched a brow, daring her to argue.

Scarlett rubbed at an imaginary scuff on the table. "About that..."

She told them everything about how she and Gavin met, about Aiden, about falling in love, and about why she ran out on him.

"I think we all knew there was more to the story than either of you were telling, but it was so much fun watching you lose your mind over that boy, we didn't say anything." Honey laughed.

"You weren't embarrassed?"

"Lord, no," Honey said.

"When that video was released we did worry for you some," her father said, "but that worked out too because it gave you and Gavin an excuse to get out of this small-minded town."

"But now you've come back without him," Joyce said.

"And that baby," Honey added.

Floyd slung an arm over her shoulder. "We only want you to be happy, Scarlett, and that rock-n-roll fella makes you happy. Any fool can see that."

"Yes, well, leaving him was the biggest mistake I've made through all of this. I left because I thought I was protecting him. The problem with that genius plan is that I need him so much it hurts. So even if it's selfish, I'm going to get him back."

"That's good to hear." Gavin pulled open the screen door and strode inside.

"Gavin." She knocked her chair over trying to get to her feet. Hope jackhammered her heart. Maybe she could fix this. "Let's go outside so we can talk."

"I don't think so, Red. I need the witness of our families to make sure you don't run again."

She gulped down a riptide of emotion. "Our families?"

Jack walked in carrying Aiden, Luanne right behind him, with Kristy pulling up the rear. The kitchen burst at the seams with *family*.

"Give me that baby," Honey said.

Luanne crossed her arms over her chest. "Good luck, Honey. Jack won't give him up, believe me I've tried."

"Honey? I'm Jack Avery. Would you like to hold Aiden?"

"Hey." Luanne swatted his arm.

"I sure would, you good-looking thing."

Luanne gagged.

Jack smirked.

Aiden squealed, "Scawit!"

"Sweetheart, I'm Joyce," Joyce said to Kristy.

"Hello, I'm Kristy."

Floyd slapped Gavin on the back. "Son, it's good to have you back."

"Thank you, sir," he said without taking his gaze from Scarlett. "I need to ask you a question."

"Yes?"

"May I marry your daughter, again?"

Her entire body vibrated with happiness.

"Do you love her, boy?"

"Boy, boy, boy!" Aiden yelled.

"Yes. I love her very much."

Her father's grin split his face from ear to ear. "Scarlett, darlin', do you want to marry this fellow again?"

"Again, and again, and again." She could barely see his smiling face through the curtain of tears in her eyes. "I love you too."

Gavin prowled toward her. When his warm hands cupped her face, the chaos of the room fell away and it was just the two of them.

"I do love you, Scarlett. I'm so sorry for the terrible things I said. Can you ever forgive me?" His gray cashmere eyes pleaded for forgiveness.

Her arms went around his neck. "I've already forgiven you. I'm the one who should be apologizing. I should never have left you. I'm yours. You're stuck with me, rock star."

He rested his forehead against hers. "Forever?"

"Forever."

He kissed her, and she kissed him, and they made promises to each other surrounded by the nutty, messy, unpredictable family they both loved.

Epilogue

The sweet smell of roses, lavender, and honeysuckle from her bouquet floated around Scarlett. If love had a smell this would be it. She stood under a vine-covered arbor with her rock star, who wore a beautiful tux that fit him perfectly. Never one to bend to convention, he'd left the collar open, revealing her favorite tattoo of Aiden's name at the base of his neck.

Though they'd been married several months, this was the official ceremony. At least according to Honey, who had the whole thing planned down to when and how Gavin would remove her garter—after the cake and with his teeth.

Jack stood next to Gavin looking drop-dead gorgeous, which only pissed off Luanne. She hadn't stopped griping about it all night.

Their family and friends were gathered in chairs draped in white and tied with red satin ribbons, on the side lawn of the farm. The trees were filled with twinkle lights and white paper lanterns, and fireflies danced just above the ground. It was a far cry from a Las Vegas wedding chapel, and her pastor, Brother Randy, was much more dignified than the Whitney Houston impersonator who'd done the honors in Vegas.

Shame.

In the last several months she'd learned to embrace the outrageous and let go of normal—because there really was no such thing as normal, and normal was boring. And if she could say one thing about life with her new husband, it was never boring.

He was about to go into the studio to record his first album for Honey Child Records, the label he and Jack started in Zachsville, even though Jack refused to live in town, choosing instead to live in Austin, *where all the cool people are*, according to him.

She'd warmed up to Jack over the last couple of months, but given that Luanne so openly hated him, it was good he was an hour away for his own safety.

Brother Randy addressed the audience. "The couple has elected to recite their own vows tonight. Gavin."

An adorable bead of sweat broke out on her husband's brow. He was nervous. This rock god, who had sung in front of millions of people, was nervous about saying his vows in front of sixty people. It made her love him even more.

"Scarlett, before I met you I lived in a very lonely world, a world of shadows and sadness, a world where I only existed. I never knew my life could be filled with so much light and love. You've done that." He looked at her in that way that always stole her heart. Like he couldn't quite believe she was real. "You breathe sunshine into my life. You amaze me every day with the way you adore our son and me. I love your beautiful heart, and I promise to guard it forever. I love you. I choose you, for always." He kissed her hands and wiped a tear from her cheek.

The pastor nodded. "Scarlett."

She took a minute to compose herself. She had to get this right, it was too important to mess up. "Gavin, I've always tried to live my life the safest way possible. I do the right things, I obey the law, I never break the rules, I return library books on time." The audience chuckled. "But I've found that love changes things. It has a way of narrowing down what's important and what isn't, and what I know now is… You are the most important thing in my life, and I would lie, cheat, steal, and break every rule to get to you. There's nothing I wouldn't do to keep your heart safe and to prove my love for you. You are everything I never knew I needed, and all I will ever want."

He didn't wait for Brother Randy to give him permission, he grabbed her, his mouth crashed down on hers, and like every other time he kissed her like this, she lost her mind. Her lips opened for him and their tongues played together, until she was panting and boneless.

Brother Randy coughed.

"Get a room," Jack and Luanne said in unison.

Honey whooped from the front row.

She reluctantly pulled back. With swollen lips and triumphant eyes, he smiled down at her, and she knew she'd never run from this rock star again.

The End

Acknowledgements

Oh, my gosh, y'all! I'm so humbled and blessed that you spent your hard-earned money and precious time to read my book. You guys are my new best friends!

Running From A Rock Star has been a labor of love for me, but it wasn't created in a vacuum. There are many people who helped me along the way.

First and foremost, I must thank my critique partners, who are incredible authors in their own right and the unofficial Scott Eastwood fan club. Carla Rossi, Stacey A. Purcell, and Melissa Ohnoutka, you've left your mark on this book and my heart. Your support, friendship, and honesty mean everything to me. I will never be able to thank you guys for all you've done.

I'd also like to thank the members of my home chapter of RWA, Northwest Houston RWA for all their support and encouragement.

To author Nina Cordoba, my rom-com buddy and mentor. Thank you for your encouragement and help in understanding the minutia of writing funny books.

A big shout out to the SAS Romance/Erotica Mastermind! There were many days I might've quit if not for your accountability and encouragement. You ladies are the best, and I'm blessed to know you and be counted among your ranks.

To Johnny B. Truant, Sean Platt, and David Wright (the Self-Publishing Podcast guys): Thank you for your podcast, the Smarter Artist Summit, and for giving me a path and direction to follow. Also to the Smarter Artist community at large, thank you for being so amazing.

I'm very fortunate to have many cheerleaders in my life and I'd like to thank my Austin friends, Kristy, Carol, Jennifer, Teri, Staci, Kathy, and Jo for always asking about my writing and for encouraging me in every way possible. I love you guys and miss you so much.

To Danielle, the most generous person I know, thank you for always being in my corner and knowing the right words to get me back on track when I freak out. I thank God for bringing you into my life, my friend.

Thanks to Laurie Starkey for giving me a job and more publishing information than my brain can hold. Your capacity to care for others, humbles and inspires me.

My beta readers: Kathy Duncan, Stacia Norris, Cambra Nelson, and Elizabeth Crownover, you guys rock. I am super grateful for your feedback. You seriously saved my bacon.

To the talented Najla Qamber, of Najla Qamber Designs, you created a kick ass book cover in spite of me. LOL! Thanks for your patience and incredible eye for beauty and what works. You're the best.

A GIGANTIC thank you to my editor, Serena Clarke, you made me look like I knew what I was doing. When you're grammatically challenged, it's good to know someone like you. Thank you for being such a great friend, even though we're continents away from one another. Ain't the internet grand?

To my parents: Thank you, mom and dad for always supporting me and believing I could do way more than I believed I could do. To my sisters, Amy, Dana, Joni, and Randi: You four are my ride or die people, and I love you more than you know.

To my three children: Thank you for caring about my writing and for forgiving me when my mind wandered to my story during our conversations. Thank you for your unconditional support. You guys are the best thing I've ever done. This includes my awesome son-in-law to be who built my fabulous website.

Finally, to my husband: I hit the matrimonial lottery with you, babe. Thank you for all the meals you cooked, for cleaning the house, for the celebratory cake you made when I won the Lone Star Writing Competition, and for watching

TV alone in the evenings so I could write. You've never wavered in your support of me. I hope I've made you proud, because this book is as much yours as it is mine. Team Albright for the win!

About the Author

Jami Albright is a born and raised Texas girl and an award-winning author who writes zany, sexy, laugh-out-loud stories. If you don't snort with laughter, then she hasn't done her job.

Jami is a wife, mother, and an actress/comedian. She spends her days writing and wrangling her adorably mischievous dog, Tug, who may or may not be human.

She loves her family, all things Outlander, and puppies make her stupid happy. She can be found on Sundays during football season watching her beloved Houston Texans and trying not to let them break her heart.

Made in the USA
Columbia, SC
31 July 2019